SEE
HER
RUN

SEE HER RUN

AN ALOA SNOW MYSTERY

PEGGY TOWNSEND

THOMAS & MERCER

Text copyright © 2018 by Peggy Townsend
All rights reserved.

Published by Thomas & Mercer, Seattle

www.apub.com

Amazon, the Amazon logo, and Thomas & Mercer are trademarks of Amazon.com, Inc., or its affiliates.

ISBN-13: 9781503949874
ISBN-10: 1503949877

Cover design by Shasti O'Leary Soudant

Printed in the United States of America

Fiction writers have a superpower that gives them the ability to build houses, create businesses, and reconstruct entire city blocks with a few taps of computer keys. Some of the places in this book are real; many are not. Meanwhile, the characters are all works of my imagination.

—*The Author*

JULY 16
12:37 p.m.

She ran through the desert with the white heat all around her.

Rocks scraped her feet. Branches stabbed her legs, leaving red threads of blood on her strong calves.

"Run," she told herself. "Run."

She had been at it for more than two hours, but it was only now that she was beginning to doubt she had the strength to save herself.

She looked over her shoulder. Still behind her.

Panic tugged at her, but she forced it away and kept moving. Heat radiated from above and below.

She tried to recall her drive to this place. Was the road to the right or to the left? Near the brown mountains or toward that small rise? If only she could get back to the highway, where a passing motorist might save her. Her skin felt too tight. A dizzying buzz filled her ears.

She pushed herself forward, stumbling now.

Another mile farther, or maybe it was only yards—she had lost all sense of place—she entered a section of rough dirt. She lurched across it, her toe stubbing against a spinelike rock. She felt, rather than saw, the serrated earth skidding up to meet her. The ground grated sickeningly against the flesh of her arms and belly, scraping the skin open. She tasted dust and bile and rusted iron.

She blinked at the shock, then summoned what willpower remained and got to her feet. Move, *she thought, but after only a few steps, a wave of nausea overtook her.*

She bent and vomited up a viscous string of yellow-green fluid. Pain knifed through her skull. Her stomach convulsed and she gagged again, but nothing came up. A shiver ran through her body. Why did she suddenly feel cold?

She straightened, felt the desert tilt around her, and staggered backward, falling on her butt.

Get up. Get up.

She groaned, rolled to her knees, and shook her head, trying to clear it. A few yards away, something moved. A ribbon of brown and black slithered across her path, disturbed from a rocky bit of shade by the vibrations of her fall. She gasped, pushed herself to her feet, and staggered away.

She could no longer see her pursuer, but that didn't mean the chase had ended.

Go, go.

Somewhere above her, a raven croaked. Ethan's favorite bird.

Her clouded brain summoned her last image of him: striding into the airport terminal for a trip from which he would never return. She missed him so much.

Before he left he had told her that, of the two of them, she was the stronger. But that was a lie. It was weakness that had brought her into this trouble. And it was Ethan's strength that had eventually killed him.

Keep the secret.

She moved again, now in deeper sand, her heart beating a thready rhythm. She tried to swallow but couldn't.

What was that ahead of her?

She swayed to a stop, peered into the desert.

Her cracked lips formed a single word: "Ethan."

There he was. A tall, dark figure in the distance, shimmering in the heat. He wasn't dead. It had all been a mistake. He had come to save her.

She raised a bloodied hand to let him know she had seen him, and saw his arms lift in return. But no.

She frowned as the figure seemed to sprout great wings and rise into the air, moving swiftly toward her. She felt a brush of wind. Ethan was flying.

She strained her sun-scorched eyes to see him, lifted her arms so he could grab her. But as she did, pain stabbed her chest. Dark spots danced in front of her eyes.

She bent, trying to stop the agony that stretched across her shoulders and down her arms. She heard a primal grunt and wondered vaguely from where it had originated. She felt herself falling. A shadow slid over her and then disappeared.

"Come back," she whispered, though the actual words didn't make it beyond her lips, beyond the dying cells in her brain that governed thought and sight and touch.

She never felt the raven that came at dusk to peck at the skin on her cheek.

CHAPTER 1

Aloa Snow sat on the Vallejo Street steps, leaned back on her elbows, and lifted her face to the sun. She could feel her stomach hollow against the heaviness of the manila envelope in her lap. It had been thirty-two hours since she'd eaten.

Her head thrummed with lightness as the day's warmth spread through her. Her hip bones pressed against her jeans like stone butterfly wings. She felt alive, perceptive, in control. Dangerous feelings.

Seven o'clock, she promised herself. Seven o'clock and she would eat.

Her unbalancing had begun at 9:00 a.m. the day before, as one of San Francisco's August drizzles fogged the front window of her house in North Beach. She'd just finished pitching a story about a new stem cell treatment for deafness to a cranky editor at *Senior Trend* magazine when her phone rang. She didn't recognize the number and, for a moment, let herself imagine it might be an unknown editor with a decent gig. Something better than "Friendly People are Happier People," which she'd written last week for a cosmetics company's blog. The truth was, she would take anything. Well, almost anything. She was down to her last $700.

"Aloa Snow," she had answered, remembering to keep the desperation out of her voice. Desperation was not an attractive quality on anybody, least of all a writer who'd become the journalistic equivalent of a bottom-feeder.

"It's been a long time," the caller said. The voice was male with the slightest trace of a Georgia accent, and Aloa's heart stuttered. She had not heard from him in more than eighteen years.

"Don't hang up. Please."

Aloa's fingers tightened on her phone.

"It's me. Michael."

"I have to go," Aloa said.

"Just hear me out, OK?"

The line hissed in the silence that followed, and Aloa pictured the boy Michael had been: shaggy-haired, a runner's body, haunted dark eyes. Michael had been in her dad's high school biology class when a police officer had summoned the teenager into the hallway one December afternoon. Michael's father, a colonel at a nearby army base, had mowed the lawn, hung the holiday lights, then turned a hunting rifle on his wife, his infant daughter, and, finally, himself. Aloa's father had gathered up the shell-shocked boy, found a substitute for his class, and brought Michael home, where he'd lived for the next three years.

"I need to ask you something first," Aloa said. It was the thing that had set off all that had followed in her life, the thing that made loneliness flood in if she wasn't careful. She thought she might never get another chance for an answer.

"All right," he said.

She took a long breath. "Did you ever feel bad for leaving him?"

Another silence, this one longer. Aloa wondered if he'd hung up.

"Every day," he said, finally.

Outside, a dog yipped three high-pitched barks.

"You know he died three months after you left."

"I didn't hear until much later. I'm so sorry."

"Sorry doesn't change what you did."

"I want to make it up to you. I know you're having a hard time."

Aloa glanced around the house her grandmother had built, at the narrow shotgun rooms, at the scuffed wood floors, at the front window with its view of the bay.

"I don't want your charity," she said.

"It's not charity."

"Then what is it?"

"I need your help. You've heard about Novo, right?"

Because Aloa didn't live in a cave in the Himalayas, she knew what Michael Collins had become: software developer, tech genius, philanthropist. Novo was an independent newsroom Michael recently had founded and financed against what he saw as an underfunded and increasingly pandering media.

"I don't do investigative stuff anymore."

"You were one of the best."

"Goodbye, Michael."

"Wait," Michael said. "This is about a girl, a runner. She died. Out in the desert. The cops said it was a suicide, but I got an email from her mother. She said her daughter was murdered, that the police didn't look hard enough. I'd like you to find out what happened."

"I know what you're trying to do," Aloa said.

A pause. "I'll pay you. Fifteen thousand dollars."

Aloa thought of her skimpy bank account, the mortgage payment due in a week. She'd never begrudged the money her mother had borrowed against the house to pay for the medical bills that were piling up around her, but the thought of losing the home her grandmother had worked so hard for made her sick. Fifteen grand would cover six months of payments with something left over for taxes. "That's guilt money, Michael," she said.

"Ten thousand, then. Plus expenses," Michael said. "That's our standard rate."

Aloa closed her eyes. "I can't."

"Just look at what I've got, please. See what you think. See if you agree with me. The editors at Novo think there's nothing there, and I told them I wouldn't overrule their judgment, but I need to do this, 'Lo. I really do. You're the only one who would understand."

Aloa sighed.

"Good." He rushed on before she could say anything. "I'll get everything I have to you."

"There are no guarantees, Michael."

"I know. Just see what's there. If you don't want to do it, I won't bother you again. I promise. Unless you want me to." A trace of hope.

Aloa rubbed a hand over her face. "No, Michael."

"All right. I understand." A pause. "Thank you for taking a look, at least."

The manila envelope had arrived that same evening at seven. Flown in by private jet from New York, the package had shown up in the hands of a young man in tight jeans and a button-down shirt who had said, "Mr. Collins wanted you to have it as soon as possible."

Aloa had taken the thick envelope and set it on her desk unopened. By then, it had already been ten hours since she'd eaten.

CHAPTER 2

It was 7:00 p.m., a full thirty-four hours since she'd eaten, when Aloa finally pushed her way through the fly-speckled door into Justus, the dive bar/blues club/North Beach hangout located on a narrow alley a few blocks from her house. Actually, Aloa would have needed a half dozen more slashes to describe the cubbyhole tavern owned by a former Hollywood costume designer named Erik and his husband, Guillermo, a chef on the run from some unnamed Colombian drug cartel. It was a place cluttered with movie memorabilia and flea-market tables. A place where it wouldn't be unusual to find Robben Ford or Cassandra Wilson slipping onto the tiny wood stage for a Monday night set, or for a discussion of poetry to end in a fistfight. A place where old men with gray ponytails and shadowy pasts hunched over glasses of cheap red wine, and where puzzling fusion dishes appeared on the chalkboard menu—hot and sour soup with pierogi, salmon confit with wasabi mayo—each one a mysterious coupling, each one incredibly delicious.

"Ah, the prodigal daughter has returned," Erik cried as Aloa stepped through the door. He was a bear of a man with a thick neck, a barrel chest, and arms that looked like they'd spent years wielding a lumberjack's ax instead of a Swedish sewing machine. "Baxter's been asking about you."

Aloa closed the door and gave a tight smile. Baxter was a fight-scarred tabby that had adopted Guillermo five years ago. Along with a stubborn independence born from being tossed out of a car on a busy highway in his first eight weeks of life, Baxter had a dislike for rules and a kind of psychic draw toward the wounded, so anyone who came into the bar after losing a job or being served with divorce papers might suddenly find a scrawny, one-eyed cat curled up in his or her lap.

Baxter, Erik always said, was the feline version of Aloa—both pushovers for anybody who needed saving.

"Where is the old boy?" Aloa asked, stepping into the bar's muddy shadows.

"Upstairs, sleeping off half a braised pork chop," Erik said.

"Well, tell him I miss him too," Aloa said. She headed for a spot in the far corner of the room but was stopped by a yelp.

"Oh my god, sweetie," Erik said. "Please don't tell me you've gone Mary-Kate 2008 on us."

Aloa looked down at her half-laced Timberland boots, her ragged jeans, the old wool sweater she'd tugged on over a too-large Clash T-shirt that had belonged to a photojournalist she'd accidentally slept with a long time ago.

"I've just been a little distracted," she said, and pulled the sweater more tightly across her chest.

"Honey, that outfit isn't a distraction," Erik said. "That's a cry for help." He finished pulling a beer for a down-on-his-luck songwriter and came out to hug her.

"I'm fine. Really," said Aloa, sliding behind a rickety table and setting the still-unopened envelope in front of her. "Everything's good."

Erik pulled up a chair. "Oh, honey, come on down off your crucifix. Tell Papa what's wrong."

"It's nothing."

"Sweetie." Erik drew out the word as a warning against a lie.

Aloa's fingers shook against the envelope and she pulled her hands into her lap. "Somebody called with a job. It threw me, I guess."

Erik frowned. "Have you been eating?"

"Yes."

Erik waited. He was one of the few who knew her history: the slide into anorexia in college, her hospitalization when she got down to eighty-seven pounds, the three months in a psych ward, the backsliding, and, finally, her stubborn hold on normalcy.

"A little." Aloa could not admit more.

"Gully," Erik called over his shoulder. "We've got a 9-1-1 here."

Gully, or Guillermo, as he was known to everyone but his husband, stuck his head out from behind the swinging kitchen doors. He was dark-haired, slender, bordering on beautiful.

"A steak. Stat," Erik said.

Guillermo came into the room. He wiped his hands on a towel he'd tucked into the waistband of his canary-yellow pants.

"She's not eating." Erik waved a hand at Aloa.

"You are *enferma*?" Guillermo asked.

Aloa could feel herself coming off the high of restriction, felt darkness settling in. "I'm fine. I just didn't feel like cooking."

"Pssssh," Erik said.

"A steak is too much. I have such a very thing," Guillermo said. "A vegetable pho *con* Peking duck. Is accurate for you." He hurried away.

"I love that man, despite his massacring of the English language," Erik said, and turned back to Aloa. He tapped a beefy finger on the envelope. "Whatever is in there, honey, it's not worth your health."

"I know," Aloa said.

"Rent your room out to horrible strangers. Sell your books. I hear Big Sue's is hiring." Big Sue's was a strip club a few blocks away.

Aloa smiled tiredly. "They'd have to rename it. Flat Sue's."

"Honey, don't disparage those two upstanding little sisters of yours." Erik nodded toward her chest. "It's your head I'm worried about. It's time to forgive yourself. Time to take off the hair shirt. And I'm not talking about whatever that is." He circled his finger at Aloa's T-shirt. "That should be burned."

"It's not that easy," Aloa said. "I let a lot of people down."

Two years before, when Aloa was working for the *Los Angeles Times*, she'd written a story about a group of Vietnamese nail salon workers living in overcrowded apartments, working seven days a week, with their expenses, including supplies, being deducted from their meager paychecks and tips so they were earning less than five dollars an hour.

Her editor told her he wanted a face on what was essentially a labor story the same day Aloa's mother had been admitted to the hospital with complications from her chemotherapy. Aloa had written the nail salon piece in one Dexedrine-fueled eighteen-hour stretch, combining pieces of stories from workers into a fictitious manicurist she called Binh Nguyen. It was a sin against the first commandment of journalism—*Thou shalt not make stuff up*—and yet Aloa had tried to rationalize the piece as being reflective of the truth and had filed the story. That same afternoon, she had asked for two weeks of family leave and fled north.

A month after her mother's funeral, Aloa had been called into the editor's office and given the choice of resigning or being fired. While her fraud wasn't at the same level as some of journalism's worst offenders, the editor said, it added fuel to the fires of those who attacked the press as manipulative liars. It also didn't help that the newspaper had recently run a series of ads touting her as its award-winning senior investigative reporter.

Aloa had gathered what small bit of pride she had left and wrote the resignation letter.

"You won't make them feel any better by dying for your sins," Erik said. "If my carpal tunnel wasn't acting up, I'd tear down those curtains over there and turn you into Scarlett O'Hara, because you're a survivor, honey. You're smart and funny and fierce and beautiful."

He touched her cheek, the way Aloa's dad used to. Emotion rose and she shoved it down.

"That would make me the best-dressed woman in the Opera Boxes," she said, referring to a series of concrete openings in the Mission District where the homeless went in rainy weather.

"Don't throw that kind of shade on yourself, honey." Erik tsked. "Life's dark enough."

"Here you is," Guillermo interrupted, setting a steaming bowl of fragrant broth in front of Aloa. It was filled with noodles, cilantro, bean sprouts, slices of crispy duck, lime on the side. "A *grande* bowl of love," Guillermo said, just as the bar door pushed open and a rumpled man with a gray ponytail and a porkpie hat came in.

"Looks like the Brain Farm is starting to arrive," Erik said.

The Brain Farm was what Erik called the group of old anarchists and rebels who came every evening around seven o'clock to squabble and complain and drink.

"Ink," said the grizzled man, nodding to Aloa. He was known only as Tick. All the anarchists gave themselves nicknames, an old habit born of years of hiding and guerrilla theater and monkeywrenching. If they liked you, they assigned you a pseudonym too. Aloa's was "Ink" for what supposedly ran through her veins after years of newspapering. Tick wouldn't talk about his, though there were dark hints about a bank bombing in the sixties.

Erik rose from the chair. "Let me get you a glass of wine before those old farts drain me dry," he said.

"Water is fine," she said.

He touched Aloa's cheek again. "It's OK, sweetie. Don't forget there are people who love you and care about you and won't judge you. Not ever."

Aloa felt a lump form in her throat and speared a piece of the duck into her mouth, chewing hard until the feeling passed.

She hated to cry.

CHAPTER 3

Aloa believed cops hid behind impersonal words in their reports in order to blunt the horrible things they saw every day: "Decedent" for the four-year-old girl who'd been starved to death, "Reporting Party" for the blind widower whose bank account had been emptied by a once-trusted helper, "Domestic Violence" when a young woman's eye socket was shattered by her husband's fist.

It had been her job as a journalist to uncloak those words, to lay bare the ugliness. She took a breath and began to read the reports Michael had given her.

In this case, the decedent was a twenty-five-year-old woman by the name of Hayley Poole. She was five foot five, 140 pounds, with brown hair and a small scar above her right eyebrow. On Friday, July 14, Hayley had gone with friends to a place called Jeremiah Valley in a remote section of the Nevada desert for a camping/bouldering weekend. She had left the campout in her Toyota pickup around 5:00 a.m. on Sunday after a confrontation with two locals who'd arrived with guns and accused the group of trespassing.

Hayley had reportedly yelled "nature is free" at the two men, causing her friends to hustle her into her truck. Everyone scattered into their cars and left, including the gunmen. A friend reported Hayley missing after she failed to show up for an appointment later that evening.

Searchers found the young woman's abandoned vehicle on a dirt track forty-six hours after the report. Her body was recovered a full day later. It was more than twenty miles from any road.

The medical examiner's report listed more than one hundred cuts on Hayley's feet and legs, along with deep wounds on her face, the inside of her left thigh, and the soft part of her belly. One of her eyes was missing from its socket, and flies had already begun feeding on her cracked lips. The examiner estimated the girl had been dead for seventy-eight hours when her body was found.

Cause of death, he concluded, was severe heatstroke brought on by 112-degree heat, a dry westerly wind, and drug and alcohol use. The wounds on the victim's body, excluding the cuts on her feet and legs, were the work of postmortem predators, although he was not sure about the missing eye.

Aloa flipped through the documents to the toxicology report. Hayley's blood work revealed low levels of potassium and sodium, along with traces of lysergic acid diethylamide, or LSD.

Aloa opened her Moleskine notebook and began a timeline, then a list of observations and questions. "Party girl or drug problem? Distance from camp to truck?" she wrote under the "Questions" heading and then added, "Background check, men with guns?"

She read on to discover that Hayley had been going through a rough patch before her death. Her longtime boyfriend had died on a climbing expedition three months earlier, and because of a shin injury, a documentary being made about her exploits as an adventure runner appeared to be in jeopardy. She'd also lost an important sponsor and was living in her truck.

Aloa frowned at the term "adventure runner," and thumbed through the documents until she came to a copy of an *Outside* magazine article she'd spotted earlier. In it, the writer described Hayley as one of the stars of a movement called FKT, a mostly solo and rebellious sport in which runners tried to log the Fastest Known Time from one point to another. There were no firing guns, no race bibs, and few witnesses. Most of the time, athletes would simply pick a mountain or a brutal landscape and begin to run.

According to the article, Hayley had set a speed record for the 211-mile John Muir Trail in the Sierra Nevada of California and went on to destroy the women's record for the fastest time running rim to rim in the Grand Canyon. She was the best in a class of women who moved through the outdoors like a strong and graceful wind.

Her latest project was a quest to win what was considered the Olympics of this obscure sport, something called the Cloudrunner Race Series. It was a string of gnarly, high-altitude endurance footraces around the globe in which runners tested not only their bodies but also their minds. For a moment, Aloa wondered if Hayley's lonely death in the wilderness of Nevada had been some kind of gesture or simply a sad coincidence.

An accompanying photo of Hayley showed her at the end of her Grand Canyon run. Her long hair was pulled back in a ponytail; a spray of freckles was scattered on her cheeks. The look on her face appeared to be one of exhaustion and joy, but there was something else beneath it. An undercurrent of wariness. As if Hayley already knew this triumph was fleeting and then she would be on to the next challenge, the next test.

Aloa understood how that felt: to have failure always lurking, to have success be as short-lived as the next day's news cycle. And yet, this woman had been used to enduring hardship, to pushing herself past pain. How could someone like that kill herself?

Aloa cleared her throat and warned herself not to get attached to the victim. That was no way to examine the facts clearly. She penned the questions, "Why lost sponsor?" and "Boyfriend's cause of death?" in her notebook, then returned to the police report.

The investigating officer described the campsite, the braided tangle of dirt roads in the area, and Hayley's drinking and drug use (half a pint of vodka followed by the LSD) before her disappearance. He also reported the discovery of a note written on a gas receipt in Hayley's truck.

It read simply, *"I'm sorry."*

"Death is presumed to be the result of suicide brought on by depression, and aggravated by drug and alcohol use," the investigating officer had concluded.

Aloa leaned back in her chair. The Brain Farm was hotly arguing. She had finished only half the bowl of soup and taken a few bites of the duck, but what she had eaten had tasted good and it now sat warm in her stomach. A culinary yank back from the ledge of relapse.

She took a long pull of water.

So far, it would seem as if the instincts of the editors at Novo had been right. A young woman had hit hard times and decided to end it all by going out into the wilderness. The only other explanation was some kind of deadly misjudgment, a walk into the desert followed by a loss of direction, confusion. And yet, according to the report, the young woman's shoes and socks had been found fifty feet from her truck. *If you were going for a hike in the desert, you wouldn't take off your shoes,* Aloa thought.

She knew it would be simple to turn down Michael's assignment, though what the ten grand would mean for her finances was harder to dismiss. Maybe she could turn her grandmother's bedroom into one of those Airbnb rentals. Maybe she could apply to a temp agency; although even if she got a job tomorrow, she wouldn't be able to make next month's mortgage. She thought about how bad it would feel to lose the house that had been part of her dad's legacy to her, but she also wasn't sure she was ready to let herself be publicly pummeled by the haters and trolls who would resurrect her mistake the minute her byline reappeared on a news story. She slid the documents back into the envelope.

I can't do it, Dad, she thought.

Her dad was the one who had named her after a genus of moth in the family Arctiidae. He was a thinker, a naturalist, a man who preferred to observe the outdoor world rather than write research papers about it. Consequently, he'd been denied tenure at the university where he'd been hired as an assistant professor of biology, and wound up at a small high school outside of Columbus, Georgia, much to the disappointment of Aloa's mother.

According to family lore, Aloa's father had taken her into the woods ten days after she was born. He had pointed out downy woodpeckers, brown thrashers, and a Cooper's hawk diving for its supper. He had described the birds' habits, their markings, and whistled their songs to his infant daughter. It became their Saturday routine, this observation of birds, this quiet conversation about nature. His death had destroyed the family's fragile financial situation and Aloa had moved to San Francisco with her angry and bitter mother, taken in by Aloa's paternal grandmother, Maja.

Aloa looked down at the documents poking out of the envelope and remembered what her dad had said about relying on general impressions to make identifications. In the world of bird-watching, that technique was called "jizz."

"You must look for the details. You must spend time," he told Aloa. "Jizz is the provenance of those who have no patience. Not scientists."

An image came into her head of her father sitting unmoving in the woods, enthralled by the movement of birds, by their color and sounds. His entire life, he'd prided himself on rigorous examination, on not letting failure stop the search for scientific knowledge. She knew if he were here, he would tell her that a single error was no reason to stop the pursuit of truth and that no material thing was worth the price of fear—not even his mother's house. Slowly, Aloa pulled the papers back out onto the table.

The bar was full now: locals coming in after work, artists clasping mugs of beer in their paint-stained hands, a lone guitarist setting up onstage while Erik mixed drinks and hustled bowls of Peking duck pho to tables.

An hour later, Aloa had reread most of the documents and jotted down a list of things that needed exploring. At the top of her catalog was the fact that one of the campers on the trip had never been interviewed, or even definitely identified, by the investigating officer. The other was the discovery of a shell casing from a Glock 19 located within twenty feet of Hayley's vehicle, which the officer dismissed as unremarkable in an area that was well known for target practice and drunken shooting parties.

Was the only requirement for being a cop in that place the ability to walk and breathe at the same time? Aloa wondered.

Her dad had warned her about glimpsing what you thought was a rare bird and then propping up your identification by filling in details based on what you wanted to see instead of what was actually there.

"Believing is not seeing," he always said.

Had the detective been so lazy and sure of his suicide theory that he'd dismissed clues that would indicate something else?

Aloa looked at the documents scattered on the table and tugged out the magazine article with Hayley's photo. She stared into the athlete's eyes.

Despite Occam's razor, which said that the simplest answer was often the correct one, in Aloa's experience, it was just as true that easy answers were often wrong. And wasn't every human owed at least the benefit of the doubt?

What if Hayley's mother was right and someone had murdered the athlete by chasing her into the desert until she collapsed? What if someone had threatened Hayley and she'd run and then lost her way?

Aloa thought of her own disgrace and the page two headline that had appeared the next day. DISCREDITED REPORTER TO LEAVE *TIMES*. If she died tomorrow, Aloa knew her obituary would carry the same descriptor: DISCREDITED REPORTER DIES. In the same way that Hayley's life would always end with the dark punctuation of suicide.

Aloa knew she would never be able to recover her own good name, but maybe taking a closer look at Hayley's death would be a small atonement for her failing. Maybe it would be a tiny payment against

19

her karmic debt. The young woman with the haunted eyes deserved a shot at redemption, something Aloa had not been given.

She brushed a hand over the photograph, felt the weight of Hayley's shame and of her own, and made her decision.

She would email Michael tonight and accept the assignment with a list of provisions: no contact between them; half her payment due within twenty-four hours; the option to quit the story at any time if she felt it was falling apart; and final approval of all headlines, subheads, and edits—if she agreed to write it at all.

She slid the papers back into the envelope.

Shit, she thought.

CHAPTER 4

Aloa had settled her bill, thanked Guillermo for the food, and was now walking up the hill to her house with a to-go cup of Macallan twelve-year single malt scotch.

"Daddy's little helper," Erik had said, and winked as he slipped the container into her hand.

Aloa let herself into her house and switched on her grandmother's old glass chandelier, illuminating the redwood-paneled living room. A floor-to-ceiling bookcase lined one wall, under which sat a heavy dining room table and a straight-backed chair: her "office."

The house was long and narrow, each room opening off an extended hallway: living area, kitchen, two small bedrooms, bathroom, and a small porch with a washer and dryer. It was sandwiched between two stucco-and-glass monstrosities that had sprung up in the last five years and would have lived in eternal shadow except that her grandmother had possessed the foresight to install a series of pyramid-shaped skylights that allowed daylight to stream in.

Aloa looked up and could see a reflection of light from a chandelier in the neighbor's living room, a sliver of moon. She went into her tiny kitchen and poured the scotch into a tumbler, licking a drop from her finger.

She unlaced her boots, retrieved her laptop, and stopped for a moment to stare out the home's best feature: a large window that offered a startling view of the San Francisco Bay. She watched a trail of red taillights stream across the Bay Bridge and then turned, put the scotch on an end table, and settled into her grandmother's favorite chair.

It was a fat, overstuffed thing that had once been upholstered in burgundy velvet but had faded to the color of cheap rosé. After her mother had died, Aloa had cleared out all the accumulated stuff: the lace tablecloths and fussy silver, the knickknacks and throw rugs. All that was left was the rosé chair, the table, and a red leather couch she'd salvaged from her apartment in Los Angeles. Emptiness was good.

Aloa took a sip of the scotch, which was smoky and yet sweet. She lifted the glass in a small toast to Erik and pulled the case files into her lap.

One of her dad's most important lessons had been that a bird-watcher must always consider habitat, behaviors, and time of year in making an identification. It was a way of observing that had set Aloa apart as an investigative journalist. That, plus a dogged determination, an instinct for spotting inconsistencies, and an uncanny eye for detail, had led some of her colleagues to nickname her "Herlock Holmes" behind her back. But it was exactly those traits that had brought her awards, pay raises, and jobs at bigger papers.

Until she screwed up.

She wouldn't do that now.

She pulled out the crime scene report: a record of what was found in and around Hayley's truck, a silver 2002 Toyota with four-wheel drive and a SnugTop camper shell.

Inside the low-slung shell, the technician had found Hayley's wallet with fifty-four dollars in bills, a tent, two sleeping bags, a backpack filled with clothes, four pairs of running shoes, and a one-burner stove. The list reinforced what Aloa had learned from the reports: Hayley was a woman who lived in her truck, an athlete, a woman who relied on herself.

The alleged suicide note had been located on the driver's seat. It was written on the back of a gas receipt from a station in Reno, and Aloa wondered if Hayley's apology had been for what she was about to do or for something else. Some sin for which she sought forgiveness? She made a note in her Moleskine and continued cataloging.

She noted the truck's high mileage, its near-empty gas tank, and a cell phone charger but no phone in evidence. She then turned to a statement taken from Hayley's ex-roommate, a twenty-four-year-old named Samantha Foster who lived in a section of San Francisco known as Dogpatch. Once home to rusting factories and crumbling Victorians, it was now filling with start-ups, craftspeople, and trendy cafés, a familiar story line in this city by the bay.

According to Samantha, Hayley had fallen apart after the death of her boyfriend, who'd died on a trip to Africa. She'd begun drinking heavily, which had led to a police complaint after a drunken scuffle with another patron in a local bar. That had been followed by an incident in which Hayley had been ordered off a Muni bus after the driver had complained about her loud inebriation—and the fact she'd vomited all over a fellow passenger. Vodka, apparently, had been Hayley's first stage of grief.

The ex-roommate said Hayley had sobered up after that and returned to training for her Cloudrunner quest, but she either didn't know or wasn't asked why Hayley had moved into her truck. The detective only noted that the ex-roomie had said Hayley had been acting "weird." The detective did not elaborate on what that meant.

"Christ," Aloa muttered at the man's incompetence.

Aloa opened her laptop, praying no one had taken down Hayley's social media sites, and was rewarded with Hayley's still-open Facebook, Instagram, and Twitter accounts. A bit of luck.

She examined photos of sunsets, of Hayley trail-running in someplace called Superstition Wilderness, of her crossing the finish line of her first Cloudrunner competition in Washington state. The posts revealed the kind of woman who'd rather be caught in a blizzard than a nine-to-five job, a woman who shunned high heels and expensive clothes for a life of freedom and wandering.

There were photos of her boyfriend, Ethan—*handsome,* Aloa thought—and one or two old shots of an aunt who'd apparently raised her for a time. There were the requisite photos of sunsets and meals (mostly vegetarian), plus a Mother's Day shot of her mom holding her as an infant.

There were also hints of darkness.

One selfie showed Hayley alone on a wind-tossed, empty beach with the message: *It's only when I'm outdoors that I can be my true self. Don't judge me if you don't know me.*

Aloa swirled the scotch in her glass, leaned her head against the back of the chair, and considered the woman Hayley had been. She had known loss, just as Aloa had. She had tried to rise above her peers, the same as Aloa had in her work. She wondered if Hayley also had eating issues. If she counted calories along with the miles. If she craved control over bodily weakness.

Behaviors and habitat, Aloa thought.

She returned to her laptop, typed in "death by heatstroke," and read how, as the body overheated, proteins and membranes around the cells in the body—especially the brain and heart—began to malfunction or were destroyed altogether. Heatstroke victims became dizzy and nauseous, then disoriented. Hallucinations were common. An autopsy would reveal muscle changes that pointed to high temperatures in the body. Like being cooked alive.

Aloa shuddered.

More results led her to stories of immigrants dying in the desert heat as they fled from Mexico toward what they believed would be a better life in the United States. Humanitarian groups reported finding the bodies of men, women, and children with cracked eyelids and swollen tongues protruding from withered lips. Worst of all were the trails of dried blood on some of the victims' faces. Those dying from dehydration would sometimes cry tears of blood.

"My god," Aloa said, and clicked out of the site.

She picked up the case file and again read through the gruesome list of Hayley's injuries. Lividity, the coroner said, indicated Hayley had died where her body was found. Aloa reached over and finished the last of her scotch, feeling the beginning of a warm buzz. She liked that spot between sober and high, between control and release. She set down the glass and contemplated pouring herself another drink, but instead flipped to the next page and found a photo of Hayley's naked body laid out on a stainless steel autopsy table.

The muscles in her belly tightened.

The fluorescent lights made Hayley look like a waxen image of herself. Her once muscled and smooth legs were slashed with cuts, her skin pale except for the places where ragged wounds dug into the flesh of her cheek, belly, and thigh. Her eye socket stared emptily while her cracked lips told the story of the flies and beetles that had arrived to feast on her flesh. Aloa imagined the living Hayley against the photo before her and looked away.

Such a horrible way to die.

She sat there for a moment, breathing deeply in and out, then returned to her work, lifting the photo to examine it more closely. She could see half-moons of dirt under Hayley's fingernails, an old scar on her collarbone, and, finally, something that drew Aloa's attention: a gash at Hayley's hairline. The cut was straight, about three inches across, and stood out when compared to the irregularity of Hayley's other injuries. Aloa's mind backtracked and she tugged the crime scene report out of the file. Item number twenty-three was a rust-colored smear on the left edge of the camper shell's hatchback. Aloa turned to the lab results. The smear had never been tested. Could it have been blood? The result of an accidental collision with the open hatchback? *Or,* thought Aloa, *a deliberate shove as the result of some kind of struggle?* More sloppiness on the detective's part. She made a note and moved on, fully awake now.

She scanned the search reports, weather conditions, and a brief note about the missing witness who the two other campers had described as a guy who'd just happened by and decided to hang out with them. The only information they provided was that he was tall and called himself Boots. She filled her Moleskine with four pages of notes and questions, made herself a cup of tea, and clicked through more websites.

At 1:00 a.m. she finally turned out the lights, brushed her teeth, and climbed into bed, but the images of Hayley's body and of immigrants' deaths rose and turned into a slide show she couldn't stop. At 2:30 a.m. she gave up, went to the hall closet, and took out the only antidote she knew for the insomnia that had plagued her for most of her adult life.

She padded into the living room, sat on a stool, and spread open her legs. She settled the cello between her knees, the instrument's neck warm against her skin.

She set her fingers, lifted the bow, and, in the darkness, began to play, the music rising, the notes vibrating through the instrument and into her body. The music filled her and drove out thoughts of horrible deaths, of Michael's return, and of mistakes that could never be made right.

She played the prelude to Bach's Cello Suite No. 1 over and over until peace came. Only then did she sleep.

CHAPTER 5

Aloa woke at 8:30 a.m., her sheets twisted around her legs, her eyes ragged from only five hours of sleep. She pulled on yoga pants and a sweatshirt, did a few stretches, and went into the kitchen. Fog pressed gray against the front window. Today would be different. No more restrictive bullshit.

She pulled her beloved Aldo Rossi French press coffee maker from the shelf next to the stove, set a kettle of water to flame, and began her morning ritual: heat water to boil and let stand thirty seconds, warm carafe with hot water and dump, grind beans, settle grounds, pour half of the hot water over the grounds for thirty seconds of what was known as bloom, then add the rest of the water, let steep for three and a half minutes, press, and pour. Leave the Mr. Coffees and Keurigs to others. This was the only way to make coffee.

When the brew was ready, Aloa poured herself a mug and inhaled, savoring the scent, the rich dark color. She took a long pull and then checked her email. The contract with Michael was sitting in her inbox as promised. She sent it to the printer, put a whole-wheat bagel into the toaster, and made herself get out a jar of peanut butter despite the quick stab of guilt that came with the knowledge of how much fat and calories it would add. She hoped it hadn't been a mistake to let Michael back into her life.

She was fourteen when Michael had come to live with them, a boy Aloa's father had treated as gently as if he were a wounded bird. Her dad had pulled the desk out of his office and moved in a double bed, which he covered in flannel sheets and a soft quilt. He spoke quietly, bought the boy new clothes so he would not have to go back to the house where his family was killed, and cooked pots of pasta and grilled steaks, even while his wife, Aloa's mother, told him his salary barely supported three of them and asked how he expected it to cover four. But she shouldn't have worried, because Michael lived like a ghost among them. He picked at his food and shunned the new clothes for what he had been wearing on the day his family died. He sat in his new room with the lights out and took showers only when Aloa's father reminded him.

A month in, Aloa's dad persuaded him to go on their Saturday nature walk, but Michael had lagged so far behind Aloa and her father, it was as if he wasn't there.

"Nature reveals herself when she is ready," Aloa's dad told her afterward. "We need to be patient."

And so they were.

As Aloa's father told the story later, he looked out the front window one evening to see Michael striding up and down the block. He thought of the way a caged leopard will pace from one side of his enclosure to the other to relieve the mental stress of its prison. He'd gone out the next day and bought running shoes and shorts for both him and Michael.

"Oh my god. Really, Ben?" Aloa's mother had said to her husband when she saw the bill for $200.

The next day her father and Michael had set off into the woods behind their house. They ran two miles on a shadowed hiking trail and came back. Michael went off to take a shower and Aloa's father smiled.

A week later, they were running three miles, then five, then seven, then ten. Aloa's dad never said what he and Michael talked about on the trail, but after a while Michael stopped holing up in his room. He ate dinner with them, joined the cross-country team, and was named the year's top scholar-athlete in the town newspaper. And, as Aloa watched, Michael became part of her father's life. The two ran a marathon together, became fascinated with electronics, and, on warm evenings, would play catch in the backyard.

Sometimes, Aloa's dad called him "son."

But Aloa's father wasn't the only one captivated by this intelligent and broken boy. Slowly, Aloa found herself being pulled into his orbit too.

In the evenings, as she struggled with calculus homework at the kitchen table, he would pull up a chair and carefully explain the beauties of math to her, never once attributing her mistakes to stupidity or incompetence, as her mother did. He lugged her cello to her recitals, listened patiently to her overwritten short stories, and once held back her hair while she vomited after a party that had featured way too much peppermint schnapps.

In the summers, he drove her out to the lake while Aloa's father, under the watchful eye of his wife, did the chores he had neglected for most of the school year. Aloa and Michael would swim out to an old raft and lie in the sun where he would open up, talking about music and life and whether it was better to live in a city like New York or in the mountains of Colorado.

She picked New York. He picked Colorado.

After, they would swim back to the shore, turn on the radio, and leave the car doors open while they ate the lunch Aloa had packed: ham sandwiches, potato chips, and, sometimes, beer Aloa stole from the basement refrigerator. Once, she had opened her eyes and caught him watching her as she lay near the lake's edge in her bikini. Their eyes had caught, and for a moment, the space between them had seemed to pulse with an energy that Aloa could, or would, not forget.

Then, on an April evening, when she was seventeen and he eighteen, they'd found themselves alone in the house. He'd suggested a movie and Aloa, feeling reckless, made them Jack and Cokes. He slid

Legends of the Fall into the VCR while the moon rose and a warm wind awakened the buds outside. Halfway through the movie, she had seen a glisten of tears in his eyes and had taken his hand. Then somehow they were kissing and their clothes had tumbled off and by the time the film was finished, they were sweating and sex-sated, Michael murmuring "oh my god" into her hair.

The next morning, when he would not look at her at the breakfast table, she had told herself their lovemaking had been nothing more than sad-movie sex, no different than her tryst with Jason Meyerson, to whom she'd given her virginity during a New Year's Eve party that same year. Only, the truth was, what had happened was much more than that because, at some point in that warm and wanton evening, Aloa had lost her heart completely to Michael.

Four days later, Michael left with no explanation beyond a note on the kitchen table, which said he had to leave and that he would be in touch. "Don't worry," he wrote, although Aloa's father did. He startled when the phone rang, hurried home to check the mail, and cornered anyone who had known Michael. He grew distracted, complained of headaches, and experienced periods of sleeplessness. Even his Saturday walks with Aloa weren't the same.

A few weeks before the Fourth of July, Aloa's father went for a six-mile run in the woods. A jogger found his body three hours later, and the coroner speculated that if someone had been with Aloa's father or had found him sooner, he might have survived the sudden and partial blockage of his left anterior descending artery.

Aloa blamed Michael for the stress he'd placed on her father and for not being there when he collapsed.

She also could not stop thinking of the note Michael had left on her pillow: "I'm sorry," it read.

CHAPTER 6

The morning fog misted Aloa's dark hair as she strode through the city. She told herself this was why she had cut it short when she'd fled to San Francisco from LA—the ease of styling in a maritime climate—but there was a part of her that admitted it may have also been some kind of penance.

She'd dressed that morning in black jeans, a white T-shirt, and a beautiful leather jacket she'd bought in LA. "Mary-Kate, my ass," she'd said as she changed, although she did not give up her Timberland boots. They were a throwback to her father, sturdy footwear that made you feel as if you were born to handle hardship.

She'd ringed her blue eyes in dark liner and slipped a platinum ring in the shape of a feather over her thumb. Four small silver hoops pierced the upper cartilage of her right ear. The piercings were all relics of her earlier life, each with a meaning linked to the time she had acquired them: the day of her release from the psych ward after she'd managed to gain ten pounds, her first reporting job, the afternoon a runaway she'd befriended while writing a story about homeless kids was found dead in an alley with a needle in her arm, and, finally, her firing from the *Times*.

Some people got tattoos. Aloa wounded cartilage.

She carried an old leather backpack over her shoulder, containing her notebook, a bottle of water, and two pens. In her pocket, her phone busily recorded her steps, her location, and her caloric output thanks to an app called HardE, which despite its overbearing name drew her like a bee to nectar. As a recovering anorexic, Aloa knew the dangers of recording movement and burned calories but thought if she could prove to herself that she consumed more than she used, it would show her stability, her resolve to live like a normal person. Yesterday's relapse had left her feeling unsteady.

She walked with long strides, her boots tapping out a four-four rhythm on the sidewalk. Her editor at the *Times*, a gruff man with tufts of graying hair, had once said Aloa looked like a heat-seeking missile when she walked. Aloa was pretty sure he hadn't meant it as a compliment.

Her steps took her past law offices and banks. Past litter-flecked alleys where life-worn humans slept under ragged blankets. Past coffee shops with six-dollar lattes. She no longer owned a car.

It took her a little less than an hour to get to her end point: a concrete warehouse in the Dogpatch neighborhood where Hayley's ex-roommate lived. Aloa frowned at the building, checked the address against the one she'd copied from the police report, and circled the structure. Could this be right?

She found three metal sliders covering what must have been work bays. At the far corner was a battered, army-green door. A stenciled sign announced 101–107. She stepped back, snapped a shot of the building with her phone, and opened the door to find a hallway bathed in flickering fluorescent light. Her footsteps echoed on a concrete floor as she followed the passageway along the building's length, locating 104. She knocked. *It's never this easy,* she thought, and it wasn't.

The door remained closed, silent. Aloa sighed and looked up and down the hallway.

As a reporter, she had always preferred the face-to-face interview, where the nervous tapping of a foot or the sadness behind a smile revealed hidden truths. An old reporter at the *Oregonian*, where she'd worked in the early days, called these forays "knock-and-talks," which had the ring of an honest day's work, which Aloa also liked. She continued on.

Apartment 105 yielded an angry young woman whom Aloa had apparently awakened; 106 held a paint-splattered man who said he knew nothing about a Samantha Foster in 104. He asked if she would like to join him in a morning whiskey. Aloa declined.

Aloa could hear music from behind 107's door. She hesitated, knocked. Waited. When there was no response, she knocked louder. This time, the music died and the door cracked open to reveal a man in a blue mechanic's coverall.

"I'm full up. Two transmissions waiting," the man said. He was broad-shouldered and looked to be in his late thirties. He had wild golden hair, what seemed like an overly large head, and a pair of too-big hands.

"I'm not here about a car," Aloa said.

"OK. Goodbye," he said, and began to close the door.

"Wait." Aloa shoved her boot into the space. Another reason for the sturdy Timberlands. "Please. I'm looking for someone. Samantha Foster."

"Gone." The big-headed man peered down the hallway.

"Do you know where she went?" Aloa persisted.

"No," the man said.

"How about Hayley Poole? Did you know her?"

His brown eyes scanned Aloa. "What's the password?" he asked.

Aloa frowned. "Sorry, I don't have a password. I'm a reporter. I mean, a researcher." It felt wrong to claim that title anymore. "I'm doing a story about Hayley, about how she died." The pressure of the door against her foot lessened slightly. "I'm looking at what the police might have missed; what was left behind."

A big hand suddenly gripped Aloa's arm and yanked her into the space. The door slammed behind her.

"That's it," the man whispered. "That's what Hayley said, that someone might come for what was left behind. I've been waiting and waiting." He let go of her arm and Aloa stepped back, her body buzzing with a quick shot of adrenaline. She took in the large man, the distance to the door.

"I knew it." The man paced away from her. "I knew you would come."

Aloa ran through her options: run, fight, or play along and see what happened. She picked "play along." The reporter who had taught her about knock-and-talks had also said the best way to deal with crazy was to step into their world. She touched the canister of pepper spray in her jacket pocket and lowered her voice conspiratorially. "She said you would have it."

"I kept it," the man said, and gestured toward a trash can filled with grease-stained rags. "Can you stand over there, please?"

"Sure," Aloa said, and watched the man make big Zorro-like slashes in front of the door.

"Auric barrier," he explained. "Nothing can penetrate."

"Good thinking," Aloa said.

He moved across the room with a limping gait and began unloading boxes of car parts and supplies onto the floor from a large metal case. Aloa kept one eye on him while she took in her surroundings. An older model Volvo with a raised hood was parked in the middle of an immaculate concrete floor. Tools hung from labeled hooks. A crisply made bed was tucked neatly into a corner with a small counter that contained a toaster oven and a sink next to it. Nearby was a blue motorcycle polished to a high sheen.

"So you and Hayley were friends?" she asked.

The man stopped. "She said it was OK. She loved Ethan best but she said I could be second."

Aloa heard the defensiveness in his voice. "I'm sure you were a good friend," she assured him quickly.

"I helped her all the time," the man said, and turned back to his task. "Big things, little things. Whatever she needed, I did it. Even with them out there."

Aloa frowned. "With who out where?" she asked.

"The watchers. But don't worry." He stopped his work and went over to a large rolling tool chest, yanked open a drawer, and pulled out a foot-long knife with a sharp, serrated blade and a leather handle.

"Jesus," Aloa said.

"I'll stop them. See? Nothing to it. Six angles of attack. Move in straight lines." For a moment, it seemed as if he was talking to the knife instead of her. "Can we keep it safe? Yes, we can. We can do it, Hayley. Roger that, I got your back. Evil things out there, Cal. But I trust you, big guy." He shoved the weapon back into the drawer. "You're my helper. My very good helper."

Omigod, thought Aloa.

She watched him go back to work, stopping for a moment to slide a piece of cardboard under a daddy longlegs and carry it to the sliding bay door. "Hurry," he told the arachnid before limping back to his task.

A few minutes later, the shelves were emptied and the man heaved aside the heavy case, his one-sided conversation resuming. "I'll fix it, Hayley," he muttered. "Don't be late. Socket set. Torque wrench. Finder-minder. Finder-minder."

He glanced over at Aloa and seemed surprised to see her there. Something came into his brown eyes. "Oh yes, she'll know what to do. Yes, she will. Stay calm, Cal."

The mechanic squatted, reached into a hollow space in the wall, and pulled out a cardboard box. He stood, and Aloa rested her finger on the pepper spray's release valve.

What the hell was in there?

The man moved toward her, his eyes darting like a hummingbird from her to the door and back to the hidden spot. He shoved the box into Aloa's hands. "Take it. You'll find what you need on Uranus. That's what she said."

"On Uranus?" Aloa asked, but it was as if the mechanic didn't hear her.

He turned and plucked a small black device with three long wires from a nearby shelf and set it atop the box in Aloa's arms.

He leaned in so close that Aloa was forced to take a step back. "I took it out," he whispered. "But who put it there? That's the question, isn't it?"

Aloa opened her mouth to ask more, but the mechanic was already reverse-slashing his auric barrier and opening the shop door.

He took her shoulder and moved her gently toward the opening, in almost the same way he had moved the spider. "Whatever you do, don't let the High Priest find you. Don't let him get you too," he hissed.

"Wait, what High Priest?" Aloa said. "What are you talking about?"

Instead of answering, the mechanic pushed her into the hall and slammed the door shut. A lock turned; then there was nothing but quiet.

"Why did Hayley want you to hide this? What's in here?" Aloa called.

Silence.

"At least tell me your name," Aloa said.

"Calvin Leroy Rabren," came a faint voice. "Don't say you ever saw me."

Aloa smelled the mustiness in the cardboard box, shuddered, and quickly set it on the floor. Once, when she was working at the *Chicago Tribune*, a cardboard box had been delivered to her desk. She'd slit it open without thinking and found a rotting rat carcass crawling with maggots. From the note the police found inside, the rat was apparently a comment about a story she'd written on the city's awarding of a garbage contract. Garbage, it turned out, was a hot topic in Chicago. After that, Aloa had had a hard time with brown cardboard boxes. Even when her mother had mailed her birthday presents, Aloa had always had someone else open the container.

She shoved at the box with the toe of her boot and glanced at the locked metal door. Calvin might have been a mechanic, but he could stand to tighten a few loose bolts in his own head. Still, if Hayley had left something with him, there must have been some kind of trust between them.

Aloa toed the box again, and felt the slightest gag in the back of her throat at the memory of that rotting carcass. Lunch was out. She'd planned to stop for soup at a place she knew south of Market Street. Dinner, she promised herself. Roast chicken, a green salad. She stopped herself before she could go further.

She inhaled a breath, squatted in front of the cardboard container, and removed the device the mechanic had set on top of it. The label read DAUNTLESS M750. A car part? Some kind of electric switch? She set it aside, fished a Swiss Army knife from her pack, and slowly slit open the taped box. No sick-sweet smells. No scrabble of insects. She lifted one side of the box's flap with a tentative finger, ready to run if needed. She peered in.

The box was cluttered with manila folders and stacks of papers. She reached for the top one, a termination notice for health insurance. The named owner of the policy was Hayley Poole. These were her things.

She crouched in front of the box, wondering why Hayley would ask the mechanic to protect what looked like a random assortment of bills and objects. Unless it was simply the product of the mechanic's overactive imagination. She debated for only a few seconds before loading the box's contents into her daypack. Better to check everything out.

She found a wooden keepsake box, one of those college composition notebooks crabbed with handwriting, a couple of Topo maps. Her fingers stilled next to the last item: a cracked coffee mug that advised LET YOUR HEART SHINE.

She hated coffee mugs with cheerful sayings.

She zipped her pack, added the Dauntless whatever-it-was to an outside pocket, and stood, considering the mechanic behind the closed door. Sometimes sources sparked more questions than answers, and there was still plenty of work to do. She needed to find Samantha, talk to the detective on the case, and locate the missing witness at the campout. But she sure as hell wasn't going to Uranus to do it.

CHAPTER 7

When in unfamiliar territory, detail is especially important, Aloa's father had always said. Aloa knocked on the doors of 103 and 102 on her way out. No answer. Outside, she squatted against the warehouse, drank from her water bottle, and jotted Calvin Leroy Rabren's name along with the rough facts of the visit in her notebook. She also recorded the results from the HardE app: 8,323 steps walked, 600 calories burned— and told herself to shut down the demanding piece of technology, which included messages like "All right!" if you reached your daily quota of steps and scolded you if you didn't. "Good job," the message read, and Aloa felt a guilty twinge of satisfaction. She stood and shoved the phone in her pocket. She would turn off the stupid app as soon as she got home.

She had moved a few yards away from the building when a thought rose: Where was 101? She turned and counted. Seven windows near the roof's edge but only six doors inside. She paced the length of the building, figuring the location of Calvin's shop/home. The extra window was at the opposite end. She went back inside. No door showed the number she wanted.

She paused, called the windows to mind, and went back to 102. She knocked more loudly this time. Nothing. She looked up and down the hallway, then twisted the doorknob. From experience, she knew not everyone believed in locks.

The door swung open to reveal a short hallway and there, to her left, was a narrow set of wooden stairs with a sign that announced 101.

Some weird remodeling job had left a misleading door. "Hello?" she called, and when there was no answer, she headed up.

Sometimes, Aloa wondered about the transformation she underwent when she was on assignment. In regular life, she sent thank-you notes, called her elders ma'am and sir, and always brought a hostess gift to dinner parties—all traditions her Southern-born mother had drilled into her. But give her a story and she had no qualms about asking questions that might be considered rude, going through someone's trash, or walking into what may or may not have been another person's home.

The stairs opened to a small living space: a galley kitchen, beat-up recliner, rumpled bed, a TV silently beaming out a baseball game. A rough-looking man with a dark mullet sat at a table scattered with papers and books.

"Hello. Hi. Sorry to bother you," Aloa said, although she wasn't. She smiled—a reporter's most effective disguise.

The man looked up.

"I'm looking for Samantha Foster." Aloa stepped into the space, still smiling.

"You and me both, honey," said the man. "Skipped without a word. Owes me a month's rent. Busted toilet, a dog I didn't know about. Dog crap everywhere."

"You're the . . ." Aloa let the sentence hang.

"Property manager. Soon to be ex–property manager." He hacked a cough, reached for a cigarette smoldering in an ashtray, and took a drag. "Some Chinese company is buying the building. Gonna turn them into start-up lofts or some nonsense. I'm waiting for the leases to expire, then gotta kick everybody out. Then they kick me out."

It was the kind of change that was occurring all over the city. Despite rent-control laws, landlords were finding ways to evict their middle-class tenants so the units could then rent for exorbitant rates, with the consequence that some people were living like Harry Potter in places hardly bigger than a closet under the stairs.

"And you are?" the manager asked.

Out of habit, Aloa started to say *reporter* but stopped herself again. "I'm a researcher," she said.

"Like a detective?" The man blew a funnel of smoke from the side of his mouth.

"I'm doing an investigation for a journalism website," Aloa said. "They're thinking of doing a story about Hayley Poole. As I understand it, she lived here for a while."

"Suicide, right?" the man said.

"That's what the police reports said."

"Too bad. Nice girl. Can't say the same for that Foster gal. She fought with everybody. Took in strays just to have somebody to argue with, I think."

"Was Hayley a stray?"

"Started out that way. She and her boyfriend . . ." He snapped his fingers. "Ethan something. Rock climber. Anyway, they lived with that Foster bitch for a year or so. He died and Hayley lost it. She was getting better, happier, you know. Then Foster kicked her out, or maybe Hayley got tired of living with that big mouth." He shook his head. "A few weeks later, Foster rabbits on me."

"Do you know where she went?"

"Say, you're not working with that other dude, are you? Some guy came in asking the same thing." The man ground out the cigarette in the ashtray.

"Somebody else was looking for Samantha?" Aloa's radar pinged.

"Big guy. Lotta muscles. Showed up all hot right after she left, wanting her info."

"Did you give it to him?"

"I didn't like his type."

"What type was that?"

"All high and mighty. Like his business don't stink or something. Did I tell you about the dog poop I found all over her place?"

"You did."

"She left most of her stuff behind too. Junk. All of it. Put it in the dumpster out back."

Aloa plastered a smile back on her face. "Would it be all right if I got a copy of Samantha's rental application? Maybe I could track her down for you?" Playing the good guy to the Big Bad Dude whose business didn't stink.

"That's right. Investigators got tricks, right?"

"We do," Aloa agreed, although her tricks were few and simple.

"Although I ain't exactly sure where the application is." The man hesitated.

"How about a pair of twenties for your trouble?" Aloa thought of Michael and his promise of expenses.

"That'll work," the man said. He got up, tugged open the top drawer of a metal filing cabinet, and began rifling through it.

"You know anything about the guy in 107? Calvin?" Aloa asked.

"Ol' Cal? Cuckoo but harmless. Needs to get out more, you ask me. Helluva mechanic, though." He pulled out a sheet of paper and handed it to her. "Here it is. You find her, you call me, you hear?"

CHAPTER 8

Aloa stopped at a Starbucks and ordered a venti Caffè Americano. Tiredness pressed around the edges of her body, but she couldn't eat yet. The sensory image of the cardboard box was still with her. She sipped the hot brew, waiting for the caffeine to kick in, then pulled a stack of Hayley's papers from her pack. Might as well find out exactly what Calvin was trying to protect.

She began to sort through the papers while, at the next table, a man in a shirt and tie argued loudly with someone on his cell phone. "I told you about the vet appointment this morning. Are you deaf or just an idiot?" he said.

Aloa tried to ignore him.

It wasn't long before her cup was empty and the papers revealed a portrait of a young woman for whom the poverty line was an aspiration. Hayley had apparently worked a couple of waitressing jobs with W2 forms that showed she'd earned $4,330 and $5,239 in each of the last two years plus about $5,000 in sponsor money. A month before her death, she'd also received $550 from some Canadian annuity. From the statement the company sent, it looked like it was to be a monthly sum.

Aloa wrote, "Annuity. Source?" in her notebook and drew a rectangle around it to mark its importance as a question. How had someone with Hayley's limited means gotten her hands on an annuity that paid that kind of dividend?

The man next to her was now loudly telling someone that the heater in his car was acting up and that, with what he'd paid for it, he expected it to be fixed. Immediately. Aloa wondered how much caffeine the man had consumed that morning. Like bartenders, baristas should be able to cut people off.

From the papers, it also appeared Hayley carried a good chunk of debt. She owed $2,000 to a hospital in Colorado for a broken wrist that had been treated in the ER, $300 to a neighborhood gym, and $4,000 on a Visa card. In addition, she had gotten four parking tickets she hadn't paid.

Hayley also had completed a backcountry-medicine course, had graduated from high school (Aloa found her diploma), wrote terrible poetry, and had attempted to pitch a book about her life in the wilderness to a dozen literary agents. "Done to death," one had written in the rejection note Hayley had printed out. Aloa shivered mentally at the prescience of those three words and skimmed the first ten pages of the manuscript as the overcaffeinated man got up and strode out the door, telling an entirely new caller about a hot girl he'd met at a bar the night before.

Hayley's story opened with her being stalked by a mountain lion on a portion of the John Muir trail. It was an incident written with a kind of Hitchcockian suspense and seemed to have some skill behind it. Aloa remembered the bad poems and wondered if Hayley'd had help writing it.

Finished with the papers, Aloa turned to the composition book, which appeared to be some kind of workout diary. There were notations of miles run, times logged, weather conditions, and comments about her life and health.

"Twelve miles, 82:10, Mount Tam, back felt better today," read the first entry. The notation was followed by: "Missing Ethan so much I can hardly stand it. Know I have to stay strong. Remember: fall seven times, get up eight."

Aloa knew loss wasn't something that could be overcome by aphorisms, yet there Hayley was, trying hard to pull herself out of her grief.

It had been almost two decades since Aloa's father's death and there were still times when the loss made her world go dark. Aloa closed the book. She would spend time with it later.

She reached for the keepsake box, which was inlaid with small turquoise stones. A headache was building behind her eyes and, for a moment, the container seemed too personal to open, but Aloa shoved the feeling aside.

She found an owl feather, its quill wrapped with colored thread, a braided hemp bracelet, and a birthday card that stopped her cold. There was a cartoon drawing of an elephant on the front with the words "Never forget that I love you" written inside. "You are the half of my whole, the owner of my heart. Soon, all the craziness will end and we'll be able to live free." It was signed "Always, Ethan" and dated six weeks before he died.

Had these been Ethan's last words to Hayley? She thought of her own father's last words to her: "Tell your mother I'll put out the trash when I get back." And hers to him: "Yeah, whatever."

She closed the box, stuffed it into her pack, and stood. Regret was a wound that bled at the slightest touch and, right now, she couldn't stand the ache of it.

CHAPTER 9

The house Aloa's grandmother had built sat nearly at the top of the Vallejo Street steps, which zigzagged their way through gardens of rose, cactus, and bougainvillea to Montgomery Street below.

There were scores of these stairway streets in San Francisco: thoroughfares that, when they ran into steep hillsides, had simply been turned into steps. The myth was that early planners in Washington, DC, had laid a grid over the landscape, either forgetting or not realizing that San Francisco was built on a series of hills. The truth was that although city planners had wanted curved streets that fit the contours of the land, greedy developers had insisted on straight streets in order to make it easier to subdivide and sell lots. These stairways were among Aloa's favorite parts of the city and the reason her grandmother had built her house where she had.

"A view even God would envy," her grandmother Maja always said.

Her grandmother, who had spent her days in a mortuary basement styling hair and applying makeup for those who would never appreciate nor complain about her work, had designed her house to snatch every bit of view it could. Out front was a small porch with just enough room for a pot of geraniums, a chair, and a tiny table where Maja used to sit with her nightly coffee. And now there was a stack of cardboard boxes on the porch and two men sitting on Aloa's front steps.

They were young, sporting chinstrap beards and glasses, and they looked up from their phones as she approached.

"Can I help you?" Aloa asked sharply.

"We're here for setup," said one of the men. He was short and pot-bellied. The other was medium height and thin.

"Setup?" Aloa said.

The potbellied man gestured at the boxes. "High-speed inter-net, MacBook Pro, thirty-inch monitor, wireless printer, hi-def TV, LexisNexis, Bloomberg, a bunch of other databases."

"And who ordered . . . ?" Aloa started.

"Mr. Collins," said the thin guy. He consulted his phone. "For a Ms. Aloa Snow. This is the address, right?"

"Wait right there." Aloa pointed. "Don't do a thing."

The men shrugged and sat back down.

Aloa strode a few yards away, scrolled through her recent-calls list, found Michael's number, and stabbed the screen.

"I wrote that I didn't want contact, and I certainly don't want your pity," she barked the minute he answered.

"I think you called me."

Aloa could hear the hint of a smile in his voice. She ignored it. "I want you to take back all this"—Aloa waved her arm at the boxes—"this junk."

"If the junk you're talking about is computer equipment, I thought you could stand an upgrade."

"I'm fine with what I've got, thank you."

"I don't think *fine* includes a laptop that was around when Bush was president, and for your information, people in the Yukon have better internet speeds than you."

She started to ask Michael how he knew, then remembered he owned a company that wrote complicated software programs for crunching big data. He'd probably hacked into her information before he'd even called her.

"We agreed on expenses, didn't we?" Michael said. Aloa could hear music playing faintly in the background. Black Sabbath, if she wasn't mistaken.

"But not all this." She waved her hand again at the boxes.

"I don't want you hamstrung by something as simple as a background search. I told those guys to give you whatever you need. They interned with my company. They're good."

Aloa knew Michael was right. A fact that might take her a few hours to track down with her current setup could be done with a few keystrokes with the right equipment. "Just until I'm done with the project," she said. "Then you take it all out."

"We can talk about that later," Michael said as a man came out of the gated apartment complex across the street. He wore a pair of Italian loafers that likely cost more than Aloa earned in a month.

Over the past years, the city had filled with these kinds of upwardly mobile hipsters, their inflated incomes and ability to spend tempting landlords and business owners to raise rents and increase prices so that one could only survive in the city by chasing after the same god everyone else did.

Aloa shifted her mind back to the conversation. "I'm not taking the television, though," she said. She needed a victory, no matter how tiny.

"Fine, but I thought it might help if you're looking at videos, photos. To see details," Michael said. He could have been condescending but he was not. "Have you found anything?"

Aloa took a deep breath. "Yes. A little."

"That's good."

"I'll need the mother's contact info."

"I'll email it to you right now."

A car started up. Expensive sounding. Probably the yuppie in the Italian shoes.

"Thanks for doing this," Michael said. "It means a lot to me."

"I need the money," Aloa said, and ended the call.

She let the chinstraps and their boxes into the house, showed them where to set up the gear, and wondered at her overreaction. The truth was, part of the reason she'd accepted the job was the very reason it was so hard to do. It wasn't the money that had finally sealed her decision, although that was certainly a huge part of it. It was the hurt she'd heard in Michael's voice during that first call, the same hurt she'd heard when he'd finally told her about his sister, the one whose murder had set off the end of his family.

Her name was Michelle and she had been Michael's twin. A rebellious and sometimes self-destructive girl who was flunking out of school and had twice been suspended for smoking weed, her body was found two months after she had disappeared during a trip to the mall. She'd been strangled.

At first, police had called her a runaway, then zeroed in on the dysfunction of the family and of her own life: evidence of an abortion shortly before her death, a screaming fight between her and her father that was overheard by neighbors, a progress report that showed she was failing two classes. The police had arrived at Michael's house with a search warrant three weeks after her body was found, hinted at evidence of possible abuse at the hands of Michael's father, and the next day, Michael's father had ended everything with three blasts of a Winchester Model 70 hunting rifle.

Michael never found out why he had been spared.

There were no arrests, no other suspects named, and only Michael seemed to think the case had not been closed. Aloa guessed the sloppy investigation into Hayley's death, a young woman who had her own troubles, had opened old wounds for Michael. The end result had her working as a reporter again with him back in her life. Either one of those things could end with a Thelma-and-Louise-like emotional crash. Once again, she wondered if she was making a mistake.

Aloa told the chinstraps to lock up when they were done and strode down the hill toward Justus. She tapped a search into her phone as she walked. Three thumbnail images appeared on her screen: a handsome dark-haired man in a tuxedo outside some fancy hotel, the same man splattered with mud on a mountain bike, and a close-up of the man with a three-day beard and troubled eyes.

Michael hadn't changed all that much since the last day she had seen him. She thought of how innocent she'd been in those years when he had lived with them, of how life had seemed full of possibilities then, and how everything had changed with the words in one note. She turned off the phone.

"Just do your job," she told herself.

CHAPTER 10

Tick waved from a back table as Aloa came in the door. The rest of the Brain Farm was in attendance, old men whose hair ranged from bald to salt-and-pepper crew cut to ponytail.

"Get over here, Ink," Tick called.

Aloa sighed internally. All she wanted was to sit down with a glass of wine and maybe a few bites of what was on today's menu. Still, having someone at the table might take the edge off the inner voice that whispered about calories and the roundness of her belly every time she ate.

A list of yesterday's food with a calorie count already sat in her notebook. *Ten ounces duck pho, two ounces scotch, eight hundred calories.* A slippery slope if she let it go too far.

"We hear you might be working on something," Tick said before she could even sit.

"I've just started," she said, settling herself at the table.

"Spill," ordered the crew-cut old photographer known as P-Mac. He had a hawklike face and sharp gray eyes. There were stories of him from the Vietnam War: running through gunfire to capture the shot of a medic giving CPR to a wounded comrade, wading into a river to take a shot of a Vietnamese family fleeing a bombing raid, disappearing for a week into the Cambodian jungle and coming back with images so troubling he said he would never show them to anybody. He always sat with his back to the wall.

"It's about a girl who died in the desert. I'm doing it for Novo."

The Brain Farm nodded approvingly.

"Just research," Aloa amended. "No promises I'll even turn in anything."

"Hair of the dog, Ink," P-Mac said. "High time you got back in the saddle."

Erik arrived in time to interrupt more mixing of metaphors. He set a glass of house red in front of Aloa, inspecting her outfit.

"*Desperately Seeking Susan* 2.0?" he said. "Does that mean you took the assignment?" He put a hand on her shoulder.

"I'm looking into it."

"You be careful."

Aloa nodded.

"Something to eat, hon?" Erik asked.

The inquiry always set off an arrow of guilt in Aloa. Her grandmother had asked the same question whenever Aloa came home from UC Berkeley for visits, trying to hide her skeletal frame under layers of clothes and excusing her twice-daily hill running as a plan to join the cross-country team, even though she'd had no more chance of making the squad than a three-legged dog. Her grandmother, raised with the stories of Ireland's great famine, could not understand Aloa's desire to starve and had placed the blame on an insufficiency of fattening food at the university. Whenever Aloa visited, her grandmother would send her off with care packages of meatloaf and brownies. Aloa's mother, on the other hand, had noted her daughter's gaunt frame and nodded in approval. "I see you've finally gotten rid of some of that baby fat, although why you can't wear something pretty is beyond me," she'd said. When it came to her daughter, there was always room for criticism.

"What's on the menu tonight?" Aloa asked Erik.

"Total America Pasta," Erik said.

"Maybe just a cup of soup," Aloa said.

Erik raised his eyebrows.

"OK, I'll have the pasta."

"That's my girl," Erik said, and hurried off.

Aloa turned back to the Brain Farm.

"Erik told us it was a murder," Tick said. His slender fingers worked the stem of the wineglass. It was said he could pick a lock in under four seconds.

"More likely a suicide or an accident," Aloa said.

"That's what the pigs say when they don't want the truth to come out," said Doc. He was six foot five and broad-shouldered, an ex–Black Panther who'd retired as a college history professor and now volunteered as a cook at a couple of soup kitchens in the Bay Area.

"There wasn't much to work with, actually," Aloa said, giving the men a rough outline of Hayley's story as Erik set a bowl of pasta, fragrant with pancetta, tomatoes, and wilted spinach in front of her—Gully's version of an all-American sandwich, the BLT.

"I put a rush order on it," he said.

The Brain Farm listened as Aloa recounted Hayley's debt, her lost sponsorship, the death of her boyfriend, and, finally, the strange visit with the mechanic, Calvin, who had urged her to go to Uranus and avoid a High Priest.

"That's some fugazi shit there, man," P-Mac said when she was finished.

Aloa twirled some of the pasta onto her fork, frowned, and set the utensil back down.

"Does the phrase 'six angles of attack' mean anything to you, P-Mac?" she asked.

"Sure, I heard of it," the old photographer said. "It's from the army close-combat manual."

"I knew it. He was army," Aloa said. "It all fits now."

"Sometimes that brain of yours scares me, Ink," Tick said.

Sometimes, Aloa thought, *it scares me too.*

"The mechanic," Aloa explained. "I'm thinking maybe that's why his brain is scrambled. PTSD or some kind of traumatic brain injury."

"You should check his service record," P-Mac said.

"I'll do it as soon as I get home," Aloa said. "I got some new computer stuff: high-speed internet, big screen, LexisNexis, and some other databases. Courtesy of Novo." She didn't mention Michael's name.

Tick whistled. "I'd love to get my hands on some of that."

"You know computers?" Aloa asked.

"He's the mayor of nerd city," said Doc.

"I could do a little driving if you want," Tick said.

"Oh yeah," Doc said.

"That's OK," Aloa started to say, but Doc was already on his feet, shouting across the crowded bar. "Hey, Erik, we need a to-go box, man."

And that's how Aloa came to be sitting in her house with P-Mac and Doc watching Tick at the computer. "Beautiful, man," Tick kept muttering. "Just pure-ass beautiful."

While Tick searched for background on the annuity, Aloa powered up her old laptop to see what she could find about Calvin Leroy Rabren. She discovered a workman's comp claim he'd filed when a lift at the car dealership where he'd worked had malfunctioned and crashed into his head. That led to a report about his army service and his ADHD, PTSD, and OCD—a whole alphabet of disabilities—and finally took her to a military blog where the story of what had happened to Calvin's platoon made her want to run back and tell him, "I am so sorry for what we and the government did to you."

According to the blogger, a member of the platoon had been abducted and his body found in an open septic tank with a gunshot wound to his head. The platoon leader, a staff sergeant nicknamed Herc, had gone all avenging angel after that, ordering one of his men to toss a grenade into the home of what he claimed were two Taliban sympathizers who'd had a role in the soldier's death. The structure turned out to house a clandestine school for girls. Seven mangled bodies were pulled from the wreckage. Herc had received a letter of reprimand and a sixty-day suspension for what he had described as "acting on bad intel."

Two platoon members had committed suicide after their discharge.

Aloa sat back in her grandmother's rosé chair and twisted the feather ring on her thumb. She'd bought the band in memory of her father, who liked to say that birds were the link between earth and the heavens; that they helped us see the connection between the natural world and something greater than us.

How much of Calvin's mutterings, she wondered, were the truth and how much were the result of a mind damaged by the country's ill-advised war? Was it possible he was jealous over Hayley's love for her boyfriend? Did the knife indicate a tendency toward violence or simply a need to protect?

A shout from Doc interrupted her thoughts. "You're looking in the wrong place, Tick," he said, tapping the computer screen where Tick worked. "It's always the money, you know that."

Tick waved him away. "I told you, I'm getting to it, old man."

"Unless it's power they want," P-Mac called out. He was lying on Aloa's couch smoking a joint he'd rolled on the walk over. He'd asked her if he could spark inside—some head injury from Vietnam required regular herbal self-medication—and had lit up. "Look at William Walker," he said. "A two-bit mercenary who went south and tried to conquer Baja and Honduras just so he could hear himself called *El Presidente*."

"You can call me King Kiss My Ass if you don't let me work," Tick said, which resulted in a noisy argument about clandestine power-grabs and whether a few investors had inside information about the 9/11 attacks that allowed them to profit from the heartbreaking disaster.

Aloa ignored their squabble, got up from her chair, and unloaded Hayley's things from her pack: the papers, the strange device, Hayley's notebook. She sat on the wood floor and thumbed through the composition book, finding a news article folded into a back page. A GRISLY DEATH IN AFRICA, the headline read.

The piece was written by Mark Combs, a reporter she'd met at a narrative nonfiction workshop a few years before her firing. He was a decent reporter, although his ego hovered somewhere between large and elephantine.

She began to read:

"T.J. Brasselet crouches on a ledge high above Horseshoe Canyon in Utah, his dreadlocks copper in the sun," Combs had written. "He is barefoot, his eyes haunted, and for a moment, I am afraid he will jump.

"I've tracked him here, to a place where he and his best friend, Ethan Rodriguez, once roamed in preparation for a trip into the forbidding Tibesti Mountains in north-central Africa. Only, no amount of climbing or trekking or deprivation could prepare Brasselet for what would happen. Nothing, he says, could have prepared him to watch his best friend die."

The story went on to describe how the pair had gone to the Tibesti to explore a land ravaged by desertification and species loss, a land of volcanic spires and land mines, of bandits and nomads.

There, they found primitive drawings of animals that had roamed the once-lush area and the remnants of an ancient tribe who had shared some kind of trippy vision ceremony with them. They climbed towering rock spires, had a brush with a poisonous viper. Fifteen days into their return trip to the city of N'Djamena, they had been attacked by bandits.

Aloa's reading was interrupted by a bark from Tick. "There it is. Right there, man," he cried.

"I told you, money is the medium," Doc crowed as Aloa's fancy new printer whirred to life.

Aloa ignored the men and turned back to the article. T.J. told Combs he had been relieving himself a distance from their camp when the robbers arrived. He'd heard a shout, zipped his pants, and hurried back only to find Ethan and their Teda guide kneeling in the sand with two men in headdresses and combat gear aiming AK-47s at them. He'd dropped to his belly behind a rough boulder and watched as the robbers shouted at Ethan and the guide and poked at them with their guns. One bandit punched Ethan in the face, causing him to sway from the impact.

Without any weapon beyond a few fist-size rocks scattered around him, T.J. could only watch in horror as one of the robbers finished some sort of diatribe and then went over, grabbed Ethan by the hair, and slashed a knife across the climber's throat. He did the same to the terrified guide.

"All I could see was his blood spilling everywhere," T.J. was quoted as saying. "It just kept coming. It was like some dream, but I couldn't wake up."

The thieves took the expedition's camels, which were loaded with food and gear, and disappeared into the desert. T.J. said he spent the night huddled in shock, then salvaged what he could from the campsite—a gallon jug of water, a multi-tool, and a Bic lighter—and hiked through the desert for a day before he found a Tuareg camp, where he was offered food and water.

The article ended with T.J. saying he would continue adventuring because that's what Ethan would have wanted.

But was that what Ethan really would have wanted? Aloa wondered. Wouldn't he have preferred to be alive? To live happily ever after with Hayley in the mountains, to grow old together, to live free like he'd written in his card? Or was there something inside people like Ethan and Hayley, where safety and the fear of death were overruled by a need to challenge themselves, to explore the limits of the human body and spirit?

She refolded the article and considered what she knew she should do next. She grabbed her laptop, retrieved Combs's contact information, and picked up her phone.

He answered on the fifth ring.

A cacophony of voices, music, and the clink of glass indicated he was in a bar.

"Mark, it's Aloa Snow. How are you?" she said.

The background sounds seemed to rise in volume for a moment. She heard a loud cheer.

"What do you want?"

She steeled herself. She hadn't expected this to be easy.

"I saw your story on Ethan Rodriguez, the climber," Aloa said. "Really nice job."

"Thanks." Distrust edged out his obvious pleasure at the compliment.

Aloa plunged ahead. "Listen, I was wondering if we could grab a beer or a cup of coffee? I'd like to pick your brain. Find out more about what happened to those guys on the trip, maybe take a look at your notes." Space and readers' time constraints meant reporters usually had to leave out two-thirds of what they'd reported from their stories.

"Why do you want to know?"

Aloa debated a lie but she'd vowed truth in everything after her disgrace. "I've got a gig. I'm doing some research for Novo. I'm looking into Rodriguez's death for a story they want to do. It's about his dead girlfriend."

"Are you frigging kidding me?"

Aloa took a breath. "No. I'm not."

"Why would Novo hire somebody like you? You've seen the people on their staff. They wouldn't let a faker like you anywhere near their site."

Among people whose business was news, the report that a journalist with a shelf full of writing awards had made up a source for one of her stories had spread as quickly and nastily as the flu. Aloa pressed down a flash of anger. "Mark, I know I made a mistake. I know what I did was wrong; my mom was dying, the editors wanted this big story, and I made a stupid decision . . . that's not an excuse, that's just how it was and I'm sorry for it every single day. All I need is some background on this Rodriguez guy, on the trip. Novo is going to vet everything. No shortcuts. I promise. Give me a hand here."

There was burst of loud laughter in the background.

"I wouldn't trust you with a sack of garbage, let alone my notes," Combs said.

Aloa pictured him as he had been when they'd met: his too-tight jeans, his styled hair, the air quotes he used to tell the conference leader how he'd been aced out of a job at the *New York Times* by a "targeted hire."

"That's OK. I doubt there's much difference between garbage and your notes anyway," she said, and stabbed off the call.

CHAPTER 11

Aloa glanced over at the address in her open notebook as she drove over the Golden Gate Bridge. She was on her way to interview Hayley's mother, who lived in Inverness, a tiny tourist town in western Marin County.

Her stomach felt raw and her head seemed to float a few inches above her body—both the result of the gut-churning conversation with Combs and another round of 2:00 a.m. sleeplessness.

She'd gone to bed at midnight, her body exhausted, but after two hours of tossing and turning, she had finally surrendered and climbed out of bed. She'd drunk a glass of water while standing at the front window and retrieved her cello. She lowered herself onto the stool, felt a shiver of coolness through the T-shirt she wore, and began to play. The complicated beauty of Mark O'Connor's "Appalachia Waltz" filled the house, taking her mind away from shame and into the memory of mountains and pines and her father. She played until her eyelids grew heavy and then crawled back under the covers.

She'd had a few hours of twitchy sleep before she'd awakened dry-mouthed and slightly nauseous with the certainty that she should email Michael and tell him the assignment had been a mistake. Combs had proved what she already knew: that it was almost impossible to make up for the sins of your past, and that she'd probably feel worse when this was over.

She would have written the email, except for two things: there was a part of her that wanted to wipe the smug judgment off the faces of people like Combs, and, if she wanted to save her grandmother's house, she really needed the money.

Now she was behind the wheel of Doc's car, a Volkswagen van so gutless he had to take long, circuitous routes to his volunteer cooking gigs in order to avoid the vehicle chugging to a standstill on one of San Francisco's famed hills. Luckily for Aloa, the bungalow where Hayley's mother lived was set low on the slopes above Tomales Bay.

"Ms. Poole," Aloa said when Hayley's mom answered the door. She was a sturdy woman dressed in a green thermal shirt and overalls. Her short brown hair sprang from her head in a tangle that didn't suggest any sort of style but rather a lack of interest in grooming.

"Please, call me Emily," the woman said. She looked to be in her late fifties, or maybe it was that the puffy, dark circles under her eyes made her look older. "Come in. Sorry, I didn't have time to clean."

The small living room was littered with newspapers, partially empty coffee cups, unopened mail, and a pile of laundry that could have been clean or not.

"It's fine," Aloa said, wondering if the house was in its normal state or if the disarray was a product of grief. A dried-up pot of macaroni and cheese sat on the floor.

"I've just been so busy," Emily said, shoving the laundry aside so Aloa could sit on the room's small couch. She picked up a stack of newspapers, put them down, then grabbed the pot of dry mac and cheese. She stopped, frowned.

"Tea," she said as if reminding herself. "And cookies."

"Tea is fine," Aloa said.

"I went to the store after you called," said Emily, disappearing through a doorway into a small and equally cluttered kitchen.

Aloa turned and peeked into a bedroom off the living room while Emily noisily prepared tea. It held an unmade bed, a nightstand piled with books, and a framed photo of Ethan and Hayley on some tropical beach.

Ethan was dark-haired and olive-skinned. He wore board shorts that showed off his taut belly and muscled arms. He looked like some Latin American god.

Hayley stood next to him in a blue bikini that gave her a look of power more than some kind of magazine-cover sex appeal. Still, they were a commanding couple. No wonder they had drawn attention from sponsors. Aloa took a quick photo with her phone, grabbed a shot of the disheveled living room, and shoved the phone back into her pack. She let her eyes drift back to the view out the house's front window, a serene stretch of wide, blue bay with open hills beyond—a natural calmness in contrast to the chaos of the house.

"Here you go," Emily said, coming back with a small plate of oatmeal cookies. She shoved them toward Aloa. "They're vegan."

In her years of reporting, Aloa had learned that accepting an offer of hospitality—no matter how unwelcome—often helped open the door to conversation. She'd drunk warm cola and bitter coffee and had once swallowed a gelatinous pickled fish at the home of a Russian gambler just to draw out confidences. She took a cookie and bit into it. It tasted like wet cardboard.

"Thanks," she mumbled.

Emily stood as if waiting for Aloa to take another bite and then, thankfully, muttered "tea" and went off to get it.

Aloa shoved the rest of the cookie into a pocket in her pack, mentally adding "one quarter oatmeal cookie" to the list of today's food, which so far included only a piece of dry wheat toast and a cup of her strong coffee. She told herself she would eat lunch and that this restrictive bullshit had to stop, although she knew that, once started, the purity of self-denial was hard to shake.

Emily reappeared a minute later with two mugs of tea, shoved aside the newspapers, and set one of the cups in front of Aloa. There was an oily sheen to the brew although the cup looked clean enough.

"I'm so glad somebody finally wants to listen," said Hayley's mom. She perched on an upholstered chair garlanded with socks and towels and took a sip of her tea. "The cops in Nevada stopped taking my calls and the *Chronicle* wouldn't talk to me. The magazines said they didn't want to glorify suicide." She huffed out a breath. "I didn't know who else to turn to. Then I read about Mr. Collins in *People* magazine and emailed him. He's a saint."

"Well," Aloa said noncommittally.

"Try your tea," Emily said. "I've never talked to a reporter before."

"Researcher," Aloa corrected, taking a tiny sip of the sharp-tasting brew.

Emily frowned. "You mean, like a detective? I thought . . ." She let her voice trail off. Her hand fluttered from her hair to her face to her knee as if she didn't know where it should rest.

"Not a detective," Aloa said, then thought she would have to come up with another way to describe herself. "More like an investigator."

"But still for Novo, right?" Emily asked.

"That's correct," Aloa said.

"OK. Well," Emily said. "Shall I just tell you what I know or do you want to ask questions?"

"Why don't you start?" Aloa said, and pulled out her notebook. "I'll ask questions as we go along."

"Sure." Emily took a deep breath. "Hayley was such a good girl. Always helping everybody, always offering a kind word. She loved the outdoors. From the minute she could walk, she was outside exploring. Her first pet was a little garter snake she found. She named it Joe and kept it in her room. One day, she brought Joe to the office in her jacket pocket. Her father and I had a start-up back then. We couldn't afford a sitter, so we always brought Hayley. Anyway, she let the snake out to play and well, you know, a few people freaked. Our best programmer threatened to sue. Said we had a hostile workplace. That's when my sister took over."

"Hayley's aunt?" Aloa asked.

"Yes. In Sacramento. She was very good with children. Hayley loved it there. Our business was at a critical juncture." Emily picked at the skin near her thumbnail.

"How long did she stay with her aunt?" Aloa asked.

"Hayley came back when she was ten, so it was five years, I think. My sister got sick. Breast cancer."

Aloa imagined what that decision had done to Hayley's psyche: One day you bring your pet snake to your parents' office and the next day you're banished to a different family.

"How did Hayley take the move?"

"She was a good girl. We talked on the phone every week." Emily squared her shoulders. "Hayley and I were always very close."

Aloa guessed there was a good chunk of revisionist history in that last statement but let it go.

"Where is Hayley's father now?"

"Who knows? Last I heard he was in Brazil, but that was nine years ago."

"What about Hayley and Ethan? How long were they together? What was their relationship like?"

"Let's see, Hayley met Ethan after high school. He was in medical school at UC San Francisco. She was working at a coffee shop. I wanted her to go to college, but she was having, um, a little trouble. Took after her father."

"What trouble was that, Emily?" Aloa asked quietly.

Emily looked up. "Do I have to tell you?"

"If you want me to help."

Emily seemed to consider. "Well, she, um, was having, I guess you'd say, a problem with drugs. Nothing hard," she added hastily. "Just that she fell in with a bad crowd. They got her into pills. OxyContin, Vicodin, Percocet. I didn't know what to do with her. Then she met Ethan and everything changed. Ethan saved her."

"Tell me about him."

"Like I said, he was studying to be a doctor, but he quit school after he met Hayley. He got her healthy again. They backpacked for four months in South America and then rode bikes from here to Alaska. After that, they went to Spain and he learned to climb. That's when Hayley started running. When they came back, they lived in a van outside of Yosemite for a while and then Ethan got sponsored. He had two first ascents, some speed records. He was what they call a free climber." Emily waited half a beat. "That means he used ropes, but only so he didn't fall. Otherwise, it was just him climbing, using cracks and little ledges, stuff like that."

Aloa nodded, even though the idea of clinging to a rock wall with your fingertips while the earth fell away around you seemed more like torture than sport to her.

"He was getting magazine profiles. One of his videos got four million views. He did some stunt work too."

"For movies?"

"Yes. That's how he hurt himself. He had a bad fall in Canada. They call that a whipper, you know."

Aloa nodded, though it was the first time she had heard the term.

"He got a terrible concussion and had to take time off. That's when Hayley set her John Muir Trail record. Ethan supported her, dropped off food and gear, new shoes. She got a couple of sponsors after that. Ethan helped her write a book about it, but those stupid publishers couldn't see how good it was."

Considering Hayley's horrible poetry, Aloa guessed Ethan did more than help.

"When he died, well . . ." Emily pressed her lips together, her eyes traveling past Aloa to the bay, or maybe even beyond it. Finally, she said,

"When Ethan died, it was like I lost Hayley for a while too. She started drinking, which an addict should never do. I told her Ethan would be sad to know what she was doing and she said Ethan came to her in a dream and told her she needed to follow the dark steps."

"Do you know what that meant?"

Emily shook her head. "Not really. But after that Hayley started acting strange. She said people were out to get her, that the world was full of hypocrisy. I think maybe it was the alcohol. Worried me sick. But then she got sober. She was a strong girl."

Aloa thought of the police report and the vodka Hayley had drunk that day. "She'd stopped drinking?"

"Yes. Thank god for Hank Tremblay," Emily said. "He's the president of RedHawk Nutritionals. You've heard of that?"

Aloa nodded. Who hadn't heard of RedHawk, a supplement company started in a small cabin in Revelstoke, Canada? Its products were now sold worldwide.

"Anyway, his company partners with a place called the Palms. It does rehab. Lots of nutritional counseling. Hank believes an imbalance in the body is what sparks addiction. Hank paid for Hayley to go there. He was Ethan's biggest sponsor. I think he felt guilty after Ethan died, but I told him it wasn't his fault."

A connection tickled Aloa's brain.

"Did Mr. Tremblay also set up an annuity for Hayley, by any chance? With a Canadian company?" Aloa asked. Tick had found details about the company the night before, but not who put up the initial money for the fund.

"How did you know that?" Emily asked.

Aloa gestured vaguely.

"It was part of Ethan's contract, kind of a life-insurance thing. Hank goes further than most sponsors. He even put Ethan on his company's health insurance plan in case he got hurt. He was giving Hayley all kinds of free nutrition products. For her project, you know."

"The documentary she was doing?" Aloa asked.

"Yes. That's why she died."

"What makes you think that, Emily?"

Hayley's mom looked over her shoulder into the kitchen, then out the front window. She leaned in. "Hayley told me."

"Before she died?" Now they were getting somewhere.

"No, after."

Aloa frowned. "And how did she do that, exactly?"

Emily stood and disappeared into the bedroom, returning with a small black device that looked like a cross between a TV remote and a voltage meter.

"It's a spirit box," Emily said, settling next to Aloa. "It picks up the voices of the dead, the voices humans can't hear. You ask a question and, if the time is right, those who are gone will talk to you." Emily looked at Aloa. "I read about it online and watched videos. I bought this on Amazon. $89.99. The top-ranked model."

Aloa gave a mental eye roll. "Go on," she said.

"It was the fifth time I used it that I heard her." Emily pressed two buttons and lifted the device toward Aloa's ear. "I saved it. Listen."

There was a hiss of air and then Emily's voice: "Who killed you, baby? Who did this to you?"

The question was followed by a buzz of what sounded like static, a clicking sound, and then something deeper, a rumble that seemed to pulse in a staccato pattern before it dissolved into another hiss of interference.

"Hear that?" Emily said.

"Sorry." Aloa shook her head.

"Listen again. That was Hayley. You can hear her," Emily said. She rewound the recording and held the small machine against Aloa's ear. "She says, 'hear me,' and then, 'she did it.' It's very clear if you know what to listen for."

Aloa closed her eyes and listened again. With a lot of imagination—supplemented by the desperate hope of a grieving parent—she supposed part of the rumble could sound a little like the words, "she did it."

Emily clicked off the device. "Hayley said it. It was that girl who killed her. I knew it all along."

Aloa tried to keep the frustration out of her voice. "What girl are you talking about, Emily?"

"Jordan Connor."

"Her friend at the campout?"

Emily sniffed. "Hardly a friend."

"And how exactly did Jordan kill Hayley?"

Outside the kitchen window, Aloa could see two cedar waxwings bobbing on the branches of a dense berry bush. Their Kabuki eyes made them appear exotic and showy.

"By giving her drugs and alcohol," Emily said. "That's why she got lost."

"You're saying it was deliberate?"

"Of course it was." Emily went on, as if explaining the obvious to a slow-witted child. "Jordan met Hayley at some big race a couple of years ago. A hundred-miler, I think. She was an ultramarathoner and did well for her first time. Got fourth place, I believe. Anyway, she attached herself to Hayley, tried to ride on my baby's coattails. She was doing those races with her."

"The Cloudrunner series?" Aloa asked.

"Yes," Emily said, "and Monica Prager—she's an adventure film-maker—decided to make a documentary about the two of them. You know, their strength, their ups and downs, their determination. But, as things went on, she decided to shift the movie to Hayley's story: how she was healing, how she used running to face grief. Jordan was getting aced out and she didn't like it. Hayley didn't see the jealousy, but I did. When Hayley died, I suspected right away that Jordan had some part in it."

"So you're saying Jordan got Hayley high and therefore she's responsible for Hayley getting lost and dying?"

"It's called manslaughter. I looked it up." Emily straightened her shoulders. "You do something negligent that causes somebody else to die. By the way, did I tell you what Hayley said the last time I saw her?"

"You didn't," Aloa said.

"She told me she didn't know who she could trust anymore." Emily stared at Aloa's notebook. "Aren't you going to write that down?"

She waited, so Aloa did.

"What about the note in the truck?" Aloa asked. "What about everyone saying Hayley was depressed?"

"I know my girl. She wouldn't kill herself." Emily got up and went to the front window. "Sure, she was having shin problems, but they would have gotten better. They did before. And, sure, she lost one of her sponsors, but when the movie came out, she would have gotten more. She was doing good. She was working hard. She was determined."

Aloa knew determination was not the lone cure for addiction, or for depression.

"Did you tell Mr. Collins what you're telling me?" she asked.

Emily came back and sat across from Aloa. "I told him nobody cared enough to find out what really happened to Hayley and how much it hurt to think my baby killed herself." A tear slipped from Emily's eye and she brushed it away. "I told him there were guys with guns and that Jordan had threatened Hayley."

"Did she? Specifically?"

"Giving drugs and booze to an addict is a threat," Emily said, her face wrinkling into grief and more tears. She scrubbed them away.

Aloa waited. Then, "Did you tell Mr. Collins about the spirit box?"

"No."

"Why not?"

"I wanted whoever was looking into her death to hear it for themselves."

Aloa couldn't help the small sigh that escaped her lips. "So you're saying Jordan Connor is the reason Hayley is dead?"

"Talk to T.J. He'll tell you. He was there at the campout. He lives in the Santa Cruz Mountains. I'll give you directions. There's no cell reception there so you just have to show up. He won't mind."

"And Jordan Connor?"

"She works part-time at this fancy bar in the city." Emily gave Aloa the name and address.

"You'll see I was right," she said as Aloa rose to leave. "Hayley's spirit told the truth."

CHAPTER 12

Aloa stepped into the roadside deli, her sleep-deprived eyes rebelling at the fluorescent light glaring off the shop's white walls and checkered linoleum floor. Bowls of potato and macaroni salad sat in glass-front cases next to hunks of honey ham and peppered turkey. The place smelled like pickles and cheese.

She waited while a family of four ordered sandwiches with such specific directions it was as if each were guiding a nuclear missile to its target and told herself to order something substantial. Maybe a veggie sandwich on whole wheat. But when the pimply faced clerk turned to her, she said, "Just a kale salad. And a water, please."

She carried her meal to a wooden outdoor table where she pulled on her sunglasses and set the plate of chopped greens in front of her. Actually, she hated kale salad. But compare 250 calories to the 575 for the sandwich and she'd ordered the salad, almost against her will.

That was the thing with eating disorders. Your mind worked like a calculator, assigning guilt-inducing numbers to every potato chip, celery stick, and hamburger that crossed your line of sight. Which, as a recovering anorexic, made you feel bad for eating and worse for not eating. She retrieved two ibuprofen from her pack, swallowed them with half the bottle of water, and choked down the salad, which made her feel like a horse chomping at the last nibbles of a dry and dying pasture.

The interview with Emily had made her tired. She wanted to lie down on the table and go to sleep. Instead, she closed her eyes and listened to the rush of cars on the two-lane road, the burbling song of a warbling vireo, the faint buzz of a small plane. Finally she got up, cleared her plate and fork to a plastic tub, and got into Doc's van.

One step at a time, she thought.

Back on the road, the van chugging along at what seemed to be its top speed of forty-five miles per hour, she called the detective who had handled Hayley's case.

"And you are?" asked the woman on the other end of the line, who identified herself as Dispatcher Norris.

"I'm a researcher for Novo. It's a journalism site," Aloa explained. "We're doing a story about Hayley Poole. She died in your jurisdiction."

"You got a case number?" Dispatcher Norris asked, seeming not to care about journalism or a girl's death for that matter. Aloa glanced at her notebook and gave the number to the woman.

"Oh yeah, Detective Walton. He retired right after that. Let me give you to Chuck," she said, and before Aloa could object, she found herself listening to Neil Young's "Old Man." Interesting hold music.

"Detective Charles Torres here," answered a gruff male voice halfway through the song.

Aloa explained who she was.

"Now why do you want to be digging up that case?" Detective Torres asked.

"We're not digging it up, Detective. We're doing a piece on Ms. Poole. She was quite an accomplished athlete."

"Not accomplished enough, apparently," Detective Torres snorted.

It had been less than thirty seconds and Aloa already disliked e man.

"Can you tell me why Detective Walton didn't interview the third witness at the campout or the men who showed up with guns?" Aloa decided it wouldn't hurt to let her claws show.

"You inferring Detective Walton didn't do his job?"

"I'm not inferring anything. I'm just asking why an investigation of a woman's death didn't include an interview with the last people who saw her alive, at least two of them in possession of guns."

"Because, Aloha—" Detective Torres gave an exaggerated sigh.

"Aloa," she corrected.

"Because, Miss Hawaiian Tropic Tan, the girl's friends didn't have a name for the third guy, only that he was called Boots, and maybe you think you've got some magic internet wand or something, but that isn't enough to find somebody. Plus, the men with guns, Carl and Pete? Well, they're fine, upstanding young men and your little runner gal and her friends were camping on sacred land. The Paiute hold that place holy, but some of those yuppie climbers don't seem to agree. You want people drinking and stringing ropes all over your church, eh? They ran off your friends like they have every right to do; then they went home. We didn't need to ask them anything."

"A sacred site?" Aloa started.

The detective cut her off. "You can look it up. There's a lawsuit, newspaper stories. Carl and Pete have had to run off people before. They're a couple of the best, you ask me."

"What about the shell casing?"

"That was from a Glock 19. Carl and Pete had rifles. Plenty of people go shooting out on those roads. We can't be chasing every bullet casing we find."

"How do you know they didn't follow the girl?" Aloa began, only to be interrupted again by the detective.

"How do I know? Because I know those guys. They don't own a Glock or a pistol or nothing like that. Plus the sister, the one who gave the alibi, happens to be my wife. I know for a fact she didn't lie. So you tell those nosy website friends of yours that we may not live in a big city, but we know how to do our jobs."

The sound of Detective Torres slamming down the phone left a ringing in Aloa's ear.

CHAPTER 13

His ribs felt as if they had been hit by a sledgehammer, the weight of the steel against his chest was a tight band. He struggled for breath and, for a moment, thought of Lopez. Shot once in the head and shoved into an open cesspool, the rumor spreading that he had not died from the bullet but from drowning in a great vat of piss and shit.

"Hey, are you listening?" said the intruder, the one who'd come in with his big silver pickup claiming to be a combat vet, saying he thought the alternator was acting up. The one who'd started asking about Hayley's stuff and making him feel all the old things he didn't like to feel and then, when he showed him the knife, had gunned the engine. The concrete wall was cold and hard against his back.

"Medic," he groaned.

Bullets hiss when they're close. Cover your ears and open your mouth after you throw the grenade. Nobody gets left behind.

"There aren't any medics. Where's the stuff, loony tune?"

"She told me to keep it, Sergeant Herc," he said.

"I'm not Sergeant Herc, you idiot. Where's the girl's things?"

Observe the target. Allow the throwing arm to continue forward naturally once the grenade is released.

"I'm not going to ask you again. What did you do with it?" asked his tormentor.

"Gone."

Throw the grenade, Private Rabren. Do it like I said.

"Gone where?" demanded the intruder.

"She took it, Sarge."

"Who took it?"

"The one who was supposed to have it. She took what remained."

"What's her name, dammit?"

"It was Snow. Snow came."

"Come on, buddy." A hand pressed his head downward against the hood of the truck. No air now.

After throwing the grenade, lie on the ground.

"Snow," he wheezed. "Her name. Reporter."

The hand pushed even harder now. Darkness pressed.

"Attaboy, Calvin. You've been a big help there, buddy."

CHAPTER 14

Aloa walked through the shadowed tunnels of the financial district, her head full of what Emily had said. She'd dropped off Doc's van at his apartment and was now headed to the hotel where Jordan Connor worked. She'd thought that, despite Emily's wild accusations, it wouldn't hurt to check out what Jordan had to say.

Above her were banks and wealth management firms. Below her were the rotting hulls of ships that had carried the same kind of fortune seekers to the city during the great Gold Rush. The fever for wealth was so infectious, it was said, entire crews would abandon their ships to look for gold the minute they arrived. Eventually, dirt and rocks were shoved over the abandoned hulls, adding land where there had been water before. Some forty ships in all were buried beneath North Beach and the Financial District.

Dreams above and dreams underfoot, Aloa thought. *So much remains hidden.*

She passed men and women talking industriously on their phones. Heard horns honk, engines rev. The smell of diesel filled the air.

Only a small sign announced the Hotel L's location. Aloa pushed her way through the front doors.

The walls were brick, in a nod to the city's past, the floors covered with thick carpet that hushed conversation. The bar was in a far corner and behind its rich wood counter was a woman who looked like a poster for the benefits of healthy living. She had a wide mouth, blue eyes, and a straight nose that hinted either of excellent breeding or excellent plastic surgery. Her long, gold-red hair was pulled back in a ponytail, and a tight black shirt showed off high breasts and a taut body. JORDAN, the nametag on her shirt announced.

Aloa watched for a moment as Jordan poured expensive scotch for two men in business suits and gave them a brilliant smile. She was the kind of woman who could set off old feelings in Aloa. "Would it kill you to try to look pretty like the other girls?" Aloa's mother had asked for most of her teenage life.

Aloa looked down at her jeans, her Timberlands, and the now-wrinkled shirt she wore and told herself she didn't need to measure herself against women like Jordan Connor, but the warning was about as useful as trying to resurrect the rotten ships from their resting places and sail away.

Jordan was smiling at something the businessmen had said. Aloa thought of Hayley's torn feet, the eye plucked from its socket, the cells in her body heating until they burst. Was jealousy enough of a motive for a death like that? Aloa thought not. Most murders that resulted from jealousy were quick: a gunshot, a stab wound, a blow to the head. She approached the bar.

"Welcome to Hotel L," Jordan said, turning away from the businessmen. "What can I get for you today?"

Her greeting was smooth, professional.

"A Diet Coke," Aloa said.

"Coming up," Jordan said, opening a can and pouring it into a tall glass filled with ice.

Aloa noticed an edge of dark ink peeking from beneath Jordan's uniform sleeve but could not make out the tattoo's design.

"Are you enjoying your stay with us?" Jordan asked, settling the soft drink on a napkin in front of Aloa.

"Actually, I live in the city. I came hoping to have a word with you."

Jordan stilled, her body language indicating wariness.

"I'm a researcher for Novo," Aloa said. "We're doing a story about Hayley Poole. I understand you were a friend of hers."

Jordan glanced down the bar toward the two men. "I'm working," she said.

Aloa followed Jordan's eyes. "It doesn't seem too busy. I just need a few minutes."

"Sorry," Jordan said.

Aloa reached a hand into her pocket and laid a fifty-dollar bill on the bar. "Keep the change," she said. She could afford to be generous. It wasn't her money.

Jordan eyed the cash. "There's not much to tell. She killed herself."

"It's the why that concerns me." Aloa took a sip of her Coke to allow Jordan time to consider.

"If someone else comes, I'll have to see to them," Jordan said.

Aloa pushed the bill toward Jordan. She pocketed it in a single move.

"Did Hayley seem depressed to you?" Aloa asked. Start out with nonthreatening questions, gain whatever trust was available.

"Of course Hayley was depressed." Jordan kept her voice low. "She lost a sponsor and her shins were a mess. She wasn't sure she was going to be able to finish our next race, which would have meant the movie we were doing would show her breaking down, quitting. That's never good."

"I guess not," Aloa said. "How about worried, a little paranoid even?"

"Maybe. It was more like she was biting the hand that fed her, saying corporations mess up the purity of sports."

Aloa cocked her head.

"You know, like professional athletes do what they do but in the back of their minds there's always the fact they have to do more to keep their sponsors happy. They have to make sure stuff goes viral, that they get likes and views, maybe even land on TV. So maybe you take chances, do stuff you wouldn't do otherwise to get noticed. Or maybe you do the opposite and back off from stuff that sponsors think is too dangerous. Lots of those guys say it doesn't happen but it does. It's part of the gig."

"And Hayley felt differently?"

"Both she and Ethan did. He blogged about how sponsorship not only wrecks creativity and judgment but also, if you take a company's money, you're accepting its values too. Like profit and greed don't belong in nature, you know. Like it's wrong or something." Jordan looked up as a well-dressed couple came through the lobby. Aloa willed them to go to their room and not stop at the bar. She needed more time.

"Did Hayley ever use the word 'evil'?" Aloa remembered the mechanic's mutterings.

"Yeah, I think. She was acting strange."

"And you're still doing the documentary?"

Jordan watched the couple glide past and get on the elevator.

"I am. The main focus now, as it turns out."

"A lucky break."

Jordan's nostrils flared slightly. "You think it's luck when your best friend dies?"

"Sorry," Aloa said, and shifted tacks. "When's your next race?"

"I've got France at the end of this month and I'm going to Italy in October."

"So you're deep in training?"

"I am."

"And dropping acid with alcohol is OK?"

Jordan's eyes narrowed. "I know what you're trying to do. Don't pin that on me. We were partying. Nobody forced Hayley to do what she did."

"I'm not pinning it on you." Aloa backpedaled. "Hayley was a big girl. She made her own choices."

"She needed to relax. Get out of her head for a while. It was no big deal."

"But you knew she was an addict, right?"

Jordan wiped at the bar with a damp cloth, not looking at Aloa. "That's the line they fed her in rehab. Not everybody who likes to party is an addict."

"Do you know if she was still high when she left the campsite?"

"Maybe a little. She went at the vodka pretty hard."

"How about you?"

"I know my limits." She lifted her chin.

"The police report said Hayley had gotten into an argument with someone."

"I think they meant T.J. He got mad because she was drinking and also they had this whole thing over her shins and whether she was overtraining." Three men in pressed shirts and expensive slacks came through the hotel's front door and Jordan looked over at them.

Aloa tapped the bar with her index finger to gather Jordan's attention. "A bad argument?"

"Bad for the two of them. T.J. and her were close."

"Did he seem upset when he found out Hayley was dead?"

"What kind of question is that? Of course he was upset. So was I."

"Sorry. Just covering all the bases," Aloa said. "How about that guy named Boots? I'd like to find him."

Jordan glanced down the bar, checking the two businessmen with their scotches. "I didn't really know the guy. He was driving by, stopped, then stuck around for a day. I didn't ask his real name."

Another dead end.

"Is there any reason somebody might be tracking Hayley?"

Jordan cocked her head. "What do you mean, 'tracking'?"

The night before, Doc had identified the device Calvin had given to Aloa as a starter interrupter with GPS tracking that could be used to monitor and also disable a vehicle. Aloa wasn't sure if the apparatus had anything to do with Hayley or if it was just another creation of the mechanic's damaged mind, but it didn't hurt to ask.

"I mean, if somebody put something in her truck that could record where she was and maybe even shut down the engine?" Aloa clarified.

Jordan glanced over at the nicely dressed men. One was gesturing toward the outside while the other two nodded their heads toward the bar.

"It's called a starter interrupter," Aloa said, trying to regain the bartender's attention.

"Oh yeah," Jordan said as the men laughed and headed for the bar's upholstered stools. "There was one in Hayley's truck. The lender put it there. Her credit was terrible." Her eyes were still on the men. "I gotta go."

"Did she ever talk about having somebody take the thing out?"

"I don't know. She called it her ball and chain."

The men settled at the bar. One lifted a finger. "Miss?" he said.

"That's it. I need to get back to work," Jordan said.

"Can't they wait another minute?"

"Are you telling me how to do my job?"

"How come you didn't stick with her? How come you let her drive off by herself?"

Jordan leaned close. "Listen, if Hayley wanted to kill herself there wasn't anything any of us could do. We all tried to help her. Go tell your journalist vulture-friends to find some other life to feed on."

She straightened, turned to the three newcomers at the bar, and smiled. "Welcome to Hotel L," she said.

CHAPTER 15

Seagulls circled above as Aloa sat on a wrought iron bench, her boots propped on a concrete railing fifteen stories above Sansome Street. It was one of those places that gave San Francisco its reputation for whimsy and freethinking, a rooftop hideaway atop a handsome office building open to whoever wanted a bit of peace. Aloa listened to the hum of traffic below, finished jotting down a few notes, and considered the feelings the beautiful bartender had set off. Annie, the counselor who had diagnosed her eating disorder, would not have approved.

Aloa pictured Annie, a tall woman with a fall of dark braids, who she'd met her first year of college. Aloa had gotten a Regents' scholarship to UC Berkeley, a place sometimes labeled a liberal outpost of do-your-own-thingness. But whoever had given it the description had never attended the school. It was filled with goal-oriented, whip-smart young people and sharp-minded professors who triggered every one of Aloa's needs to prove herself. She spent hours in the library, finished every required reading, and turned in papers days before they were due. It was two months into classes, after Aloa had spent four hours studying in her room and devouring a package of chocolate chip cookies, that her roommate, a seasoned bulimic named Sloan Morgan, had introduced her to the world of eating disorders.

"I wish I was like you and didn't care what other people thought about how I looked," Sloan said when she came in and saw Aloa surrounded by books and scattered crumbs.

It was the kind of camouflaged attack Aloa had lived with for most of her life. "She has her great-grandmother's build," her mother, a former Miss Georgia Peach, would tell her friends as she eyed Aloa's frame, her own slender body the product of celery-stick lunches and a never-ending parade of Virginia Slims cigarettes. "That woman pushed out one baby after another and was back in the fields the next day."

As a little girl, Aloa had worked hard for her mother's approval, but when she grew older she realized she would never satisfy a woman whose bitterness rose from her own failure in life—the winning of a handsome young man who she believed would become a university professor but instead ended up a high school biology teacher—and yet, Aloa tried.

She tried with good grades, as the editor of her high school newspaper, and with a cello scholarship to the prestigious Idyllwild summer music program.

"Why do you have to play such an ugly instrument?" her mother had said.

Perhaps that was why having a girl she barely knew point out the imperfection of her body allowed Aloa to fall so easily into restriction. Or perhaps it was the other thing she'd never told anyone about.

Sloan had been more than happy to share her own secrets: the fingers down the throat, the syrup of ipecac taken in just the right dose, the herbal laxatives, the powders with names like Colon Cleanser when that didn't work. The vomiting and continual quest for bowel movements had been too much for Aloa. But standing in front of the spaghetti and chicken potpie in the cafeteria a few days later, she thought if she restricted what went in, it would accomplish the same caloric effect of her roommate's purging. She put a few leaves of lettuce and a tomato slice on her plate and watched others eat, feeling pious and punished at the same time.

Aloa lost five pounds fairly quickly, then three more. She liked how her stomach flattened and her jeans loosened. But, even more, she liked the sense of achievement and the peace that being in control gave her. People began to tell her how good she looked and her mother eyed her frame without her usual frown. Aloa told herself she was just getting healthy when she began jogging and lost seven more pounds. She set timetables for when she would eat and then pushed herself past them. Her mind felt clear, her body like a feather. Ten pounds. Then fifteen.

Aloa made excuses to herself when her hair stopped growing and her period stopped. Her breath turned rancid and she shivered with cold. Aloa told herself to stop but she couldn't. Starving was her accomplishment. Starving was the thing she could do well.

When Aloa came down with pneumonia toward the end of her freshman year, the physician at the health clinic took one look at her and called in Annie.

Annie sat on one of those rolling stools while Aloa shivered and coughed on the exam table. "What you have is a disease," she said. "Your brain is acting like a bully. It's feeding you a line of crap because of its own insecurity. Bullies need to be ignored. They need to be put in their place."

The logic appealed to Aloa's need for accomplishment, but Annie warned her things weren't as straightforward as they might seem. It took Aloa all summer and daily support group meetings just to learn how to eat again. But then school resumed and, by February of her sophomore year, Aloa was eighty-seven pounds and in the hospital with a heart that fluttered in her chest like a frantic bird. Two weeks later, she was in a psych ward her mother had found. A place filled with girls who threatened suicide or cut their skin with razors or talked to people only they could see. Aloa had escaped only after she'd used the willpower she'd relied on for restriction to push through the nausea and shame that filled her with every bite of food. They'd let her go when she had gained ten pounds, and she vowed never to go back.

She'd relapsed twice since then—the second slipup just before her firing from the *Times*, with her mother gone and all the guilt and old feelings piling up.

She would not let restriction rule her life again.

She had a job to do and questions to answer, even though Hayley's mother had left her wondering at the gullibility that grief could inspire. Still, Aloa thought there was something wrong with the picture the cops had painted of Hayley's death, something in her gut that told her the runner's demise was more than suicide. Instinct was one of the things Aloa still trusted in herself.

She rode the elevator down, strode into a nearby coffee shop, and bought a chocolate croissant, almost slapping the money onto the counter. Then she walked into the sunlight, taking a deep breath of the city Paul Kantner of Jefferson Airplane had once called "forty-nine square miles surrounded by reality," and bit into the pastry.

She tasted butter, the sweetness of dark chocolate, felt golden flakes of crust tumble onto her hand. She wiped bits of chocolate from the corners of her mouth.

All around her, the city moved and breathed.

CHAPTER 16

Aloa's father always said that when you walked into a forest or meadow or slough, the first thing you needed to do was be still and let the habitat recover from the shock of your arrival. Birds that had wheeled into the sky would settle, animals that had scurried into the brush would venture back, and insects that had frozen in their tracks would move again. She'd let that advice guide her now. She'd wait and see what developed.

She had just balled up the bakery bag and tossed it into a trash can when she heard a text alert chime.

Need to see you tonight if possible. Something important has come up. It was Michael.

I'm not flying to New York, she texted back.

At my SF house. Had a meeting. Will send a driver for you at 9, came the almost immediate reply.

"Dammit," she muttered under her breath.

The city was settling toward evening and Aloa sensed the fog sitting just offshore. She climbed the last hill to her house, her lungs, as always, rebelling at the steep incline. She thought that if you wanted to live in San Francisco, it would help to have a little bit of mountain goat DNA.

As she approached, she fished her keys out of her pack, looked up, and groaned. There on her front porch was the Brain Farm, mugs in hand, a box of Cabernet beside them.

"Ink," Tick said, lifting his cup in salute.

"What are you guys doing here?" Aloa put her hands on her hips.

"When you didn't show up at Justus we got worried," Doc said. "We came here to wait."

"I had a long day," Aloa said. "I just want a shower."

Doc lifted up a brown paper sack. "We brought food. Guillermo insisted. Ginger-carrot soup with pork dumplings or something."

They were like old dogs who limped and farted and accidentally peed on the carpet, Aloa thought: lovable but energy-sucking.

"Look, I appreciate all you guys did, the computer search and the van and everything," Aloa said. "But I can handle things from here on out."

"Yeah, but you haven't heard this part yet," Tick said. He drained his cup and clunked it down on the step next to him. It was obviously not his first mug of wine.

"We've been doing a lot of thinking," Doc said.

Uh-oh, Aloa thought.

"Remember how I couldn't find anything about Samantha Foster?" Tick said.

Aloa nodded.

"Well, that just doesn't happen anymore. Credit cards, prescriptions, cell phones, social media. We all leave technological bread crumbs, so to speak."

"True that," Doc said.

"But this gal's trail stops a week or so after your girl died. I called her sister and then her mother."

Aloa put her palm to her forehead. "Tick, you didn't."

"Hell yeah, I did. And guess what?"

"What?" Aloa asked tiredly.

"They haven't heard from her. Not a word. And she usually checks in every other day, even when she's traveling."

"And something else. How'd Hayley's truck end up so far from the highway?" P-Mac chimed in.

"She was coming down from her high and the roads are a mess out there," Aloa said. "It wouldn't take much to make a wrong turn."

"But who slipped her the acid?" Tick asked.

"They were partying," Aloa said. "I talked to her friend, Jordan Connor, this afternoon. She was at the campout. She said Hayley wanted to relax."

Tick lifted a finger. "Or maybe somebody there wanted her compliant."

"Yeah, just like at Edgewood Arsenal," P-Mac said, continuing when he saw the blank look on Aloa's face. "That's where the army fed drugs to so-called volunteers in the name of national defense. Acid, ketamine, BZ. They wanted to study enhanced interrogation and gas warfare."

All three men nodded.

"Maybe she knew something. Maybe somebody wanted her gone," Doc said. "Tick looked up her boyfriend's blog. He was writing about how corporations buy the lives of extraordinary people as masks for their corruption. Athletes hawking for pharmaceutical companies, actors shilling for crooked banks, musicians selling out to carmakers, even climbers like him."

"They buy you and then call it freedom," P-Mac chimed in.

"It's how corporate America runs our lives," Doc continued. "They have us by the balls."

"And the only way out is to hit back. Kick 'em where it hurts," Tick said.

"Like Ethan did," Doc said.

"And look what happened to him. He wound up dead," P-Mac said. "Killed by bandits? My ass."

"Hayley must have known something, and they came after her too," Tick said. "Ever heard of The Syndicate? A secret society of corporate types trying to take over America. Very clandestine. All undercover."

Aloa took a deep breath. "This isn't a Dan Brown novel, guys."

"What about Uranus and the High Priest? That's code, man," Tick said.

"And what about the annuity, huh?" Doc said. "That stinks like my grandfather's socks."

"Ethan's sponsor bought the annuity. It was in Ethan's contract. Like life insurance," Aloa said.

"Oh." The men's faces fell.

"What about that starter interrupter?" Doc asked.

"Subprime lender. Hayley knew it was in her truck."

"Then how did the mechanic get it?" Tick pressed.

"Not sure. Maybe he took it out for her. It's on my list of questions."

"What if . . . ," Tick started.

Aloa held up her hand. "Just stop. Please."

The three men looked at each other. "Are we off the case?" P-Mac asked.

"I don't remember you guys being on the case."

"Implied contract," Doc said.

"Could we at least look for that Samantha girl? Her mom is real worried," Tick asked.

"Maybe check out those crime scene photos too?" P-Mac said.

Aloa looked at their lined faces, their hopeful eyes. This was the most excitement they'd had since the Occupy movement, which had broken their anarchistic hearts when it fell apart.

"All right, but just for a little while," Aloa said. "I have an appointment at nine."

The men stood, dusting off the seats of their faded and baggy pants. Tick tucked the wine box under his arm.

"And no more conspiracy stuff, all right?" Aloa asked.

The men didn't answer.

CHAPTER 17

Aloa came out of her room, spiking her damp hair with her fingers. "Good enough," she told herself, even though she'd changed three times: from jeans and a shirt to a knit dress over tights, and then back to jeans and a black pullover with her Timberlands. Did she look too much like Steve Jobs? *This is ridiculous,* she told herself. She would wear whatever the hell she wanted.

She was stopped from more fashion musings by a yelp from P-Mac. The Brain Farm was on her couch, studying the crime scene photos on the obscenely large TV she'd grudgingly accepted. They had obviously hacked into her email and found the file she'd requested from Michael yesterday. She wanted to tell them her email was private and not to be tampered with, but what good would it do to set rules for anarchists?

P-Mac moved toward the TV in a half crouch. He pointed triumphantly. "There it is, baby. Right there," he said.

In front of him was a wide-angle photo of the crime scene, Hayley's body splayed in a sandy wash. One arm was spread outward as if reaching for something, the other folded almost protectively across her chest. Her wounded body and missing eye belied the appearance of someone at peace.

"Crank it up, Tick." P-Mac tapped the screen. "Zoom in right there."

Tick tapped commands into the laptop, causing the photo to enlarge and shift and then enlarge again.

P-Mac pointed to a corner of the TV. "See that? That's your evidence."

Tick and Doc got up from the couch and joined P-Mac. They squinted at the screen. "Hell, yeah," Doc and Tick chorused.

"I don't see anything," Aloa said.

P-Mac waved her over and pointed to a grainy image of a spiky creosote bush located five or six yards from Hayley's body. There was something under it, something small with a curved shape to it. "See that?" He tapped the screen again. "That's your answer."

"Your big fat answer," Tick echoed.

Aloa wondered how much of the wine box the old boys had emptied.

"What is it?" Aloa asked.

P-Mac straightened. "If that's not a sapper tab, I'll eat my hat."

"The leading edge of America's sword," Tick cried.

"I have no idea what you're talking about." Aloa leaned closer to the TV. She could just make out the small, arched shape. It was pushed against the base of the bush, most of it covered in sand. One edge curled outward to reveal what looked like the top half of the letter *S* or a *C*.

"Comes from the French word, 'to dig,'" P-Mac said. "Sappers were brave sons of bitches, the guys who dug trenches under enemy fire so the attacking army could get close to a fortification. Nowadays they blow up stuff, clear landmines. There are only three skill tabs in the army: Special Forces, Ranger, and Sapper. You've got to be badass to wear them."

"So you're saying . . . ?" Aloa asked.

"I'm saying, somebody associated with the army, a sapper, was near your girl's body when or just before she died," P-Mac said.

An eerie tickle ran down Aloa's spine, the sense that something dangerous had just tapped her on the shoulder. She'd had the same feeling once, hiking in Montana with her father. Circling back a short time later, they'd found the paw print of a grizzly over their own footsteps.

"Her killer?" she said.

"Exactly," said the Brain Farm and nodded their collective gray heads.

"If that thing is what you say it is, how come the police didn't take it as evidence?" Aloa asked.

"Look at the shadows," Tick said. "It's late. The cops probably wanted to get out of there. They scooped and scrammed."

"Plus something like that would wreck their suicide theory," Doc said. "Pigs see what they want to see. That's why you've got those white cops shooting black people for felony possession of the wrong skin color."

Aloa remembered the surliness of Detective Torres, his disdain for campers like Hayley who came into his jurisdiction and caused trouble with the locals. And wasn't the lead detective a few weeks from retirement when he caught Hayley's case? Maybe he wasn't a bad guy, maybe he wanted to do his job. But wouldn't it be easier to pick the obvious answer instead of leaving with an unsolved murder on your conscience? A last failure?

"I'm thinking that girl didn't go into the desert voluntarily," P-Mac said.

The Brain Farm nodded their heads.

"It was a death march," Tick said.

"You can run but you'll only die tired," P-Mac said ominously. "That was something they said in Iraq."

"But at some point, your girl fought back," Doc said. "She tore that tab off her killer's shirt."

"She wanted us to find her murderer," Tick said. "She gave us a last clue."

Aloa lifted a hand. "Hang on a minute, please."

A lesson she'd learned as a reporter was not to immediately dismiss a theory but also not to embrace it without question.

"So you're saying Hayley was killed by a sapper, by someone in the army?"

The men looked serious.

"Are you thinking it was the mechanic, Calvin?" Aloa said.

"Maybe he followed her there. Maybe he got triggered. You said he was in love with her," Tick said.

"No one who goes to war ever comes back the same," P-Mac said.

"Was he a sapper?" Aloa asked.

"I'll see what I can find," Tick said.

"You should eat your soup," Doc said, handing Aloa the container the men had brought from Justus. "Erik said we shouldn't leave until we saw you eat it."

Aloa pried the lid off the take-out container. Smells of ginger and citrus rose to meet her. She thought of Calvin. Had war planted the seeds of violence in him? Enough to kill a friend?

"Wine?" Doc asked and held up the box.

"I'm good," Aloa said, and took a spoonful of soup, her mind running.

A few minutes later, Tick sagged back in his chair. "Infantry. Not a sapper."

"A wannabe then," P-Mac said. "I've seen it. He could have washed out of the program but wouldn't let go of the idea."

"He seemed more like a guard dog than somebody who was jealous," Aloa said.

"And what happens when you mistreat a dog? He bites back," Doc said.

"Or it could have been PTSD, a triggered blackout," P-Mac said. "I've seen guys lose days after something as simple as a car backfire or a scene in a movie."

"Maybe something set him off out there in the desert," Doc said. "Maybe he thought she was the enemy."

"We need to find out if he was there," P-Mac said. "You know, look at credit cards, cell phone records."

"Can you get hold of them, Tick? Maybe find Hayley's cell phone records too?" Aloa asked.

"I can try," said the grizzled anarchist.

"How about VA records for Calvin, psychiatric reports?"

"Those are tough," Tick said. He looked up as a grin split his face. "But there are always back doors to what they don't want you to know."

P-Mac began shimmying his shoulders in a lewd way and singing an old blues tune. "You gotta open doors, on what they don't want you to see."

"Shut up, old man," Tick growled.

"Ladies in the dark, little girls in their finery," P-Mac sang.

Tick lifted a fist. "How'd you like a bite of a knuckle sandwich?"

"Wait. Wait. That's it," Doc said. "'Little girls in their finery.' 'What they don't want you to see.'" He snapped his fingers. "What if Calvin is also the reason we can't find Samantha? What if that goofball is out murdering women he befriends?"

"Jesus," Aloa said.

She thought of the serial killer she once had interviewed in prison, a cell-phone salesman named Jimmy Anderson who'd abducted five women over the course of three years and, after raping and torturing them to death, cut off their index fingers to wear as a necklace. Anderson had seemed completely normal as he talked to Aloa about growing up in Oklahoma, about hunting with his contractor father, and dropping out of TCU. And yet, there had been something in his eyes that gave away the sickness inside him: a flat deadness that made Aloa feel as if she were sitting across from the devil himself.

She had felt none of that with Calvin and yet . . . She thought of him waving the knife, of his warning about staying away from the High Priest. What if the High Priest was an alter ego? What if he was out there murdering women? A ripple of nausea passed through her as she imagined him standing over Hayley's body. She set the soup aside.

She was saved from considering more by a discreet knock at the front door.

She stood. "You guys do what you can. I'll be back in an hour or so." But it was as if she hadn't spoken. The Brain Farm was already deep in argument, zooming in and out on crime scene photos and dissecting investigations into serial killers who had haunted California: the Grim Sleeper, the Night Stalker, the Trailside Killer. Aloa hated the way the media turned murder into movie titles, the way it tried to titillate with death. She'd covered enough trials to know murder was neither sexy nor entertaining. It was ugly and evil and the very darkest part of humanity.

CHAPTER 18

Sunk in the soft leather seat of a black Porsche SUV, Aloa was whisked to a three-story house in the Marina District across from the Palace of Fine Arts.

It was a neighborhood of expensive homes, built on a former marshland that had been covered with the rubble of bricks and stone from the city's devastating 1906 earthquake and later converted to housing by developers. Its boggy, hodgepodge foundation would come to haunt the neighborhood in 1989, when the Loma Prieta earthquake returned the neighborhood to a tumble of shattered walls and fallen chimneys. It was quickly rebuilt and now housed the city's newest and most hip millionaires.

The driver pulled up in front of a sage-colored stucco house accented with rich wood and tall windows. Its straight lines gave it a more modern feel than the Mediterranean Revival–style homes around it.

"I've notified Mr. Collins of your arrival," said the man. He had a ramrod-straight back and brush-cut hair and had identified himself as Vincent. She guessed he was ex-military.

He led Aloa across the sidewalk and through a pair of wood-and-frosted-glass gates to the house's front door. The air here smelled of salt and sea and money.

Vincent held his cell phone up to a recessed reader and escorted Aloa through a pair of hammered-copper doors to a vestibule of wood and stone where an elevator awaited.

Aloa stepped into the paneled cubicle and Vincent leaned in and tapped a button. "There you go, miss," he said.

Aloa did not believe in stereotypes, but as the elevator doors closed with an almost reverent hush, she suddenly wished them to be true. She hoped Michael had turned into the hackneyed geek—unwashed, scruffy beard, sweatpants, ratty shirt—and that this beautiful house would be filled with rumpled couches, Star Trek posters, pizza boxes, a pool table.

Instead, the elevator doors opened to an expanse of wood and glass. Expensive parquet floors, sleek furniture, and a handsome blaze in a floor-to-ceiling fireplace filled the space. Rock music played softly from hidden speakers. She stepped out and there he was near a bank of windows: dark-haired, feet bare, wearing jeans and a cream-colored thermal top that showed off buff pectoral muscles and biceps. Aloa could not help the ripple of want that tickled low in her belly.

"Aloa," he said.

"Good to see you, Michael," she answered, though they both knew it was a lie.

For a moment, there was no sound except for the faint thrum of rock music, like an erratically beating heart, and she wanted to step back into the elevator, push the buttons, and go.

"Shall I take off my shoes?" Aloa asked instead, looking at his feet on the beautiful floors.

"If you want," he said. "I lived in Japan for a while and just got in the habit, but I don't ask others to do it. I have slippers if you want."

"I guess I'll keep my boots on," Aloa said, remembering the socks she'd pulled on with their threadbare heels.

"Please. Come in," he said, and Aloa moved into the room. Awkwardness was a wall between them.

"That's a nice view." Aloa nodded her head toward the front windows, which looked out onto the Palace of Fine Arts. It had been built for the 1915 Panama Pacific International Exposition and now was one of the city's most popular tourist destinations. At night, its soaring columns were golden with light.

"Maybeck is one of my favorites," Michael said of the building's architect.

"I'm more the Julia Morgan type," Aloa said.

"Can I get you something? Wine? A martini?" asked Michael, ignoring her challenge. He swept his arm toward a beautiful coffee table dotted with small plates of sushi and bowls of edamame and pickled vegetables. "I ordered a few things. I didn't know if you'd be hungry."

"No thanks. I just ate," Aloa answered, guessing he didn't know her history. People usually pressed plates of fattening foods on former anorexics. Pastas, cheeses, cakes—as if not eating was simply due to not having enough hearty food in front of you.

"Well." Michael looked toward the fireplace where a blaze crackled against the evening chill.

"I'll take a glass of wine, though," Aloa said.

Michael seemed relieved to have something to do. "Pinot?"

"Sounds good," Aloa said as he went over to a curved bar made of some kind of exotic wood.

She stood, her eyes roaming the space as he opened the wine: gleaming kitchen, a staircase descending to the floors below.

"Your home is pretty impressive," she said.

"I guess," he said. "I bought it a year ago. I needed something near the office. We're transitioning most of our folks here."

"But you live in New York," Aloa said.

"Most of the time. I also have a place in Montana." He said it almost apologetically.

He poured two glasses of wine and moved toward her. He smelled faintly of soap.

His eyes moved from her hair to her lips, which she'd painted a dark burgundy. "You look good, Aloa," he said quietly.

"Stress and poverty do wonders for a girl," she said.

He smiled. "I appreciate that you came."

"You're paying me, aren't you?"

A pause. A slight dilation of his amber eyes.

"I suppose I am," Michael said. "Shall we sit for a few minutes?" He gestured toward the couch.

"You're the boss," Aloa said. She took the wineglass, careful that their hands would not touch, and waited for him to settle. She perched on the opposite end of the sofa.

He swirled the wine and took a sip, not pretentiously but appreciatively. Aloa did the same. The wine tasted of blackberries and mineraled soils. Exquisite, of course.

She set the glass aside and cleared her throat. "Listen, before we go any further, I need to clear something up."

"Sure," he said.

"Exactly what made you hire me? You and I both know there are plenty of journalists out there who'd jump at the chance to write for you. Plenty of reporters who aren't carrying around the baggage that I am," she said. "If pity is the reason, then I'm out of here. I don't need some prince swooping in to save the ruined reporter from the streets."

"That's not how it is," he said quietly. He swirled his wine in the glass. "I asked you to check out the story because you're a good reporter, Aloa," he said. "The people at Novo are great, but they only want the big story. They don't see why anybody would care about some woman who walked off into the desert. They don't understand that she's somebody's daughter, somebody's friend."

Aloa saw his jaw work. Bruce Springsteen leaked softly from the speakers.

"Or somebody's sister?" she asked.

He tossed back his wine and poured himself another glass. "Yeah, that too."

Aloa knew what Michael's sister had meant to him. He'd told her out on the raft one day when the heat was like a blanket and even the frogs wished for a breeze.

"You had no part in Michelle dying," Aloa said.

"The hell I didn't." He stood up and went over again to the window. "The reason she ended up where she did is exactly my fault. I told her not to push him, but she did. I should have gotten her out of there."

He shoved a hand in the pocket of his jeans.

"When she died, people said, 'Oh well, just another dead delinquent. So what?' She wasn't cute enough, not all-American-girl enough—until my father shot himself, and then the press descended like flies. You want to know why I wanted you to do this story?"

He turned back to her.

"That's what I asked," Aloa said.

"Hayley's death felt the same way to me. Like nobody cared enough to look beyond the obvious. Did you know Hayley had a miscarriage five months before Ethan left?"

Aloa felt a wave of lightheadedness. "Nobody told me." She took another sip of wine.

"She was only about eight weeks along, but Emily said she and Ethan had already decided the Africa trip was going to be his last. They were going to move to Wyoming, to live off the land instead of living off sponsor money. He even built her a cradle, for Chrissake. Hayley told her mom it took feeling a life inside her to understand that simply walking the earth was a miracle. When she lost the baby, it was more than a month before she accepted it wasn't inside her anymore. Then Ethan died."

He moved away from the window toward her. "She was somebody, 'Lo. I knew you would get that. I knew you would see Hayley as more than a headline because I've read the stories you've done. I also knew that, given the opportunity, you would work twice as hard as anybody else. I trust you to do this right."

Aloa's hand shook as she set down her glass of wine. *Change the subject,* she told herself. *Change it now.*

"You know the mom is a little off," she told him.

"I gathered that."

"She told me she talked to Hayley's ghost."

"Grief is grief, 'Lo."

He stood halfway between her and the windows, a distance that seemed to stretch from the past to the present and made them quiet.

"I never told you why I left."

Aloa suddenly felt like she needed air. If they started talking about his leaving, there was no guarantee it wouldn't lead to what had been between them . . . and the aftermath of that. What happened was her secret.

"It doesn't matter. It's the past; let it lie," she said.

Michael opened his mouth, but she lifted a hand.

"How about if we keep this professional? Just tell me why you wanted to see me."

"All right. If you want. Let's get to it," he said, and came over to the couch. He cleared his throat and checked his phone. "We've got a few minutes," he said, and lowered himself onto the cushions.

She could feel the heat coming off him. "A few minutes before what?"

"I've got a friend. He's going to leave his access open for a few minutes while IT does its weekly backup. He told me what to look for."

"And who's this friend?"

"It's better you don't know."

"I'm not doing anything illegal. I've already had my professional ass kicked once and I'm not wild about having it kicked again."

"That's why I'm going to do it," he said. "Your fingerprints won't be anywhere near this thing."

"Michael," she said, and started to rise. "You know why I can't do this."

"Wait."

He touched her arm and she pulled away.

"Listen, Aloa, I wouldn't do this if I didn't think we needed to. My friend called it a 'smoking gun,' some kind of report the government wants buried."

"Why can't we just file a FOIA?"

"I'm not sure you could get what we're going to see. If we need to, we can go back and do FOIAs to back up what we already know, maybe get someone to comment on the record." He turned to her. "I think the boyfriend, Ethan, might have been mixed up in something."

Once, when Aloa was eight, her father had caught her on the upstairs extension listening while her mother complained to one of her friends. "I don't know what I did to get such an ugly thing for a daughter," her mother had said. "Lord knows I've tried, but when God hands you a turd, you can polish it all you want and it's still a turd, if you know what I mean."

Her father had gently hung up the phone, wiped Aloa's tears, and told her that curiosity was a fire for some people, but that they needed to be careful not to get burned. He'd been right, of course. Aloa's intense curiosity had made her good at her job but had also gotten her into more than a few scrapes.

Slowly, she sat back down.

Michael picked up a tablet from the table and tapped a few instructions into it. A television screen above the fireplace came to life. "OK. So here's a map of Africa, and there's Chad smack in the middle of it. It's a pretty rough place. Infrastructure is bad, water is scarce, the average age at death is forty-nine. They've got oil but not much else, and there's a lot of disputes over that." He was businesslike now.

"They've also got political trouble all around them," he continued. "Sudan, Nigeria, Libya, Mali. But one of the things Chadians are good at is fighting. Back in the eighties, their army took on Muammar Gaddafi with pickup trucks and machine guns. Beat his ass. Some historians call it 'The Toyota War.'" Another tap of the tablet screen. "Now, there's this: the Chadian army's Special Anti-Terrorism Group. It's called SATG. The US gives it money to help secure their borders, catch terrorists and prosecute them, spy."

"And that's what this document is about?" Aloa leaned toward the screen.

"I think so. When I started digging around for the background you said you wanted on Hayley's boyfriend, I came up with an obscure reference to SATG and the Tibesti Mountains. It rang a bell so I got in touch with a friend who owes me a favor from a long time ago."

"Homeland Security? CIA? State?" Aloa asked.

"Better not to know."

"But if I need to know later?"

"We'll figure something out."

Michael swiped his finger across the tablet. A map, this time of Chad, appeared with a dotted black line running jaggedly through it. "That's part of the path Ethan took. It's an old trading route, developed by Idris Alawma in the 1500s. He was a devout Muslim, a smart ruler, and a brutal war commander. Some people call him the godfather of the scorched-earth policy." Another image rose, that of a rugged mountain range lifting from a desolate landscape. "And that's the Tibesti. There's talk of terrorists being trained there. From what I can tell, Ethan and his partner went straight into a region where certain cells are suspected of operating."

"You're not telling me Ethan was CIA or something, are you?" Aloa remembered stories of the agency trying to recruit aid workers as covert operatives, of spies posing as journalists.

"I don't know," Michael said. "I do know there was some activity in that area around this guy, Amine Mokrani, at about that same time." Michael flashed an image on the screen of a man in fatigues with a black headscarf. The man was bearded with a narrow face and gray eyes. "He ran a terrorist faction. An extreme group of Wahhabi Muslims who called themselves The Bloody Hand Brigade. They attacked a couple of hotels, killed an aid worker, then started kidnapping Westerners for ransom. His group was thought to have a training camp in Mali and then in Chad. There's another group in play, too, one that's even worse. They've named themselves the Holy Army. Besides blowing up a couple of gas plants and slaughtering a convoy of UN observers, they've kidnapped and sold girls as young as ten as sex slaves. They've cut out women's tongues if they weren't submissive enough, put out their wives' eyes if they caught them even glancing at another man."

Aloa shook her head at the barbarism.

"They've called for holy revenge against anything Western."

"You're talking about Ethan being killed by terrorists?" Aloa asked.

"I don't know. My friend said the document we're going to see is very interesting. Something that either fell through the cracks or was deliberately hidden."

The old reporter who had taught her about knock-and-talks also told her that if something smelled fishy, you'd better look around for sharks. Why had Ethan decided to climb in a place haunted by terrorists? Had no one bothered to warn him about that? Or was that the reason he'd gone?

Michael glanced at his phone. "Time to see what we've got."

"So he lied," Aloa said, leaning back in the webbed chair in Michael's office. On the wall behind her were photos of turquoise waves, a misty jungle, a Japanese shrine. In front of them was a long cherrywood table that held a quartet of computer screens.

Michael swiveled his chair toward her and steepled his fingers under his chin. "Tell me."

Aloa recounted the story Combs had reported: How robbers had sliced the throats of Ethan and the Teda guide as T.J. Brasselet watched in horror. Then, how T.J. said he had managed to make his way through the desert to safety. But the document they'd seen, which appeared to be a report from two SATG operatives, told a different story.

Combs would freak out when he discovered he'd fallen for a lie, Aloa thought.

The spies detailed how they'd stumbled on two bodies while checking out a report of suspicious activity in the area and began following the tracks of two camels and three men.

By 1:00 a.m., they'd located the three men at a makeshift camp. Two were in headdresses and combat gear while the third appeared to be a foreign male with his hands bound. The spies believed they'd come across kidnappers working with either the Holy Army or The Bloody Hand Brigade. They'd hoped the men would lead them to a camp belonging to one of the groups, but a hyena pack arrived and spooked the camels, which sent the kidnappers scrambling after the escaping animals. Their captive ran, and the operatives decided it was more important to discover a terrorist camp than save one guy and went after the men in headdresses. The report never said whether the suspected kidnappers were arrested or whether a terrorist lair had been discovered, but the bodies of the two men were later identified as Ethan Rodriguez, thirty, of California, and Atahir Hassan Bello, age approximately thirty-four, a native of Chad, which meant the kidnapped foreigner had to be T.J.

Aloa tapped her pen against her teeth. "The big question is why the government never said anything about an American being killed by suspected terrorists."

"Probably because they don't want us to know the extent of our involvement in the area," Michael said. "Boots on the ground but not really on the ground, if you know what I mean."

Aloa nodded, remembering covert operations the US government had undertaken: Iran-Contra, Operation Fast and Furious. Playing dangerous games without rules. She knew there were scores of these secret actions that had never come to light.

"And the second question is, why would T.J. lie to Combs for the article? Why didn't he say he was kidnapped?"

"The government has ways of persuading people to keep quiet: threats by the IRS, plant a pound of cocaine, and, boom, it's jail time."

Aloa knew the Beltway had a way of turning regular people into power-hungry hucksters. "OK, here's another thing. If those guys were really terrorist kidnappers, why would they kill Ethan? Wouldn't they get more ransom for two people than for one?"

"Maybe Ethan fought back or something."

"I guess that's possible. Right now, I don't know what's the truth and what isn't."

"I'm sure you'll figure it out." He smiled. "You've got what others don't."

"A star on journalism's walk of shame?"

He shook his head. "You've got tenacity, Aloa. I saw it the minute I met you."

"We'll see about that. Right now, I should be going." She pushed herself out of the chair.

"Stay for coffee? We could catch up."

"It's late," Aloa said, although it wasn't.

"Maybe another time?"

"Sure," she said, despite the fact she had no intention of ever coming back. "I'll show myself out."

"Vincent will meet you at the end of the hall. He'll get you home safely," he said.

CHAPTER 19

Gray tendrils of fog fled past the towers of the Bay Bridge as Aloa jogged toward the Embarcadero. The day was going to be warm. She'd slept surprisingly well the night before, but then, her insomnia had always been a trickster, striking without reason or pattern as if daring her to figure out how to stop it.

She breathed in the salt air, lengthening her stride down the nearly empty sidewalk. She thought of the questions that swirled around this case, of Michael and what had happened between them a long time ago. A mourning dove moaned its song from a window ledge above her.

Early on, her father had taught her the difference between birdsong and call. Calls were the exclamations of life: Hey! Hawk! But songs were the stuff of sex and territory. Birds sang for courtship, for attraction. They sang to mark real estate: I am here.

It was what all living things had in common, her father had said: the need to affirm their presence in the world. It was what Aloa had lost, what her mistake had stolen from her. She picked up her pace, straightening her back, pumping her arms, trying to erase the list of her regrets. This was no time for a pity-fest.

At the waterfront, she turned toward Cupid's Span, the giant bow-and-arrow sculpture that evoked the god Eros who ruled this city, interspersing her sprints with breath-returning jogs. The HardE app on her phone recorded her workout. By the time she climbed the steps back to her house, she was drenched in sweat and her legs quivered. "Eight hundred calories! Keep moving!" the app proclaimed.

"Screw you," she said.

She took a long shower, soaping herself from head to toe and letting the hot water pound her skin. She toweled off, catching a glimpse of herself in the mirror: small breasts, long legs, a slight washboard of ribs under her skin. She turned away and dressed quickly.

A shaft of sun fell from the kitchen skylight, leaving a rectangle of brightness against the dark wood floor. Aloa made her coffee and ate a toasted bagel standing at the counter. Her laptop was live-streaming NPR's *Here & Now. Exactly where I need to be,* she thought.

She wiped the counters, swept the floor, stowed the French press and the coffee grinder, and went to her desk to work.

She looked through her notebook, found the info she needed, and phoned the lender that held the papers on Hayley's truck.

"It's perfectly legal. She knew what it meant," said the man in answer to Aloa's request for confirmation that he'd installed a Dauntless M750, serial number 04756GA, in Hayley's truck.

"How about if you tell me what it meant," Aloa said. "It's not exactly a feature, like leather seats or cruise control, is it?"

"It meant if she missed a payment, I could shut down her vehicle until she paid me. I got the right to make a living."

"Would you know if she took the device out of her truck?"

"Sure I would. I'd get a signal telling me the thing was off-line. I always tell people not to try it 'cause if they do, I send the tow truck. Boom, the car is gone."

Which meant that since Hayley still had her truck, she'd either asked Calvin to remove the device and rabbited before the lender could repossess her vehicle or that the nasty little piece of technology had still been in her vehicle when she died.

Aloa doodled little squares in her notebook as she thought. "Was the starter interrupter still tracking on July 16?" she asked.

"What?"

"I said, was the device still tracking on the day Hayley Poole died? July 16."

A pause.

"That's confidential information."

"Let me ask this then: Did you trigger the device on July 16?"

"Like I said, that's confidential."

"You know I could file a complaint with Consumer Affairs, don't you? You'd have to disclose the information," she said.

"Be my guest," the man said. "And give me a call in five or six months when they finally get around to what you want."

Aloa knew the guy was right. Like most watchdog groups, the agency was overburdened and understaffed.

"It will look worse if you don't answer my question. Like you have something to hide," she said.

"And here's my answer to that," the man said. He hung up.

Aloa flipped her pen onto the table and ran a hand through her hair. At times like these, she wished she were a cop with real threats to issue and the power to back them up. Even though she'd confirmed the Dauntless device had been installed in Hayley's truck, she was still no closer to answering the question of why Calvin had had it in his shop. Or why he had wanted her to have it.

Aloa waited for her frustration to cool and then dialed an old source in the State Department. A burst of staticky buzz made her hold her cell phone away from her ear. Was her phone dying now? Of course it was. If there was one thing you could count on, it was that technology was about as hardy as a head of lettuce when it came to shelf life and that your equipment would die at the worst possible time.

She was saved from considering the prospect of shelling out cash for a new phone, which then required the purchase of a charger, a protective case, and a doomsday lecture from a sales clerk on the need for insurance because, who knew, you could drop your expensive new phone into a puddle the minute you walked out the door, when her source, a data-recovery expert named Steve Porter, came on the line.

"How's it hanging, girl?" he bellowed.

"It's hanging, Steve," Aloa said.

A forty-year-old desk jockey with a degree from Harvard, Porter always sounded like he believed himself to be a twenty-year-old street tough. He'd been devoted to Aloa ever since she'd written a story that helped exonerate him from accusations he'd cyberstalked a woman who was later found murdered. It turned out Porter's identity had been stolen, a case of a savant being so sure of his security skills he'd forgotten to lock his own back door. The real perpetrator had used Porter's identity to lure the woman into a false relationship that ended with her money gone and a bullet in her brain.

Aloa told Steve she was looking into the death of an American who'd possibly been killed by terrorists in Africa.

"That's some serious shit, man," Steve said.

"I know."

"I gotta tell ya, I just ain't comfortable in front of that particular eight ball," he said.

Aloa knew better than to push and lose a source forever. "What can you give me, then?"

A run of computer keys. "I could give you his tax info for the last five years, travel records, his birth and death certificates."

"I'll take all those. Thanks."

"You stay cool now," Porter said.

Aloa promised she would.

The tax records and travel records revealed nothing unusual for a guy in Ethan's line of work, but the death certificate made her hesitate. From her time covering murder trials, she knew the law required a doctor's presence or some kind of concrete evidence, like a photo, in order to make a finding about a cause of death. But Ethan's body had never been recovered, so how had the medical examiner concluded that an incised wound to the neck was what had killed the climber?

She copied down the medical examiner's name from the certificate, found he lived near the Canadian border in Maine, and gave him a call. No strange noises this time. Maybe her phone would be all right after all.

The doctor was just readying himself for his postlunch walk but said he would help Aloa when she told him she was researching the death of a climber named Ethan Rodriguez as part of a story for Novo.

"Ah yes," he said, his voice a melodious blend of countries she didn't recognize. "I have enjoyed that website very much. Just a moment," he said, and Aloa listened as he clumped into another room and awakened his computer. There was a rustle of papers, the opening of desk drawers. "Just a moment. I need my glasses."

Aloa waited.

"Yes, yes, here it is: Incised wound to the neck with an apparent transection of the trachea and both internal jugulars," he said. "A cutting wound, estimated to be nineteen centimeters in length. The direction of the pathway appeared left to right and slightly upward. I would say Mr. Rodriguez bled out rather quickly."

"And how did you determine this, sir?" Aloa asked.

"A report from an eyewitness, confirmed with a photo. The body was not recovered," the physician said.

"Where did the photo come from?" Aloa asked.

"I received it from the insurance company as part of an annuity claim, but beyond that, I do not know." He chuckled, a quiet heh-heh. "I only ask questions of the dead, not the living."

"And you sent your report to the company?"

"I did."

"Is it public?"

"I'm afraid it is not."

Things are never easy, Aloa thought.

"But this I can tell you: The manner of this young man's death was not suicide. The poor boy was murdered. Thus, the annuity was put in force."

Aloa chewed the end of her pen.

"Does the wound give you any clues about the killer?"

"Ah yes. A wound can tell many secrets," said the doctor. "From what I saw, I concluded the killer was right-handed and that he stood above our unfortunate young man. The victim was either seated or kneeling. This would indicate a ritualized killing, which was confirmed by the witness's declaration."

"A death that was also a statement to the world," Aloa said.

"Or to someone."

The medical examiner paused. *An invitation,* Aloa thought. "What kind of statement?"

"I would say a threat."

Aloa knew this was the delicate part, the dance between a source and an interviewer where the source wanted to provide some information but needed to be asked in such a way that the revelation wouldn't violate their moral or professional code.

"Was the threat obvious?"

"I would say not."

"Would it indicate the killer?"

"Perhaps."

"Did it have to do with the style of the killing?"

"Not that."

"The body position?"

"No."

Such a fragile game of twenty questions, Aloa thought. "Some mark on the body, then?" she asked.

"The mark was not on the corpse." The medical examiner's words were chosen carefully.

Aloa paused.

"Something was in the photo, then?"

"You have said it, not I."

Aloa's mind ran through the possibilities. "Something scratched in the dirt? A note pinned to his clothes?"

The medical examiner was quiet.

"A document left behind? A talisman?"

Finally, he continued, "Do you know, Ms. Snow, that I once wanted to be a cryptologist?"

"An interesting field," Aloa agreed warily.

"One symbol can convey a variety of meanings, yes?"

"True."

"Take the Chi-Rho."

"Sorry, I don't know what that is."

"It is a *P* with the letter *X* across the vertical axis. It is most often referred to as a Christian symbol that evokes the crucifixion of Christ. It was also used by Greek scribes to denote something important."

"Yes?"

"As I was saying, it would be interesting to find the Chi-Rho appearing as a ghost image on a photo of someone's violent end, would it not?"

"Extremely interesting," Aloa said. She could feel her pulse ratchet up a notch.

"Especially if there was some attempt at scrubbing the symbol and yet, it was spotted as a faint apparition when examined through an exemplary computer program. In death, details are important."

"Just like in life," Aloa said.

"An insurance company is only interested in numbers, actuarial tables, but people like myself—and perhaps you—wonder about the significance, the meaning, of symbols and words, do they not?"

"I do."

Another long pause.

"I'm sorry, Ms. Snow, but if I do not leave for my walk now, I will be late for my afternoon nap, which will put off my evening sherry and thus dinner. Perhaps you will let me know what you find?"

"I will," Aloa promised and clicked off the phone.

Aloa knew of killers who left forensic boasts in order to taunt investigators. In some cases, the signatures—a specific wound on a body, words scrawled in blood, the position of a corpse—led police to the murderer. In other cases, like the Zodiac killer, whose identity still stymied detectives in San Francisco, the calling cards remained a vicious taunt.

But what did the symbol on the photo of Ethan's body mean? For that to be answered, she needed context. She needed origin and history. That was the job of both a cryptographer and a journalist: to decipher.

She got up and walked twice through the house in an effort to order her thoughts, but she couldn't yet see a path through the questions that seemed to be piling up around her.

CHAPTER 20

He watched her run past him on the sidewalk, her arms pumping and her back straight. Good form. He'd give her that, at least.

She was tall with dark hair that was shorter than what he'd seen in the photos online. But her eyes had the same kind of intensity. Like they could burn a hole right through you if you were caught in their gaze long enough.

He turned and watched her back as she weaved around an old lady with a Chihuahua, her movements smooth and precise. What the hell had she been doing snooping around that mechanic's shop?

He'd read her history once the cuckoo, Calvin, had given up her name and thought there wasn't a newspaper or magazine that would hire a reporter like her. Not with her baggage. Not with her mistake. Which made her a guard dog without a bite, a bitch without a bark. He shouldn't even worry about her. Yet he did. The people who were paying him expected him to do exactly that.

His clients were powerful people, people who swam in the shadows but whose every move could cause ripples in markets and governments and, yes, even in wars. Screwing up with them wouldn't net you a letter in your personnel file. Instead, you'd wind up with a toe tag in the morgue.

It was what you had to accept if you wanted to play the big game, which he did.

He shoved his hands in his pockets and watched the reporter turn the corner and disappear. He thought it was best not to make any sudden moves but, rather, to listen in on her calls—you could tap almost anyone's phone without even having to touch it these days—and figure out what she knew and why she'd turned up at Calvin's place.

And if she got close?

He turned and headed back toward his car. Well then, she wouldn't be running for her health. She'd be running for her life.

CHAPTER 21

Aloa had just let herself into the house with a bag of groceries—yogurt, fresh fruit, a baguette, some sliced Bayonne ham, and two bottles of Pellegrino—when her phone rang.

She set her purchases on the floor and fished her cell phone from her pocket. "Aloa Snow," she said.

"How are you today, Ms. Snow?" said a woman's efficient voice.

"Who is this?" Aloa asked. Had the government already discovered Michael's intrusion? Was it the CIA? The State Department?

"This is Hannah Ramundi calling on behalf of Mr. Tremblay at RedHawk Nutritionals."

"Oh. Yes." Aloa let out a breath and moved toward her notebook on her desk.

"Mr. Tremblay would like a word. Would you hold?"

"I guess," Aloa said. She hated this corporate ritual: your work interrupted by someone who then forced you to wait while they finished their tasks, which, it was insinuated, were infinitely more important than your own.

Finally, "Ms. Snow, this is Hank Tremblay. I hope I'm not disturbing you." The voice betrayed a hint of his Canadian birthplace and had a slightly hoarse quality to it.

"No, it's fine."

"Good. Good."

He sounded distracted, or maybe he was simply a man who didn't do small talk. "Hayley's mother called me yesterday," he said. "She said you were looking into Hayley's suicide."

"That's true, Mr. Tremblay."

"Please, call me Hank."

"That's true, Hank."

"And you're a writer for Novo? Collins's bunch?"

Aloa reminded herself of the adage about catching more flies with honey and tried to put a more personable tone into her voice. "I'm doing research for them at the moment."

"Splitting hairs," Tremblay said. "The fact is they must have some suspicion that Hayley's death was more than suicide, otherwise they wouldn't be looking into this. Correct?"

"At this point, I'd just say there are a few questions. I'm tying up loose ends."

"I'd like to discuss those loose ends with you," Tremblay said.

"I'd rather not."

"Playing your cards close to the vest. I get that, I do. But Hayley was like family to me. Her and Ethan."

"I'm sorry, but this is the way I work."

"As you may know, I'm not a fan of reporters. Always putting their noses where they don't belong."

Aloa said nothing. Journalism was one of the few professions where people felt free to insult you as soon as they learned what you did.

"But I, too, wondered why Hayley would kill herself," he went on. "She was training hard, focusing on her movie. And yet, sometimes we extinguish our own light for fear of being awash in abundance," Hank Tremblay said.

Aloa wondered what self-help book he had been reading. "Do *you* think Hayley killed herself?"

"As her friend and a believer in goodness, I want to think Hayley went into the desert and simply got lost, but with the note, I think suicide is hard to deny."

"Murder is another possibility," Aloa said. She wanted to test the waters with him.

A pause. "The two men with guns?"

"Alibied by a reliable witness."

"Are you saying there was someone else, then?"

"I'm looking into every possibility."

The squeak of a chair, a pulse of breath. "You're not going to tell me, are you?"

"I'm afraid not."

"I like your spunk, Aloa."

Of the things Aloa had been called—and there were many—the words "spunky" and "cute" were at the top of her list of hated adjectives men used to undermine a woman's power.

"You know what, Aloa? I think I'd like to hire you. We could work out an arrangement."

"I've already been hired by Novo."

"Name your price. I'll double whatever they're paying."

"I'm fine with my paycheck."

"How about I pick your brain, then? I'd like some answers."

Aloa was not about to let her brain be picked, but she had questions for him too. She wondered about his agenda. This didn't feel like an innocent call.

"Come out to the ranch," he went on. "I think you'll find it interesting. Plus you'd be the first reporter to set foot in RedHawk's headquarters. Three o'clock today works for me. I'll have my assistant set it up," he said, and before Aloa could object, the efficient Hannah was back on the line.

As Hannah laid out instructions, Aloa wondered if he'd skipped the chapter in whatever self-help book he had on the dangers of arrogance.

Aloa glanced at her scribbled directions as she steered the rental car past horse ranches and hills of oak and golden grasses. According to the ever-efficient Hannah, RedHawk's headquarters were in the Nicasio Valley, not too far from George Lucas's Skywalker Ranch.

"The gate code is 3247," she had said. "Proceed north for one-quarter mile. Park in one of the designated guest spots to the east side of the main building. Someone will meet you there. Mr. Tremblay does not like to be kept waiting."

From Aloa's recent experience with Tremblay and with other corporate types, that meant it would be she who would be twiddling her thumbs.

RedHawk's headquarters looked like a sprawling ranch house set against a backdrop of rolling hills. The structure was two stories with gabled windows and a wide veranda with pots of colorful flowers. Wicker chairs cushioned with red and yellow pillows dotted the porch, and an Australian shepherd sat at attention at the top of the front steps. For a moment, Aloa wondered if the canine was real or simply another prop to make the place look authentic. She pulled her car into the designated area and was greeted by a handsome blond man in khaki shorts and a polo shirt.

"This way, please," he said as he escorted her toward an outbuilding that resembled a stable.

As Aloa walked, she caught a glimpse of a blue pool with swimming lanes and what looked like an adult-size jungle gym behind the main house. Two blonde women in purple-and-pink Lycra were doing pull-ups from its jutting metal bars. Aloa wondered if part of everyone's job description was to look beautiful.

The competent Hannah, petite and dark-haired in a pantsuit and heels, was waiting in front of the stablelike structure. "Thanks, Justin," she said to Aloa's escort. Then to Aloa, "Mr. Tremblay thought you might like to join him for his afternoon ride."

Aloa felt a pinprick of dread. She did not like horses nor could she understand how you were supposed to control twelve hundred pounds of animal with a pair of thin leather straps. To her way of thinking, it was the horse taking you for a ride and not the other way around.

"I'm not a rider," Aloa began, but Hannah was already through the barn doors and Aloa had no choice but to follow.

The stable was lined with handsome stalls. Overhead fans circulated the air above a herringbone brick floor. A grizzled older man in jeans and a cowboy hat was saddling a spotted Appaloosa while a pale guy in a faded Hawaiian shirt, mismatched plaid Bermuda shorts, and cowboy boots brushed a regal-looking chestnut. *The only two normal-looking people in the place,* Aloa thought.

"Aloa Snow to see you, Mr. Tremblay," Hannah said.

The man in the Hawaiian shirt turned. His nose was slightly hooked, and his wavy dishwater-blond hair hung almost to shoulder length. "Aloa," he said, and came toward her, his arms outstretched.

Aloa saw what was coming and thrust out her right hand while sidestepping left, a maneuver that had saved her from more than a few unwanted embraces.

Tremblay stopped. "Not a hugger, Ms. Snow?" He cocked his head and wiggled his fingers in invitation. "Come on. I'm told my hugs have a wonderful energy, very healing."

"No, thank you," Aloa said firmly.

Up close, Aloa could see the provenance of Tremblay's shirt: vintage silk. His boots were ostrich skin and clearly handmade. He was not what Aloa had expected and yet, it was the appearance of a rare bird that called out for attention, her father said. Was Hank Tremblay's imperfect appearance a deliberate act to throw off people who tried to pigeonhole him? Or was it simply that he was arrogant enough to not care what others thought?

Tremblay dropped his arms. "Well," he said, and Aloa assumed he wasn't used to being rebuffed. "Did you have any trouble finding us?" he asked.

"Hannah's directions were excellent," Aloa said.

"I don't know what I'd do without her." Tremblay laid his palm on his assistant's head and gave it a stroke. If Aloa was right, Hannah didn't appreciate being petted like a dog.

Tremblay looked at Aloa and frowned. "I was going to take you for a ride around the property, but you look exhausted. Traffic must have been terrible."

"I just have a lot going on," Aloa said.

"I know what will fix that. Follow me," he said, and set off down the stable's wide corridor. "Hannah, switch my four o'clock to three thirty and tell my four thirty to meet me in the stable at three forty-five. Garrett won't mind a little cowboy conferencing." He leaned toward Aloa, who matched his long stride. "Off the record?"

Aloa opened her mouth to say she didn't do off-the-record, but apparently Hank Tremblay believed all a source had to do was say the magic words and the information would be private. "Garrett is leading the team on an endurance product we're developing. A complete food source that, when mixed with water, will not only sustain an adult indefinitely but may actually ward off heart disease and cancer. We're still fine-tuning the formula but, if all goes well, we hope to launch in eighteen months, then go international eight months after that. It will be huge. T.J. and Ethan were part of our product development."

Aloa opened her mouth to let Tremblay know off-the-record needed agreement from two sides, but he was already rushing on. "Just think of what that will mean for the average American with diabetes, cancer, and obesity. We also see a use for it for populations in Third World countries, or for those in natural disasters or wars. Easily transported nutrition that will not only sustain but will make its consumers healthier than before. The world is changing, Aloa. Drought, floods, famine, rising sea level, war, refugees. We're on the cusp of a troubled time. We at RedHawk are quite proud of what we're doing."

Aloa added mania as another possibility for Tremblay's behaviors. "Can we talk about Hayley, Hank?"

"Oh yes, sorry. Sometimes my passion carries me away. My father used to say, 'Hank, I don't know where you came from,'" he said, lifting his hand to the jungle-gym women who waved back enthusiastically. In contrast to the colorful Lycra and the neat Hannah, Tremblay looked like the weird uncle who showed up for free meals and a shower.

"Ah, here we are," Tremblay said, and flung open the door to an extravagant farmhouse kitchen of marble, tile, and gleaming white cabinets.

"Would you like something, Hannah? Immunity? Protein?" he asked, going over to a bank of blenders.

"A protein shake, please, Mr. Tremblay," Hannah answered, typing alternately on her phone and her tablet.

Tremblay turned and studied Aloa. "I'm thinking energy with a dash of immunity plus balance. I can see a lot of stress."

Did she look as bad as he made it sound?

"Water is fine," she said.

"Please," Tremblay said, opening a cupboard filled with containers of powders and pills. "I like to help people."

"He does," Hannah affirmed.

"Make yourself comfortable." Tremblay gestured toward a timbered table with heavy benches on either side of it.

Aloa sat and watched him create three concoctions that included handfuls of kale, slices of pineapple and mango, and powders she couldn't identify. His hands shook slightly and his movements had a forced quality to them. Nerves or some neurological problem?

Finally, he loaded a bamboo tray with three glasses that brimmed with a neon-green sludge and brought them to the table.

"Sorry, Mr. Tremblay. I need to meet with Chef for your client dinner," Hannah said. She took her drink and excused herself. Aloa wished for some pretext to leave and dump the brew into the bushes outside.

"Try it," Tremblay said, sliding in across from Aloa. "It's really tasty."

She took a sip and found, to her surprise, he was only slightly off the mark.

"Good taste, good health," he said, saluting her with his glass.

"Mrs. Poole said you took out an annuity for Ethan. Like life insurance," Aloa said, wanting to tether him to the reason she was here or risk leaving without a single question answered.

"I did. He was like a brother to me. I felt a responsibility for him and for Hayley too. I never married and both my parents are gone. We were family." His eyes grew damp. "The guilt over Ethan's death is something I'm going to have to live with for the rest of my life. It was my idea, my plan to explore the Tibesti. The evidence of climate change there is remarkable. There were great meadows, giraffes, elephants, lions. I had such high hopes."

Aloa interrupted. "You planned the expedition?"

"I did."

"Did anybody tell you how dangerous it was? That there were terrorists in the area?"

"Of course. There are bandits and wild animals and sandstorms and dry wells. The whole thing was dangerous, but we took precautions."

"But not enough."

"That's correct." Tremblay closed his eyes for a moment. "There are . . ." He swallowed. "There are always things beyond our control. Things we can't anticipate. That's life, right? All we can do is learn from our mistakes."

Unless a mistake ends in your death, Aloa thought. *Then, learning is not an option.*

"I told Hayley I would take care of her. I had to fight, but I got the annuity put in force. It was too late by then, though. Our relationship was strained and I wasn't the only one. She was lashing out at everyone. Poor girl."

"So you got the death certificate in order to claim the annuity?"

"Of course."

"I'm just curious. Where did you get the photo? The one that showed Ethan's throat cut?"

Tremblay's gaze darted toward the kitchen windows then back to Aloa. "Well, I didn't personally get it. It was my lawyers. I let them handle things like that. You would have to ask them."

"May I have their number?"

He licked his lips. "Of course. Let me just check with them first. There might be privacy issues."

"For whom?"

"You sound like you don't trust me."

"I'm just asking questions."

Tremblay took a glug of his drink. "Just like a journalist. Always thinking the worst of people." He stood. "Come on. Let me show you what we're doing. Maybe you'll realize I'm not the enemy."

Aloa followed him down a long hallway, discreetly setting her glass of green sludge on a shelf behind a tall vase. Her lips buzzed and her fingertips tingled, which did not connote health to her way of thinking.

"Did Hayley seem depressed to you before she died?" she asked.

Tremblay stopped and considered the question. "I think she was," he said. "Things had gotten better, but then she started having issues with her shins and that bothered her a lot. I tried to be encouraging. I sent her a canister of Performance-3, that's our protein powder, which is super important for healing, and I had my nutritionist talk to her. I even offered her a place here to regroup, but she insisted on living in her truck. She said she needed her independence; that everyone was trying to control her. She withdrew from everybody, so I was happy about the Nevada trip. I thought it would be good for her. Instead . . ." He bit his bottom lip. "Instead, it all ended there."

"By her going into the desert?"

"Hayley liked grand statements."

He pushed open a set of heavy double doors, which revealed a large conference room paneled in dark walnut and festooned with banners that urged guests to **BE YOUR BEST SELF** and **LIVE HARD. LIVE LONG.**

"So now it's Jordan who's the focus of the movie?"

Tremblay glanced at her. "Hayley's mother can be a bit over-wrought, as you may have noticed."

Aloa didn't respond.

"Let me tell you this, Ms. Snow. Jordan is many things—competitive, tough, determined—but she loved Hayley. They were friends."

"She gave Hayley drugs."

Tremblay sighed. "Jordan is an individualist. She wanted to have a good time; she was trying to help Hayley relax."

"By offering drugs to an addict?"

"Our perfection is not a guarantee that we will accept it."

Aloa had no idea what he was talking about.

"Did Hayley ever tell you about her friend Calvin? The mechanic."

"She mentioned him, yes."

"If he said Hayley had warned him about someone called the High Priest, would that mean anything to you?"

Tremblay flicked a hand in the air. "I would think a reporter like yourself would know better than to listen to a man as damaged as he is."

Aloa pushed down a flush of irritation. "I'm just trying to rule out the possibility that Hayley was murdered."

Tremblay's eyes narrowed but he held her gaze. "Let me tell you this about Hayley," he said. "She was not as sunny and bright as people on the outside might think. She could slip into melancholy, and after Ethan died, that melancholy shifted into paranoia. Her counselor at the Palms—you know about that, right?"

Aloa nodded.

"Her counselor said Hayley talked about conspiracies, about corporations using athletes to hide their corruption. That hurt me deeply."

"Ethan wrote the same thing on his blog," Aloa said.

"The truth is, Aloa, athletes like Ethan and Hayley are like racehorses. They are things of beauty, born with extraordinary bodies, but they can also be temperamental and single-minded, living outside the normal world. They didn't understand that kind of talk would ruin their careers, that without sponsors they could not do what they loved. Hayley was a very troubled girl."

"You were trying to help her, then?"

"In any way I could. I understood what Ethan was saying, but I also know how the world works. It's not black-and-white. Companies aren't necessarily evil. They often do good. I've tried to keep that at the forefront at RedHawk: serve the world and profit will follow. Hayley couldn't see that, the big picture. But I forgave her." He turned. "Come on, let me show you the heartbeat of our company."

Aloa trailed him into an open office where twenty people toiled over their computers. A snack station was in one corner, its refrigerated shelves filled with energy drinks and colas. Next to it was an espresso machine and shelves of power and protein bars. There was so much energy-inducing nourishment, Aloa wondered how any of the workers managed to stay in their chairs.

"This is where it all happens. This is our team. Scientists, innovators, communicators. From Stanford, MIT. Robert over there is from Yale."

The man named Robert glanced up.

"It looks like your company has lost a few employees." Aloa tilted her head toward a section of ten empty workstations.

"Or, perhaps, we are readying for a great expansion." Tremblay lifted a finger into the air. "Optimism, Aloa."

"That photo doesn't exactly suggest optimism to me." Aloa pointed to a framed photograph on the wall showing the same office bursting with employees.

"There you go again, Aloa." Tremblay wagged a finger at her. "Where you see negativity, I see that we are shifting company focus and are in the process of hiring new people to reflect that. It won't be long before every one of these stations will be filled."

"What's your new focus?" Aloa asked.

"I thought you were looking into Hayley's death."

"I am."

"Then why are you asking questions about my company?" He frowned.

"You invited me for a tour. Questions are what journalists do when reality doesn't match up with what's being said."

A shadow crossed Tremblay's face. "I'm not sure your interest in RedHawk's finances is appropriate, Ms. Snow."

"Why not?"

"Because it has nothing to do with Hayley's death."

"So things aren't tight right now?" Aloa waved her hand to indicate the empty desks.

Tremblay shook his head and opened his mouth, but before he could answer, the same employee who had greeted Aloa in the parking lot came up and tapped him on the shoulder.

"Excuse me, Mr. Tremblay," the man said, "but you're needed upstairs. They said it's important."

And maybe it was the fact that Aloa was still cataloging the half-filled office, or reading a sign on the wall that advised **Loose Lips Sink the RedHawk Ship**, but before she could react, she sensed Tremblay turning and then his arms wrapped her in an embrace.

Aloa felt the dampness of his shirt against her cheek, the press of his pelvis against hers. She tried to pull away, but Tremblay held her tight.

"That's enough," she said into his shirt.

"Relax, Aloa." One hand pressed against the back of her head, pushing her into him.

"Let go," Aloa said, this time more strongly.

"Oh, Aloa, just let yourself be," Tremblay crooned. "Feel the energy, the moment."

But Aloa did not want to feel the moment a second longer. She moved her hand and placed the pad of her thumb at a spot between two of Tremblay's ribs—a maneuver she'd learned from a female cop she'd known in LA—and then she pressed and twisted. Hard.

"Ow. Shit," Tremblay said, stumbling backward. "What the hell was that?" He held a hand to his side. His face was flushed red.

"That," said Aloa, straightening her shirt, "was a reminder that when a woman says 'that's enough' she means that's enough. And that if someone doesn't want to be touched, you shouldn't touch them."

Tremblay looked down at his shirt as if expecting to see blood or some mark to account for his pain. "It was just a hug," he said.

"And that was just another way to say 'let go,'" Aloa said.

CHAPTER 22

Aloa let herself into her house, sorting through her conversation with Tremblay and wondering what it was inside some men that made them unable to hear the word "no." She thought she would finish her notes, then reward herself with an extra-dry martini at Justus before coming home and making herself an omelet. Dust motes danced on the light coming through the front window.

She put away the keys to the car she'd rented—it was parked four blocks away in the only legal spot she could find—and was just checking her messages when there was a knock at the door.

She opened it to find a man in a gray suit who looked like he spent a little too much time at the gym. His white shirt pulled tight across his chest, and above his bullish neck, his head was shaved. He sported a ridiculous little soul patch, plus the kind of mirrored sunglasses cops in B movies wore.

"Can I help you?" Aloa asked.

"Yes, hi. I'm a licensed real estate broker with one of the city's best firms and, well, I have a client who's interested in buying in this neighborhood." He took off his sunglasses and gestured outward toward the street. His eyes were chocolate brown. "As you know, there aren't a lot of homes available right now and the market is going completely insane. Houses here are going for twice their worth. Anyway, I saw your place and thought, 'Now there's somebody who looks like they could use a windfall right about now.'" He gave a grin that showed a piano-row of white teeth. "Am I right?"

"No, actually, you're wrong," Aloa said.

The man leaned in. Aloa could smell his spicy aftershave. "My client is prepared to offer one and a half million dollars cash. One-week close."

This wasn't the first time a realtor had showed up on Aloa's doorstep. San Francisco's real estate market was like a pirate convention: everybody competing for the same treasure with throats being cut, ethics slashed, and truth embellished into lies.

"Not interested," Aloa said.

The man leaned backward as if inspecting the house. "How can you not be interested? Look at this place. Wood rot, termites. I'll bet every appliance in there is at least fifteen years old."

Actually, the stove was forty years old, but Aloa didn't tell him that. "Really, I'm not interested," she said, and began to close the door.

The man stepped into the doorway so Aloa would either have to shove him backward onto the porch or risk hitting him in the nose if she shut the door.

"You should be interested," he said.

"Excuse me?"

"I said, you should be thinking about selling. I looked up your records, and you were thirty days late paying your last property taxes, and your fire insurance is delinquent. The bank's not too happy."

Aloa's eyes narrowed. "Get off my porch," she said.

"Look, you sell this place, move somewhere where houses are cheaper, and you'll be set. You could travel, buy yourself a great car, get some nice clothes." His eyes ran down her frame: the white T-shirt, the faded jeans.

"Listen, Baldy, I'll tell you what: you get off my porch, and I won't burn your ass by sending a video of our conversation to the Bureau of Real Estate and/or the Department of Justice." Aloa gestured to a small security camera mounted in a corner of the porch. No need to mention it hadn't worked in four years.

The man raised his hands and took a step backward. "I'm just saying that this is a great deal for you, but if you don't want to listen, I can't force you." He slid on his sunglasses. "But, you know, life has a way of throwing curveballs, and there might be a day when you'll wish you'd taken my offer."

He waited just long enough for Aloa to tell him to get off her porch again; then he turned and stomped down her front steps.

Aloa watched him stride down the sidewalk until he disappeared from view.

"Asshole," she muttered.

Now she really wanted a drink.

"Thank god you're here," Erik said as Aloa pushed her way through Justus's front door. "Those Groucho Marxists of yours are out of control."

"How are they mine now?" Aloa asked, her head pounding. Talk about a day that had pushed all her buttons.

"That case of yours has them all riled up. I swear to god they're in rut." Erik pointed to a corner of the bar where the Brain Farm occupied two tables. Papers were spread, wineglasses filled, and the men were in full anarchist mode, pointing fingers and arguing loudly with three other patrons, with the consequence that a fistfight seemed not only likely but also imminent.

"Can I use your basement?" Aloa asked. All she wanted was a drink.

"Is Cher fabulous? Of course you can." Erik pointed. "Just get them out of here before one of them has a stroke."

"Will do," Aloa said, wading through the tables toward the voluble gray-hairs. "And could I get a martini, please? Extra dry?"

"I'll do better than that. I'll have Gully bring down today's special. I think you might need it." Erik raised his eyebrows at the gray-hairs, who were stabbing the air with their fingers and gesturing their arms in propellerlike motions.

As Aloa neared the Brain Farm, she could hear Tick loudly proclaim, "You'll be measuring freedom by the number of drones outside your window, baby."

"Are you denying technology?" asked a bespectacled young man the next table over.

"We're denying the brain-dead robots who use safety as an excuse to accept the taking of our freedom," Doc said, equally loudly.

"Guys, guys," said Aloa as she reached the area the Brain Farm had commandeered. She looked at the tables the men had shoved together. "What the hell?" she said.

The surface was spread with copies of the police reports on Hayley's death, maps, and printed copies of the crime scene photos Michael had emailed to her.

"Ink! You're finally here," cried Tick, standing up with a stagger that indicated more than a few glasses of wine had already been consumed.

"What are you doing with my stuff?" Aloa demanded. "Those things are private."

The Brain Farm looked at the mess of papers as if seeing them for the first time.

"We thought we could help," Tick said, chastened.

P-Mac and Doc nodded their heads solemnly.

"We might have found something too," P-Mac said.

"Yeah, something we didn't see before," Doc said.

"You guys can't be stealing police reports and hauling them around for anybody to see. That information is intended for me. Not for half of North Beach," Aloa said.

"We didn't think . . . ," Tick started.

"That's right. You didn't think," Aloa said.

"But we did find something," P-Mac said. "Something that nobody else noticed."

"Yeah," Doc said. "Another thing that casts doubt on your girl just walking into the desert."

Aloa put her hands on her hips. "What did you find?" she demanded.

"You want us to say it? For everybody to hear?" Tick said in his most innocent voice.

Aloa rolled her eyes. No wonder she didn't want children.

"Get that stuff and follow me," she said. "And don't leave anything behind."

The Brain Farm gathered the papers, stuffing them into old leather satchels and worn daypacks, grabbing their glasses of wine.

Behind the bar, Erik shook his head as Aloa marched past with the Brain Farm in tow.

"I'll make that a double," he said.

Justus's basement was a dimly lit cave with rough whitewashed walls and an old-fashioned skylight of iron and thick glass designed to let in sunlight from the alley above. Right now, Justus's blinking neon sign was creating a Morse code of blue and yellow through the glass.

"Sit," Aloa ordered.

P-Mac flipped on an overhead light and the men settled at an old Formica table surrounded by cases of booze and shelves of industrial-size canned goods. Baxter the cat had followed them downstairs and now jumped into Aloa's lap. She gave him a rub behind his ears as he settled. She could hear a purr begin deep in the feline's throat.

Guillermo arrived moments later, announced by scents of cilantro and peppers. He carried a tray laden with food and drink.

"Sashimi taco in the *estilo* Jalisco," Guillermo said, setting a plate with three delicate corn tortillas brimming with raw tuna and topped with a green sauce in front of Aloa. Her taste buds awakened in response to the sight and smell of the dish. *Tremblay's all-in-one nutritional powder would never compete with real food,* she thought, *although it could be an anorexic's dream.*

"*Muchas gracias*, Guillermo," she said, meaning every syllable.

"*Por nada,*" he said, and added a large martini to the table. "My *esposo* say you need a twice drink."

"Double *gracias*," Aloa said.

"And for these elderly, a bread to soak their wines," he added, putting a basket of sliced baguette and a bowl of olive oil on the table.

Aloa wondered if the double entendre had been intentional.

Guillermo hurried back upstairs and, for a few minutes, there was no sound but eating. The sweet fish paired with the crunch of corn tortilla and a spicy sauce made Aloa's mouth tingle with pleasure. It was almost enough to forget the rude real estate agent.

"All right. What did you guys find?" Aloa finally asked, the rhythmic purr of the cat and the martini taming her earlier frustration with them.

"Well," said P-Mac as the men dug out the documents and scattered them on the table, "if you look in the reports, you will notice there was no analysis done of tracks around Hayley's truck."

Doc picked up the stack of police reports. "I checked twice. Nothing."

"And see here?" P-Mac said, thumbing through the crime scene photos Michael had emailed and Tick had printed. He set a photo of the area near the back of Hayley's truck in front of Aloa.

"It looks like a bunch of tire marks. You can't tell one from another," Aloa said.

"That's right," P-Mac said, "but see what it looks like after Tick got hold of it."

He sorted through the photos again and pulled out a blown-up print of what looked to be a small section of tire track. "That's a motorcycle tire near Hayley's truck," he said, and touched his finger down on the shot. "A motorcycle tire has a more U-shaped profile. Car tires are flatter."

"And look here," Tick said excitedly, scrabbling his fingers through the stack of shots.

P-Mac slapped his hand away. "Jeez, Tick. Hold your horses, man."

P-Mac organized the photos, laying out a series of shots into a 360-degree view of Hayley's vehicle. It was the first time Aloa had seen close-up shots of the scene. She'd pulled up satellite views of the area, but it was not the same thing.

She saw an image of Hayley's dusty truck, its hatchback open. Then, a shot of a long stretch of a rough dirt road, a photo of the shell casing, and, finally, an image that made Aloa sit up straighter: Hayley's running shoes and socks set neatly next to a jagged black rock.

For some reason, as she'd read the police reports, Aloa had gotten a picture of Hayley's shoes flung into the wilderness in a kind of desperate statement, but the deliberateness of their placement rattled her. An image came to her of the mentally fragile Hayley walking away from her truck, unlacing her shoes, and carefully placing them next to the stone, then beginning to run. A ritual of strength but also of despair, if the cops were to be believed.

And yet, there were always two ways to look at things, and the placement of the shoes could also mean someone had forced Hayley to remove them and then run her into the desert.

She moved the photo closer to her. "Those shoes sealed her fate, didn't they?" she said.

"It's a wonder she lasted as long as she did," P-Mac said.

"But look here." P-Mac tapped a finger on one of the photos. "Remember what we said about the sapper tab?"

Aloa nodded and stroked a hand along Baxter's bony back.

"Look at the dirt off to the right, in the corner of the shot," P-Mac said. "That's a track from the same motorcycle, and it's heading into the desert in the direction where Hayley's shoes and body were found."

Doc rapped a knuckle on the table. "More evidence for a death march."

"Were there motorcycle tracks near Hayley's body?" she asked.

"None noted," P-Mac said, "but there was wind and the soil was much finer in the wash. You saw how the sapper tab was partially covered with dirt."

Aloa stopped petting Baxter, and he leaped from her lap. "Calvin had a motorcycle," she said, remembering the shiny machine parked in the corner of his shop.

Tick nodded. "I found a DMV registration for a 2006 Kawasaki in his name." He glanced at P-Mac. "I also found a charge for a gas station in Reno on Calvin's credit card. It was for the day Hayley disappeared."

Aloa felt a ripple of memory and waited for it to surface, shoving her half-finished meal away. "When I went to Calvin's shop, he said something about 'fixing it for Hayley,' about tools. Wrenches or something. It seemed like a bunch of nothing, but what if her truck was having engine problems and she called him?" She let her mind run. "What if he went on his motorcycle to help?"

The room fell silent. The background music of every bar in America—glasses clinking, conversation humming, chairs thumping—drifted down the steps.

"What if that capitalist-pig lender triggered the starter interrupter and Calvin found it when he got there?" Tick said. "Then something happened and he killed her."

Doc snapped his fingers. "And he took the interrupter with him afterward to cover up the fact he'd been there. The cops wouldn't know the truck had quit and even if they found her phone and saw a call to him, he could say that she'd phoned to say goodbye."

"But why would he give the Dauntless thing to me?" Aloa asked.

"Guilt," Tick said.

For a moment, they were all silent.

"If he killed her, it's the government's fault," P-Mac said finally. "The Pentagon trains killing into those guys and then sends them into a war where they can't tell a friendly from the enemy. Then, when the guys come back with PTSD, the government says there's no connection between its own violence and what happened; they say that kind of thinking hurts veterans, but the only thing it does is shove the problem underground where the government wants it." P-Mac's voice rose. "These guys need help, and all the VA gives them is crap."

Doc put his hand on P-Mac's shoulder. "Steady, man."

P-Mac's hands fisted on the table.

"What he's saying is that Calvin was triggered," Tick said. "That something happened in-country that set him off. It's probably not a coincidence Hayley was killed in a place that looks a lot like Iraq."

"I need to get a look at the tires on Calvin's bike, see if they match the tracks in the photo." Aloa stood and felt the kick of the alcohol. She'd only had a few sips, but it was enough. "I'll head over there tomorrow."

"Not a good idea, Ink," Tick said. "What if the same thing happens to you that happened to Samantha?" His watery blue eyes took on a new shine.

"We don't know for sure that Samantha's dead." Aloa put her hand on the old man's shoulder. "But I'll be careful anyway."

"I'd just hate anything to happen to you."

"I can take care of myself, Tick."

Tick scrubbed at his eyes. "Damned dust down here."

CHAPTER 23

Aloa was just reaching for the doorknob at the warehouse where Calvin had his shop when the door swung open. It was ten o'clock, another morning that followed a restless night, including a dream in which a huge bird was trying to peck her face with its razor-sharp bill. She'd awakened in a cold sweat.

"Well, hey there, young lady," said the property manager, giving her a grin. Apparently he believed forty bucks had made them friends. "Did you find that Foster gal?"

"Not yet."

His eyes ran up and down Aloa's frame. "Say, I'm headed to the Patch for an Irish coffee. Care to join me? I can tell you more about Foster if you want." He gave her a wink.

Not even if I were in a coma, Aloa thought. "Actually, I'm here to talk to Mr. Rabren about Hayley Poole."

"The one who killed herself?"

Aloa gave a noncommittal nod.

"I tell you what, ol' Calvin was cuckoo for her. Mooning after her, following her around."

"Like stalking her?" Aloa could smell cigarettes and stale sweat coming off the guy.

"More like a puppy dog, you know. Kinda pathetic, you ask me. Tell you what, let me make the introduction for ya. Calvin don't like strangers too much."

"I've already met him," Aloa started to say, but the property manager had turned and gone back inside. She had no choice but to follow and hope she could accomplish what she'd come to do, which was to get a photo of the tires on Calvin's motorcycle and ask some questions about him being nearby on the day Hayley died.

The property manager gave a loud pound on the door. "Cal, it's me, Horace," he hollered.

They waited.

"He don't always answer," the property manager said. "Gets caught up in what he's doing, but don't worry, I'll get you in." He pulled a ring of keys out of his pocket and began to insert one in the lock.

"I don't think that's legal," Aloa said. "As a property manager you have to give notice."

"How's this for notice?" He grinned. "I'm coming in, Cal," he yelled, pushing the key into the lock and shoving open the door.

His scream was high and piercing.

Calvin's body was slumped over the hood of a large pickup that had pinned him to the concrete wall next to the shop's bay door. His face was swollen grotesquely, his eyes bulged from their sockets, and a trail of blood ran from a mouth that appeared open in a scream. Aloa could smell the faint scent of feces, hear the buzz of flies. She looked away, but not before she'd seen the way Calvin's arms were flung across the truck, as if he were embracing the very thing that had killed him.

Aloa finished giving her statement to a detective on the scene and began to move toward the exit. She'd overheard one of the police officers saying something about positional asphyxia and never leaving a vehicle in neutral when you were working on it, but she didn't say anything. She would let the evidence and other witnesses lead the cops to what she thought she already knew. Calvin's death was no accident.

After they'd discovered the body, she'd ordered the shaken property manager to go upstairs and call the police. While he was gone, she'd snapped photos of Calvin's shop, trying not to look at the mechanic's crushed body. She'd captured his living space, the tools (three of them on the floor), then a close-up of the tires on his motorcycle, and, finally, a set of wheel chocks a few feet away from the truck.

She hadn't had the opportunity to take photos the first time she'd visited Calvin, but she remembered with clarity the neatness of his tools, the way he'd emptied the shelves and placed each item in the same pattern he'd removed it, the orange chocks placed carefully in front of the wheels of the Volvo he was working on. She was pretty sure the mechanic was the kind of person who would never begin a job without first securing the vehicle. The methodical way he kept his shop along with the mention of his OCD in the lawsuit reinforced the idea that, even with a disordered mind, discipline ruled his work.

Behavior and habitat, as her father would say.

The near certainty that Calvin was murdered shook her. One person missing and three now dead? It also seemed clear that even if Calvin had been at Hayley's truck at some point, he wasn't the person to chase her into the desert. The treads on his motorcycle's tires plainly didn't match.

A lump formed in her throat at the thought of the gentle but damaged mechanic, his body splayed across the truck hood. He was collateral damage in a war he never stopped fighting and probably didn't understand. He certainly didn't deserve what had happened.

A squad car and a fire truck had arrived quickly after the property manager's call, and within thirty minutes the place was full of crime scene processors and a detective who wanted a statement from both her and the property manager. When she was done, she watched the evidence tech take photos of Calvin's toolbox, knowing the shots would reveal more evidence of a homicide.

Because, while the property manager was making his call, she'd pulled her long-sleeved T-shirt over her hand and slid open the toolbox drawer. Calvin's big knife was missing.

CHAPTER 24

Ask any reporter who's worked long enough and they can tell you about the slide show in their head: The dead man whose arms had been chain-sawed from his body, the skeletal remains of an eight-year-old girl who'd been chained in a closet and starved to death by her mentally ill mother. The body of a teenager in an alley with a needle in her arm.

The image of Calvin slumped over the truck was now a permanent part of Aloa's montage and, though it wasn't as horrible as some images she carried, she knew it would always haunt her.

The day was hot, and Aloa could feel sweat trickling down her back as she walked toward home. She considered stopping for a cold beer, but the thought of sitting in a room full of people who needed a drink at noon in order to get through the day made her rethink the option.

She turned down a side street, finding a rough patch of dry grass between a parking lot and the bay. The water was calm, a dusky emerald green, and she lowered herself onto the ground, leaning back against a chain-link fence.

A ragged line of pelicans glided by, three of the birds turning suddenly and dive-bombing into the water, the force of their impact stunning the fish before they were scooped up into the birds' oversize bills. A container ship steamed slowly by.

She watched for a while, her mind searching for calm. She heard the first notes in her mind, raised her left hand to shoulder height, cocked her fingers, and took up an imaginary bow. She played Leonard Cohen's "Hallelujah" silently, although the music filled her head.

A seagull landed nearby and cocked its head as if waiting for notes to materialize. A breeze freshened her face.

Finally, she dropped her arms and considered her next move. She dialed Michael's cell.

"How's it going?" he asked. From the background noise, she guessed he was in his car.

"It's going," she said.

"You sound like something's wrong."

Aloa watched a sailboat tack upwind.

"I just came from Hayley's old building. Apparently, her ex-roommate is missing, and now her friend, this sweet but totally scrambled combat vet she took under her wing, is dead. Murdered, I think."

"Jesus, Aloa," Michael said.

"He was smashed into a wall. By a pickup." Aloa told him about the scene.

"Are you all right?" he asked when she finished.

"As good as you can be after seeing a dead man." She breathed in the salt air.

"You're sure it was murder?" Aloa could hear him asking Vincent to pull over.

"Pretty sure."

"I don't like this."

"Neither do I."

"I mean I'm worried about you. It sounds like things are getting dangerous. Maybe we should tell the cops what you know."

"I don't have enough yet. They'll laugh me out of their office."

"OK, then I'll call Dean, the editor, and ask him to assign somebody to help you with the story."

"You mean a guy?"

"I was thinking Cameron Brady. He did that story on Chinese drug cartels. He's as tough as they come."

"You do realize that's an extremely sexist thing to say."

"All I meant—" he began but Aloa interrupted him.

"Listen, Michael. I can do this. I want to do this."

"What would your dad say if I let you get hurt?"

"My dad would say, 'I raised her to take care of herself.' He trusted me."

There was a long pause. "If this is about money, I'll still pay you for your time."

Aloa pushed herself to her feet. "This isn't about the money, Michael. This is about three people being dead and me needing to find out who did it. This is about me proving that I'm still a journalist."

She could hear a car door open on his end of the line.

"What if, as your publisher, I ordered you to drop this?"

Aloa looked toward the bay. "Sorry, you're breaking up. I can't hear you," she said as she clicked off the phone.

CHAPTER 25

Aloa steered the rental car up the narrow mountain road. She was glad she wasn't in Doc's van. His wheezing vehicle would never have made it up the steep, curving drive. She would either have had to abandon the van to the raccoons and coyotes or try to back it down the treacherous track. She was not good at reverse. In driving or in life.

She glanced at the directions from Hayley's mom and turned into a driveway that was basically two tracks in the dirt marked by a yellow arrow painted on a block of wood. Redwoods rose around her, their stately carmine-hued trunks a monument to the passage of time. Leafy ferns sprouted near their base.

She'd come home after her phone call with Michael, drank a Diet Coke, and took a few minutes to research Ethan's climbing partner, T.J. Brasselet. She found photos of him climbing heart-stopping rock walls, a Facebook page that hadn't been updated in seven months, and a mention of him in an article about his mother driving her van into Elliott Bay, killing her and T.J.'s baby brother.

Aloa then found the story in the *Seattle Times*: A woman named Cheryl Brasselet had cleaned her apartment; wrapped her two sons, ages six and four, into blankets; and loaded them into her ancient minivan. Engine roaring, the van had crashed through a wooden barrier at a ferry terminal and plunged into the 51-degree water.

The article said Cheryl Brasselet suffered from clinical depression, had just been diagnosed with brain cancer, and was about to be evicted for not paying rent for the last three months. Police speculated suicide, although they allowed a seizure might also have been to blame.

The only reason the six-year-old boy, Tyler Joseph Brasselet, had survived was that his mother, in what would turn out to be a case of beneficial neglect, had failed to buckle her children into their car seats. When the car sank into thirty feet of murky water, the oldest boy had been shoved into a tiny pocket of air. Rescue divers found him with his mouth pressed into that lifesaving bubble, his arms holding his little brother against his chest. The brother, Peter David Brasselet, had died of hypothermia, but T.J. had survived.

Was climbing T.J.'s way of lifting a middle finger to the death he'd already eluded once, or did he carry the same darkness as his mother?

She hoped, for his sake, it was the former.

The track hugged a steep hill, its edge falling into a canyon so deep Aloa did not want to think about what lay at the bottom. She followed the path around a blind curve and up another incline. Finally, the track dead-ended at a structure that looked like it might have come out of an episode of *Tiny House Builders*.

The home was rectangular and made of steel, as if it might have once hauled freight, but large windows cut into the metal made it seem open and airy. A deck with a stack of firewood at one end of it cantilevered over a steep ravine.

An old red Saab was parked out front, along with a rusting motorbike that didn't appear capable of driving more than twenty miles without falling apart. Aloa got out of the car.

"Can I help you?" came a woman's voice.

Aloa looked up to see a tall woman with red-gold hair step out the cabin's front door. What the hell was Jordan Connor doing here?

"Oh, it's you," said Jordan, the dislike in her voice unmistakable. She came to the edge of the deck. "What do you want?"

Aloa squared her shoulders. She knew where this was coming from. A background search on Jordan Connor the night before had revealed that her father, a Texas oil and gas inspector, had been arrested when Jordan was twelve for accepting money in return for turning a blind eye to problem oil wells. He'd gone to prison for seven years, causing the family to lose everything they owned, and chances were, the dad would have escaped notice if not for a series of articles in the *Dallas Morning News.*

"Listen, I'm sorry for what I said the other day," Aloa said, although she wasn't entirely.

Jordan crossed her arms over her chest. She wore yoga pants and a tank top, which revealed the tattoo Aloa had noticed before: an ornate cross entwined with thorns.

"I'm just trying to help. Hayley's mom is having a hard time with the whole suicide thing," Aloa said.

"We're all having a hard time," Jordan said. "What good is it to dredge everything up?"

"Because," Aloa said, "Hayley deserves to have her story told."

"A story that will only make things worse."

"Why is that?"

"Because you'll just write all the bad stuff about her."

"It's not that way."

"Reporters are all alike. All they want is dirt."

Aloa swallowed the urge to argue. "I'm not looking for dirt. I'm trying to understand Hayley, understand what happened."

Jordan shook her head.

Aloa knew she was getting nowhere. "Is T.J. here? I'd like to talk to him."

"You can't," Jordan said.

"He's not here?"

"I didn't say that."

Aloa pushed down her impatience. "Where is he, then?"

"He went up Pollux. It's an old Douglas fir. A hundred yards that way." Jordan nodded her head north. Aloa could see a faint trail through the shadowed forest.

"When will he come down?"

Jordan shrugged. "Who knows? He goes up there to meditate. He's been having a hard time. I'm hanging out with his dog." As if on cue, a blue heeler with a brown snout trotted from the house and came over to sniff around Aloa's ankles.

Aloa looked in the direction Jordan had indicated.

"He won't talk to you anyway," Jordan said. "He doesn't like reporters."

"I'm guessing you don't either." Aloa decided to tackle the issue head-on.

Jordan lifted her chin. "Not really."

"It's not the reporter's fault your father did what he did," Aloa ventured.

"My dad was getting help, trying to make things right—even before the stupid articles," Jordan said. "The reporter never wrote about that, did he? He made my dad this total villain."

Aloa didn't want to debate the finer points of fraud. "How is your father doing now?"

"All right. He's working in the oil fields. He just bought a house."

"Good to hear," she said.

"Not really. He should be retired now, not busting his butt in 105-degree heat."

"He made a choice."

"Are you saying my father deserved what happened?"

"I'm just saying we never know where a decision might lead."

Jordan's eyes narrowed.

"I'll bet your dad is proud of you, though." Aloa switched tacks. "Your running, the work you do with She Soars."

She Soars was an after-school program Jordan had cofounded to help girls learn the joys of exercise.

"I love those kids," Jordan said.

"I'll bet you do." Aloa nodded her head toward the forest trail. "Listen, is there any way to talk to T.J.?"

Jordan considered her. "I don't think that's a good idea. Like I said, he's not doing so hot right now."

"I won't push him."

"Just like you didn't push me at the bar?" Jordan shifted position, her feet in a wide stance, her arms folded across her chest.

Aloa gave an inward sigh.

"You should just go," Jordan said.

"I'm afraid I'm going to have to hear T.J. tell me that," Aloa said, and turned, heading toward the trail in the woods.

"Leave him alone," Jordan called.

"I just have a few questions," Aloa said over her shoulder as she trotted along the path into the forest. Shafts of sunlight cut through the trees. The smell of fresh growth and old decay filled the air.

She arrived a few minutes later at the base of a large Douglas fir. A blue climbing rope hung from unseen branches. She craned her neck upward. "T.J.?" she hollered. "My name is Aloa Snow. Emily said I should talk to you."

"She's a reporter," Jordan called, coming up behind Aloa. The blue heeler at her feet gave one sharp bark.

Aloa ignored her and shouted up into the tree. "I'm doing research. I'm with Novo. We want to tell Hayley's story."

A disembodied male voice came down through the branches. "I don't talk to reporters."

"I told you," Jordan said.

Aloa had lots of experience persuading reluctant sources to speak, but she'd never done it at a throat-scraping shout before. "Listen, I just want to get the facts straight. You were her friend, like a brother," she hollered.

"Go away," T.J. called down.

"There's so much judgment around suicide. So much pain for those left behind," Aloa yelled back, remembering the suspicions about T.J.'s mother. "Think of Emily's pain, her suffering. She deserves to know what really happened."

"Emily told you to talk to me?" came T.J.'s voice.

"She gave me directions to your house," Aloa called.

"Think about what you're doing, T.J.," Jordan hollered up.

"What did Emily say?" T.J. said.

"Can you come down?" Aloa said. "I don't want to keep shouting."

"Come up. Jordan will help you."

Aloa estimated the tree was more than a hundred feet in height. Fifty feet, she'd read, was redline, the height at which a person would most likely die if they fell to the ground. But less was needed if you landed headfirst, which was what an old cop had told her as they stood outside a hotel where a young starlet had ended her life out a third-story window. "You see, the head's heavy," the cop explained. "Essentially, it turns your body into a lawn dart."

Aloa shook off the image. "Can't you just come down for a few minutes?"

"She doesn't want to come up," Jordan hollered.

"That's not true," Aloa called, although it was. She and her father had sometimes ascended the pines near their house to get closer to the creatures they studied. But none of the trees were as tall as this one.

A corkscrew of limbs rose up the trunk. Shafts of light stabbed through the leafy boughs. Besides curiosity, Aloa had another character trait that often got her in trouble, and that was stubbornness.

"All right," she yelled to T.J. "I'm coming up."

"Get her some gear, Jordan," T.J. hollered back.

Ten minutes later, Aloa was snugged into a climbing harness with a helmet secured on her head.

Jordan, shaking her head, set an aluminum ladder against Pollux's trunk. It was just tall enough that a person could stand near the top and grab hold of the tree's lowest branch. But then what? Did you have to pull yourself up with pure arm strength? Aloa vowed to begin a regimen of push-ups when she got home.

Jordan clipped one end of the climbing rope to Aloa's harness and ran the other end through a belay device attached to her own harness. "Top of the ladder. Grab that branch to the left. There's a small spur coming out of the bark. Put your left foot on it and step on the branch to your right. That is, if you can."

Jordan's directions were like gunfire. Quick, loud, and meant to wound.

"Don't worry about me." Aloa looked up into the branches of the tree. "How tall is Pollux?"

"A hundred and twenty feet. A baby could climb it. I don't know why I need to have you on belay."

"Let's just get this over with," Aloa said, and put her hand on the ladder. She knew it would be painful if she slipped—even with the belay. She wouldn't put it past Jordan to exact a bit of revenge on the media by giving her a little too much slack. What had Emily called it? A whipper?

She set her Timberland firmly on the ladder and began to climb. "I'm coming up," she hollered to T.J.

"Stay on this side of the tree," Jordan said. "If the rope gets tangled in the branches, you're in trouble."

At the top of the ladder, Aloa sucked in a lungful of air, fitted the toe of her boot on the spur Jordan had indicated, and began to climb. The fir gave off a sweet, fruity scent.

She monkeyed up the tree: Reach, step, pull. Reach, step, pull. At about eighty feet up, she stopped to rest and looked down. Jordan was staring off into the distance, her hands seeming slack on the rope. Should she holler down and tell her to pay attention? Aloa wondered, but then decided against it. She would not show weakness.

"How's it going?" came a masculine voice. Aloa looked up through the branches to see a stretch of green canvas and a ruddy male face, shadowed by a trucker cap and a three-day stubble. He had a boxer's nose, close-set brown eyes.

"You must be T.J.," she said.

"One and the same," he answered. "Not too much farther. You're doing fine."

"Thanks. It's not as hard as I thought."

Ten feet later, Aloa would change her mind.

She'd traveled upward, finding her way through the branches while admiring the view over the treetops, but then found herself at a spot more difficult than the rest of the ascent. It required a stretch and a slight lean forward over open space to reach the next branch, and Aloa pushed down a tickle of nerves. What had Jordan said? Even a baby could climb this tree?

Aloa glanced toward the ground, took a breath, and lifted herself on her tiptoes. With a hand on the tree trunk to steady herself, she leaned outward and began to place her boot on the branch. But at the same moment she stepped, there was a sudden tug at her hips and a loud shout from below. "Wait!"

"*What the . . . ?*" she thought, but there was no time for an answer because, in an instant, she was off balance and her foot was slipping.

The fall into empty space was like those dreams where your car is suddenly plunging off a cliff and your heart and stomach are shoved sickeningly into your throat.

Aloa grabbed for air, a scream exploding from her mouth. Then, as suddenly as it began, she was yanked to a halt. Her body swung, her hip crashed into the trunk of the tree, and the next thing she knew, she was suspended almost upside down from the rope like some horrible mobile.

"The belay snagged," Jordan yelled from below.

"Are you OK?" T.J. called down to Aloa.

"I don't know," Aloa yelled back. There was a roaring in her ears.

"Just relax. Use your abdominals to pull yourself up," T.J. said. "Grab the rope. You'll be fine."

The rope twirled her in a slow circle. The view to the ground was dizzying.

Aloa inhaled a deep breath and tried to calm her mind so she wouldn't think of the ground, of the way her body would crumple into a broken mix of bones and organs if she smashed into it from this height. She counted one-two and then lunged. Her fingers grazed the rope but then slipped away so that she fell backward again.

"Shit," Aloa cried. The detective had been right about the heaviness of the human head.

Now the rope swung again. She crashed into the tree trunk and then heard a loud crack, followed by a second sickening plunge. She was yanked to a halt, her head snapping once more. The sudden deceleration forced another cry from her.

From above, she heard T.J. yell, "Headache!" Then, the sound of hollow wood snapping through branches.

"I'm OK," Jordan called as the limb thumped to the ground.

Bile rose in Aloa's throat.

"OK. Listen," T.J. called down to her. "Some of those branches on that side are pretty manky. You've got to be careful."

Oh, now you tell me, Aloa thought.

"If you can just swing yourself toward the trunk and take hold of that knob that's sticking out, you can use it to help you grab the rope," T.J. called.

"I see it," Aloa said.

"Then, if you can brace your foot against the trunk, you should be able to lift yourself up to that branch above you."

"Just give me a second," she yelled.

She willed her breath to calm, for the blood to stop pounding in her ears. Every part of her brain told her not to move, but she knew she couldn't spend the rest of her life dangling upside down from a tree branch like some bizarre Christmas ornament.

She counted one-two-three and swung herself toward the tree trunk, feeling the wood scrape against her skin as weight and momentum pulled her hand away from the knob. She cursed and, on the third try, managed to hang on and pull herself up to the rope the way a child pulls itself to her mother.

"Good job," T.J. called.

Aloa's breath came in raspy bursts. Once again, she thanked her father for the sturdiness of her Timberlands.

With one hand on the rope and the other on the knob, she pushed the sole of her boot against the trunk's rough bark and thrust herself upward just as T.J. yelled, "Pull, Jordan."

The tug at her harness was just enough to help get her onto the branch above her.

"There you go," T.J. said. "The rest of the way is easy."

Aloa flopped onto an eight-by-eight square of canvas stretched taut between Pollux and a similarly sized fir a few feet away. Below her, a sea of green washed outward to the distant Pacific Ocean.

"Christ," she swore.

"You know, the more you do it, the easier it gets," T.J. said.

"I think my tree-climbing career is over, thanks," Aloa said.

She sat up and brushed bits of bark and a few needles from her hair. "Could I have some water?"

"Have at it," T.J. said, and handed over the gallon jug he'd stored next to a mesh bag of oranges and a jar of cashews. He was shirtless and barefoot, wearing a pair of ragged jeans.

The water was on the warm side but it tasted sweet and good, and T.J. watched her drink while she also studied him. His hands were large and knotted; his muscled forearms looked like there were rocks under the skin.

She handed back the jug, wiped the back of her hand across her mouth, and felt her heart finally slow.

"So Emily told you to talk to me?" T.J. said, settling the jug on the canvas.

"She did."

"And you're writing a story about Hay? About Ethan?"

Aloa dodged the question. "I'm in the early stages."

"Have you found anything?"

"Maybe you could tell me about Hayley first. What was she like? What was she going through before she died?"

T.J. took off his trucker cap and ran a hand over his dreads. "Well, if I had to say one thing about Hay, I guess it would be that she was really strong but she was soft, too, you know. Like once, she totally gave away her bike to this old guy. He was like seventy and had to walk six miles to work every day. He lived in some kind of storage shed and he was a dishwasher and sent all his money to his grandson so he could go to college. Hay said he was the toughest person she knew and if she had the money she'd hire a limousine to drive him to work every day."

T.J. slid his trucker cap back on his head. "She just had a lot of feelings for people, you know."

"Do you miss her?"

He frowned. "Sure I do. Hay was special."

"Hayley's mom said you two were close."

"Pretty much."

Aloa waited half a beat. "She also said you might know who killed Hayley."

"Hayley didn't . . ." He stopped. "Wait. What? Nobody killed Hay."

Aloa leaned forward. "Emily doesn't agree. She says the police didn't do a good job. That Hayley was murdered."

T.J.'s eyes darted out over the view then back to Aloa. "Listen, Emily needs to accept what happened," he said. "Hay was messed up. Everything was going bad. Her shins, the movie, Ethan. She relapsed. The end. Emily doesn't know anything."

"It must have been hard to lose two friends like that."

He cleared his throat and gave a slight shake of his head. "It sucked."

Aloa waited. A late-afternoon breeze whispered through the trees.

He plucked at a thread in his faded jeans. "Sometimes, things are going along fine, you know, and then you think you want something big and awesome, and so you go for it, but it turns out when you get there it's not what you thought at all."

"Are you talking about life in general or the Africa trip?"

"I don't know. Whatever. Just forget it." He tossed the denim thread over the edge of the canvas.

"I read Ethan's blog," Aloa said. "He talked about being afraid of the Tibesti trip but said something like he needed to do it to bring change."

"Sometimes Ethan thought too much."

Again Aloa waited. Silence often drew more than questions did.

"He was all weirded out about stuff that happened, about Hank being in Africa."

Tremblay had never mentioned being in Africa. Aloa stored that bit of information.

"What stuff are you talking about?"

"So we went there on this private jet, and there was this guy Hank brought along—some right-wing dickhead. Archie something-or-other."

"No last name?" Aloa asked.

T.J. shrugged. "I don't remember if he told us, but he was all on our case. He called Ethan and me cowards for not joining the army. Said global warming was a lie designed to kill jobs. Our trip was supposed to be about species loss and climate change, you know. He and Ethan started arguing, Ethan shoved the guy. Hank told Ethan to calm down, that Archie was there with Hank for some important mission and that Ethan would understand later."

"What kind of mission?" Aloa asked.

T.J. shook his head. "Who knows? Hank was always into different stuff. He just kept calling himself a warrior for good and said we'd understand later, but Ethan didn't like it. He said he didn't want to be part of anything that Archie guy was part of. He and Hank argued some more. Then Ethan disappeared for five or six days."

"Disappeared?"

"He left the hotel. Told me he needed to get his head together. Hank freaked but I told him Ethan was like that. Sometimes he'd pull a hermit, go off by himself, but he'd be fine when he came back."

"And was he?"

"Sort of. He was all jacked up. He said he'd followed that Archie guy back to the airport and watched all these boxes get unloaded from the jet we'd been on—not our gear but cartons with Chinese writing on them. There were these shady dudes there too. The boxes got loaded on a truck and then the shady dudes left. Ethan got in Hank's face after that, and he said Hank told him all about the mission and that it would blow my mind if I knew."

"He didn't tell you what it was?"

T.J. shook his head. "He just said everything had changed, that he was going to leave RedHawk after the trip."

"He was going to quit climbing?"

"Not completely, but the miscarriage shook him up. You know about that, right?"

Aloa nodded.

"He was going to write a book."

"About climbing?"

T.J. shook his head. "I think it was about this tribe in the Tibesti. Ethan told me that a few months before he left for Africa, he'd pitched some big-time agent about writing a book about them. They lived for like a hundred years and were all mystical and stuff. She said books on mystical tribes could sell like a million copies and maybe he'd even get a movie deal. Ethan signed up with her. He called it his declaration of independence. He always talked like that."

A crow flapped onto a nearby branch with a rush of wings. It eyed the two humans invading its territory and let out a raspy, scolding call. Aloa remembered how her father had admired crows but said you never wanted to get on the bad side of one. He liked to tell the story of a bunch of researchers being dive-bombed months after they'd stopped catching and banding crows. And it wasn't just the abused crows who'd been set on revenge, her father said. It appeared the birds' friends and family were out for frontier justice too.

For a long moment, both T.J. and Aloa studied the bird. Finally, T.J. spoke. "I wish we'd never gone to Africa," he said. "None of this would have happened."

"Ethan wasn't killed by robbers, was he, T.J.?" Aloa asked gently.

T.J. bowed his head.

"It's OK," she said. "You can tell me."

She held her breath.

"I didn't think," he said finally.

"What didn't you think, T.J.?" Aloa kept her voice low.

"I didn't think they would kill him."

Aloa moved closer, stilled herself. Waited.

The story came out in half-finished sentences and stuttered words. The arrival of the men in headdresses, the threats, the poking with guns. T.J. had been so frightened, he said, he'd blurted out that their sponsors would pay good money to have the three of them returned safely.

The men's captors had paused, asked each man his name, and then sliced the throats of Ethan and Atahir, their guide. They'd bound T.J. and forced him to walk. He'd been in shock so he didn't remember what else they'd said, only that they'd stopped for the night, his captors had broken into the whiskey the men had brought, and, when the hyenas came, he'd gotten away.

Aloa knew that just like the followers of any religion, not all Muslims adhered to prohibitions against alcohol. Still, she wondered if the two Chadian spies had been wrong.

"I never meant for that to happen," T.J. said, his voice cracking. "I wanted to keep all of us safe."

"Why didn't you tell the truth, T.J.?" Aloa asked.

T.J. sighed. "I don't know. People expect you to be this hero when you're not."

Aloa thought of T.J. holding his sibling but not being able to save him.

"Plus, that reporter, Combs, kept showing up everywhere, asking questions. Hay said I should lie so he'd go away. She said she was going to finish what Ethan started and that she needed everything to be kept quiet for a while."

"What did Ethan start?"

"I guess it was that book."

"About the tribe?"

T.J. nodded.

"But how could Hayley finish Ethan's book if she never met the tribe?"

Aloa watched T.J.'s mind slowly churn. "I don't know, man. Maybe it wasn't even that. I know he tried to call her once from this village, about two weeks into the trip. There was a guy there with a satellite phone."

"What did he say to her?"

"I don't know. I was outside. When he came back he just said she wasn't there." T.J. blew out a breath. "Then, later, he sent her a letter."

"From the middle of the desert?"

"He gave it to a trader who was going to Bardaï. That's a town a few hundred miles north of where we were," T.J. added when he saw Aloa frown.

"And you didn't know what it was about?"

T.J. shook his head. "He didn't say. I figured it was private."

"Did you ask Hayley about it?"

"By the time I got back she was acting weird and said I should keep my mouth shut about anything Ethan told me. I told her that was easy because Ethan didn't tell me anything. I just wanted to forget that trip. After that, Hayley got dark and down, you know. She kept saying Ethan would have been so disappointed."

"About what?"

"I don't know. I thought the same thing, though. That I let Ethan down by freaking out." He pressed his lips together and swallowed hard. "It was all my fault. If I hadn't gotten Ethan killed, Hay wouldn't have killed herself."

He pulled in a long breath and scrubbed at his eyes with the back of one hand. "Shit," he said.

Aloa gave him a minute to compose himself. "Did you see anybody take a photo of Ethan's body?"

"What? No. That's sick."

"How about Calvin, Hayley's friend? Did you know him?"

"Sure. I met him a few times."

Aloa took a long breath. "His body was found this morning."

T.J. looked up. "Ah, man."

"And Samantha, Hayley's ex-roommate, is missing."

"Wait. She's not dead. She's at this cattle ranch called Wind River. What happened to that Calvin guy?"

Aloa ignored the question. "Why did Samantha leave, T.J.?"

"I shouldn't have said anything."

From below came a rustle of branches. Aloa looked over the edge of the tarp. Jordan was about twenty feet below, moving smoothly as a dancer. She turned back to T.J.

"Who's Boots?"

"Boots?" T.J. frowned. "I don't know anybody named that."

"He was at the campout," Aloa prompted. "The cops never interviewed him."

"Oh." T.J.'s eyes darted left. "Um, I don't know. He, um, just showed up. Just a guy. He, um, was tall."

"Is that what somebody told you to say, T.J.?" Aloa remembered the exact same description in the police reports.

"No." He shook his head with a little too much earnestness.

"Look, I'm not the enemy, T.J. I'm here to help."

"I don't want to talk about it," the climber mumbled.

"Think of Hayley. Think of Ethan. You don't want to let them down again, do you?"

T.J.'s chin dropped to his chest. Another rustle of branches came from below. Jordan was closer now.

Aloa leaned in. "What was going on, T.J.?"

"I don't know. I don't know, man."

"Tell me," she whispered.

T.J. rubbed a hand over his face. His voice came out strangled and low. "I think it was Hank. I think Hank pulled the strings."

CHAPTER 26

At home, Aloa made herself two soft-boiled eggs that she spooned over slices of the Bayonne ham and toasted baguette and sprinkled with sea salt and spicy Piment d'Espelette.

She ate standing at the front window, watching sunset color the bay. The climb had made her ravenous and the conversation with T.J. busied her mind with thoughts of details and connections instead of with calories. Work had always been good for her.

Some of the yolk dripped down her fingers, and she licked it off. After, she washed the dishes and made herself a strong pot of coffee in preparation for the work ahead.

At her desk, she read about Tremblay's degree in mathematics from UCLA and the years he'd spent as a bass player in a series of B-grade rock bands in Southern California. He'd done a little acting (a couple of commercials) and spent two dissolute years in Europe and then India—years he called "enriching" in an interview but which seemed to involve a lot of drinking and drugs—and then had been summoned home after his father was diagnosed with a rare neuromuscular disease. He found his father's company at the brink of bankruptcy following a lawsuit by three men who claimed one of RedHawk's products had caused them to suffer debilitating strokes. The lawsuit had been settled and, to almost everyone's surprise, Tremblay turned out to have a talent for business. He rebranded RedHawk's products and hired the daughter of a powerful conservative legislator as his marketing director when a bill designed to regulate the supplement industry was introduced. He also produced two TV shows—*American Mercenaries* and *American Bounty Hunters*—whose chief audience members were those most likely to buy RedHawk products: young, testosterone-driven males.

Aloa considered Tremblay. He was arrogant and insufferable but also smart. Outside, darkness had fallen.

She made a few notes and added what she knew to her timeline— Tremblay arriving in Africa, Ethan sending a letter to Hayley from the desert, Hayley insisting T.J. lie, Calvin dead—and wondered what she'd missed. What did it mean that Hank pulled the strings?

She was just getting up and deciding whether to go for a walk or pour herself a glass of Pellegrino when her phone rang.

"What the hell, Ink?" said a sandpaper voice.

"Hello to you, too, Tick," she said.

"We've been waiting. What gives with the . . ." He stopped. "Wait. Did you hear that?"

There was a tinny echo on the line as if either she or Tick had stepped into a cavernous room.

"Oh, that," she said. "I think my phone's dying."

"Dying, hell," Tick said. "That's Uncle Satan on the line."

Long before the revelations of Edward Snowden, Tick—and the rest of the Brain Farm—had been firm believers in the intrusive reach of the US government. Which is why only Tick had a cell phone, and it was so antiquated it barely qualified as a communications device, let alone one that could be monitored.

"Could be, but I think it's the phone. It barely holds a charge anymore," Aloa started to say, but Tick was already barking orders. "Not another word. We'll rendezvous at twenty-fifteen hours. Usual place."

"At Justus?" Aloa asked.

"Jeez, Ink, don't say it out loud." He groaned. "OK. New plan. We'll meet you at Maja's," he said, and disconnected the call.

The men were out of breath from the hike up the hill when they arrived forty-five minutes later. They flung themselves into the rosé chair and the couch with noises that sounded like the last gasps of a steam engine.

Aloa fetched them water, which they drank greedily.

"So there's been a new development," she started to say when the men had caught their breath, but Tick held up his hand.

"Not another word until you take the battery out of your phone," he said.

"Yeah, Uncle Satan is everywhere," Doc said, and glanced out the window into the evening.

There was a bird in Africa, the drogo, that could mimic the alarm cries of its avian brethren and even of meerkats. It would sound a warning, then swoop in to eat while other birds fled. An article she'd read about the drogo said it would be as if a dog could yell "fire" in a crowded restaurant and then settle in for dinner when everybody ran. And while Aloa didn't believe in overreaction, she also knew inaction had its dark side.

"How about if I put my phone in the fridge?" she said. "I heard Snowden did that."

The gray-hairs nodded vigorously.

"You guys want coffee?" she asked.

"We're too old," P-Mac said. "We could die before that fancy coffee of yours is ready. You got any red lying around?"

Aloa shook her head, put her phone next to the yogurt in the fridge, and dug up a bottle of wine. She settled the men with glasses, then broke the news. "I'm pretty sure Calvin's motorcycle tires didn't match the crime scene."

The men grumbled a mixture of relief and disappointment.

"But this news is worse," she said. "Calvin is dead. Murdered, I think."

P-Mac's head snapped up. "Gun? Knife? Garrote? Blunt instrument?"

"None of those," Aloa said, and described Calvin's death scene.

"That's some sickness there," Doc said.

The old war photographer's eyes shimmered. "I'll see what I can do about getting him into a military cemetery. He deserves that much from his country."

"Damn straight," Doc said. "He also deserves what guys like him don't get and that's justice."

Tick stood. "He's right, boys. We got us some work to do." He pointed. "Doc, I want you to run down and get us a box of cabernet. P-Mac, I'd like you to go through the crime scene photos again and check the shots Ink took at the shop. I'll hit the computer and see if I can track down the truck that killed our mechanic friend, and find the witness the cops conveniently couldn't locate."

P-Mac and Doc heaved themselves to their feet while Tick settled himself in front of the computer. From his shirt pocket he pulled out a pair of orange zebra-print reading glasses he'd appropriated from the lost-and-found bin at the library and slipped them on. The glasses were a direct outgrowth of his belief in freeganism: the avoidance of consumerism and the use of salvaged or discarded goods. All the men were adherents of this philosophy. Consequently, they often looked like a yard sale on six legs.

Aloa watched the men move and mutter and went to the kitchen to heat up a bowl of leftover ginger-carrot soup. She could have told the Brain Farm that she could handle the story herself, but with the image of Calvin's body fresh in her head and the feel of her vertiginous fall still in her body, it was good to have living, breathing people around.

She returned to the living room with her soup and went to work.

She borrowed Tick's antiquated phone and made a call to the property manager, who sounded like he was well past buzzed and headed toward full-on drunk. Nope, he didn't have the surveillance tapes from the building, the cops had taken those, he told her, but if she wanted to join him at the Patch, he'd buy her a drink. She declined.

She then moved to a check of Tremblay's property holdings, where she uncovered the fact he'd sold a four-bedroom townhouse in Vail and an apartment in Barcelona in the last year and also that he lived, not in the Nicasio Valley as she had assumed, but in a fancy Nob Hill apartment with a view of the bay and rents that hovered around $10,000 a month. She guessed, for the rich, cutting back was selling your vacation homes. She wrote down the apartment's address.

She looked up as the Brain Farm erupted into shouts. Their discovery that the pickup truck that had killed Calvin had been reported stolen from an Oakland store owner two days before the mechanic's death had apparently sent them into a rant about the disproportionate arrests of young African American men and how politicians blamed it on poor moral values of the community instead of on their own policies, which denied these young males equal education and good jobs.

Aloa sighed. The problem with loneliness was that when you fought against it by inviting people to your house, you often realized it was actually quiet that you liked.

She turned her attention to finding the man named Archie whom T.J. had mentioned. Two hours later, she had two possibilities: a cameraman on one of the military shows named Archer Prescott, who could barely afford his child support payments let alone a private jet, and a former bandmate of Tremblay's named Pat Archibald, who'd become a songwriter for a rather famous country singer until he plowed his car into a bridge abutment three years ago. His wife blamed the music industry for her husband's problems with drugs and alcohol.

Not the right Archie either. She set aside her laptop.

She'd just come back from a trip to the bathroom when she heard a knock at the door, followed by Doc's voice.

"Michael Collins in the house," he exclaimed.

Aloa's heart gave a quick skip.

She ran her hands through her hair, fingernailed a bit of dried soup from her T-shirt, and took a calming breath. She came out to find

Michael standing in her living room with the Brain Farm pumping his hand and slapping him on the back. Their eyes caught.

"Hey," she said.

"Hey," he said back. "Sorry to just show up, but I wanted to finish our talk. I called but you didn't answer."

Aloa had seen the three missed calls earlier but had ignored them.

"Sit down, Mike. Take a load off." Tick gestured toward the couch. "Wine?"

"I can't stay long," he said. "Can I have a moment, 'Lo?"

"Sure," she said.

"Alone?"

"How about if we go out to the porch?"

Disappointment registered on the Brain Farm's faces.

"I'll be back in a minute, guys," she said, and stepped outside, Michael following. Lights shining from a multitude of windows created a Klimt-like portrait of the city.

Michael leaned against the railing. "So you know how I feel about you continuing with this story."

"I'm not quitting," she started to say.

"I hear you loud and clear," he said. "But can you humor me and tell me what you've found so far? I'd feel better if I knew what we were dealing with."

"I guess that's fair," Aloa said.

By the time she'd finished, Michael was frowning and had his arms crossed over his chest. "What the hell did we dig up?" he said.

"I don't know, but there's something going on, something that isn't as simple as a woman committing suicide."

"Any ideas what?"

Aloa shook her head. "I still have a lot of work to do."

He looked out toward the bay. "And you won't quit, even if I ask nicely?"

A faint smile. "I don't think so, no."

"You always were stubborn."

"You used to call it tenacity."

"How about if I ask Vincent to stay here with you for a while, then?"

"I'm not a two-year-old."

"I didn't say that. I'd just feel better if he was around."

"I can handle myself, Michael. I've done stories way more dangerous than this. I spent six months in Juárez, for Chrissake. They had twenty murders a day there," she said. "I know how to take care of myself. I'm not going to do anything stupid."

"You can't control everything, you know that."

"I'll tell you what, Michael, if anything gets weird, I'll lift my little petticoats and come running so you can save me."

"'Lo, don't," he started, but before he could say more, Doc opened the door. "We found something, Ink. Something we don't like."

Aloa threw Michael a glance and went inside to find Tick frowning at the computer screen.

"What did I tell you about being careful, Ink?" he said. "It looks like you've got a stalker."

Aloa wrinkled her forehead and went to stand behind Tick.

"I found this on the cloud," he said, tapping the screen. "Lists about where you went and how long it took, with threatening notes like, 'What are you waiting for?'" Tick pulled off his glasses. "Looks like you tried to delete them but they're still here, see?"

Heat flushed Aloa's face. She glanced at Michael, who was watching her intently.

"That's a workout app, Tick. I had to install it on my phone to get a discount for my health insurance. I just haven't deleted it yet."

"But it tracked you yesterday—" Tick began.

Aloa interrupted. "Say, did I tell you I found out where Hayley's ex-roommate went?"

CHAPTER 27

The call Aloa made the next day to Samantha Foster at Wind River cattle ranch was short and hardly sweet. Samantha apparently didn't like being found, and liked even less that Aloa was a reporter doing a story on Hayley Poole.

"Like I told the cop, she was acting weird," Samantha said after Aloa gave her name and said T.J. had been the one who tipped her off to Samantha's new home.

"Weird how?" Aloa asked.

"Like all paranoid and stuff."

"Do you know why?"

"Let me get out my psychology book. Um, here it is, maybe because her boyfriend got killed?"

It took every trick Aloa knew—not reacting to sarcasm, direct but simple questions, the repeated use of "uh-huh" and "sure" to indicate understanding—before she got what she wanted.

A week or so before Ethan died, a letter arrived from Africa containing a flash drive and, no, Samantha didn't know what was on it, although Hayley had made an offhand reference to a book project, which Samantha guessed was about this tribe in Africa that had found the secret to long life. She'd overheard Ethan and Hayley whispering about it one day.

Exactly what T.J. had described.

Then Ethan died and Hayley's subsequent drinking had caused Samantha to wonder about the state of her roommate's liver. Hayley had gotten into a bar fight. One night, she had broken into Tremblay's office, where she was found drunk and asleep in his chair, a discovery that brought on an abbreviated stint in rehab, which was followed by sobriety, a return to training, and hours in front of her laptop. Doors were closed, hushed conversations were held on the phone, and a stack of papers was locked in a trunk. Paranoia had risen, arguments between roommates had occurred, and Hayley moved out.

"She didn't even tell me she was going," Samantha complained. "Left a bed and a bunch of stuff for me to get rid of."

A week later a guy claiming to be a lawyer from RedHawk had showed up asking for everything Ethan had left behind, including computers, videos, and notes. He told Samantha if she didn't cooperate, she could be jailed for theft of corporate property, and that whatever Ethan had produced from the Africa trip belonged to RedHawk and Hank Tremblay. Samantha told him to get the hell out of her apartment. Next, a formal-looking letter arrived that said her name would be turned over to the San Francisco district attorney for prosecution of grand theft, larceny, and accessory to burglary unless she called a certain number to resolve the issue of the missing computer and notes.

"Do you still have the letter?" Aloa asked.

"Are you kidding?" Samantha said. "I threw it in the trash, took my dog, and got the hell out of there. I'm not into prison, and besides, I didn't have what they wanted."

Now, as Aloa walked toward Nob Hill, she wondered why Tremblay had wanted the manuscript so badly. Did the story of a long-lived African tribe have anything to do with the wonder drink he bragged about?

Above her, the sky sparkled with sunlight. Around her, the neighborhood spoke of the wealth that had built this city: the railroad barons, the bankers, and those who pulled gold and silver from the ground.

She passed the venerable Fairmont Hotel, the gray splendor of Grace Cathedral with its gilded bronze doors, and continued on to the apartment building where Tremblay made his home.

Aloa came through the building's twin doors into a lobby that looked like Louis XIV on steroids. Huge gilded chairs sat on shiny, marble floors. Chandeliers waterfalled light, and gold pillars held up a two-story ceiling while two full-size palms stood sentinel next to a set of mirrored elevator doors. Nearby was a reception desk behind which sat a doorman—a detail that the description Aloa had read of the twenty-unit building had failed to mention.

"Can I help you?" the doorman asked.

He had a moustache, a wedding band that cut tightly into the flesh of his ring finger, and a belly that spoke of big home-cooked meals. His nametag announced him as "Tony H."

Aloa did a quick reshuffle of her plan. "Hi, I'm looking for Hank Tremblay. He lives here, right?" she said, and gave him a smile that she hoped spoke of innocence and honest intentions.

"I'm sorry. We can't give out the name of our tenants," the doorman said.

His own face hinted at sincerity and also curiosity as to why a woman in Timberlands and spiked hair was asking about Hank Tremblay.

"Is he a friend of yours?" Tony H. asked.

"I met him once. I'm not sure I'm in the right tax bracket to be a friend," Aloa said.

Tony H. lifted his chin in homage to a fellow working stiff. "You and me both," he said.

Aloa saw her opening. "He's kind of different, right?" she said, allowing the question to be whatever Tony H. wanted it to be.

The doorman leaned forward. "Last Christmas, instead of a bonus, he gives us all a case of some kind of muscle powder. Tasted nasty. Then, the guy starts bragging how he's giving all this money to put solar in some hospital in Africa. What about us? What about Americans who can't afford to go to the hospital?"

"I hear you," Aloa said.

"Plus, he's always telling us how we should lose some weight."

"It's called fat shaming," Aloa said.

"Hey, that's a good word," Tony H. said.

"Let me ask you this: Have you heard anything about Hank Tremblay having money troubles?"

Tony H. considered the question. "Not really. He's always bragging about how his company is gonna wipe out all the competition. But like I said, he's cheap when it comes to people who work for him, guys like me. Is that why you're here?"

Aloa sidestepped the inquiry. "What about other tenants? He have problems with them?"

"A few noise complaints. Mrs. Sullivan next door to him went to the super about him and some woman making a ruckus." He winked. "A little too much enthusiasm in the bed, if you know what I mean."

Aloa suppressed a mental retch.

"Any interesting friends? Guys coming here who don't look like they fit?" She nodded her head in the direction of the marble and gold leaf.

"There was a couple of guys that came by a few weeks ago. Tony Soprano types."

Aloa had just opened her mouth to ask another question when the phone on the reception desk rang.

"Speak of the devil," Tony H. said, and picked up the receiver. "Yes, Mr. Tremblay." He listened for a moment. "Sure. I remembered. Your car is out front, waiting for you." He hung up. "He's headed for the elevator."

Aloa glanced out the lobby doors, not sure she wanted Tremblay to know she'd come to his apartment building asking questions, but what she saw made escape impossible.

Coming up to the front doors was a man she recognized: the rude real estate agent, Baldy. *In a city of 864,000 people,* she thought, *what are the odds?*

She knew if she tried to leave, Baldy would corral her and then Tremblay would want to know why she was in his apartment building.

"Is there someplace I can duck into? Hank might not be too happy to see me, if you know what I mean." Aloa made a face as if to confirm every negative word Tony had uttered about Tremblay.

"Sure thing," the doorman said, and tugged open a discreet handle set in the wall behind him just as the elevator dinged to announce the arrival of its cage at the lobby.

Aloa darted into what turned out to be a small supply closet filled with old mops, buckets, and a damp pile of rags. It smelled of mildew with a faint undertone of vomit. So much for the glamorous life of a journalist. She opened the door a crack.

"Good afternoon, sir," she heard Tony H. say.

"Hey there, Mr. T. How's it going, man?" Tremblay's voice had that false bonhomie the rich used in an effort to erase the class differences between them and their servants, even though it usually had the opposite effect.

"Good, sir. And how is your day?" Tony was moving away from the station and toward the front doors.

"Not bad," Tremblay said. "You know: people to see and places to go." He pointed a finger at Tony's ample girth. "Looks like you're not doing those exercises I told you about. Nine minutes a day. That's all you need."

"I'll get right on them, sir."

Aloa guessed Tremblay couldn't hear the undercurrent of dislike in Tony H.'s words.

At the sound of the front doors opening, Aloa pressed her eye to the door crack but all she could see was a sliver of golden pillar. She held her breath, prayed no one would turn to look back at the doorman's desk, and pushed the closet door open a couple of inches.

"Right on time," Baldy said to Hank Tremblay as Tony H. swung open the door to admit him.

174

Baldy and Tremblay knew each other?

"I hope this won't take long," Tremblay said.

Baldy clapped a hand on Tremblay's shoulder. "It'll be quick, I promise."

"I thought we'd taken care of this," Tremblay said, petulance creeping into his voice.

"Just a small snag, Boots. I can call you that, right?"

Tremblay shook off Baldy's hand as they walked through the front door. "No, you can't."

"Enjoy the day, gentlemen," Tony H. called after them.

CHAPTER 28

The detective called right as Aloa threw herself back in her desk chair with a curse. Energized by the discovery that the missing witness Boots was actually Hank Tremblay, she'd done a vehicle search the minute she'd gotten home. There was a Tesla sedan, a brand-new Escalade, and a BMW convertible under Tremblay's name along with two Mercedes vans registered to RedHawk—but not a single motorcycle on the list. He didn't even have a motorcycle license.

When the phone rang, she barked, "Snow here."

The caller identified himself as Rick Quinn with the Major Crimes Unit of the San Francisco PD and asked if she minded coming down to his office. He wanted to follow up on some of the statements she'd given to his partner at Calvin's shop.

"What did you find?" she asked, pushing herself up from her desk.

"We're looking at every plausible alternative," Quinn replied.

"Which means you're suspicious. I was a crime reporter. I speak cop." She dropped the name of the homicide detective she'd dated for eight months in LA, although she didn't mention the exact nature of their relationship. Law enforcement was a secret society where you needed a reference to even peek through the clubhouse doors.

"I guess you could say there are a few things that don't add up," Quinn said. "I'm here until eight if you want to stop by."

He had a nice voice, an absence of the macho blustering some of the old-school officers carried, and she was curious to know what he knew.

Two hours later, she was dressed in jeans, a white T-shirt, and her leather jacket and seated in a hard chair next to Quinn's desk. He was well groomed with studious hazel eyes, enough muscle to let you know he worked out but wasn't a fanatic about it, and a platinum wedding band on his left hand.

He offered her coffee, which she declined.

"Good choice. That stuff will kill you," he said.

He shifted through a few papers and got down to business.

"I don't normally do this, but Colm told me you were OK," he said. Colm was the detective whose name she'd mentioned, and "OK" was high praise in the language of detectives.

"He's closed more homicides than the rest of the LAPD combined," she said.

"Which is why I'm going to tell you that I don't think Mr. Rabren's death was accidental," he said.

Aloa nodded.

"Tell me why you agree."

He is good, Aloa thought. She told him about the wheel chocks, the missing knife, and about the disorder in what had been a meticulous shop.

"What about you? Why do you think Calvin's death wasn't an accident?"

He said the extent of the mechanic's injuries seemed to indicate the truck had been driven, not rolled, into the victim. He picked up a piece of paper. "Your witness statement said you came to see Mr. Rabren because you're doing a story on a former neighbor, Hayley Poole." He looked up at her. "Miss Poole is dead, a suicide, apparently."

"That's right." She waited.

He raised his eyebrows. "So is there a reason I should be wondering why two people in the same building are dead?"

There was always an uneasy dance between law enforcement and reporters. On one hand, each could be of benefit to the other. On the other hand, distrust was the hallmark of both professions.

"Let me ask you this," Aloa said. "Did the surveillance tapes show who drove the truck that killed Calvin?"

"You first," Detective Quinn said. "I'll show you the photos after."

She considered the advantages of possibly being able to identify Calvin's killer and then told him about Calvin's crush on Hayley, about her asking Calvin to help her, and his belief that "the watchers" were spying on him. She didn't tell him about the box or mention Uranus or the High Priest.

"Do you know who was supposedly watching Mr. Rabren and why?"

Aloa told him she didn't.

"How about Miss Poole's death? Was it suicide?"

Aloa debated the benefit of having a contact in the police department against going prisoner-of-war and not telling him anything beyond the obvious.

She told him about the tire marks and the sapper tab, which she knew he would find if he looked closely at the photos from Nevada—and he was the kind of detective who would. She also said she believed Hayley had been run into the desert by someone who wanted to harm her, but she didn't know who or why. She wasn't ready to mention the book about the African tribe or that Hank Tremblay had been at the campout.

"Why does it feel like you're not telling me everything you know?"

"Because it's your job to think the world is full of scumbags and everybody's lying to you." She smiled. He did not. "Really, that's all I can tell you for certain," she said.

"Journalists," he said, and shook his head.

"Cops," she said, and shook hers.

He let out a breath, then handed her a photo of the truck pulling into Calvin's shop through the bay door. The only thing the photo revealed through the vehicle's tinted windows was a dark shape behind the wheel. Aloa wasn't even sure whether it was a man or a woman.

"Are you kidding me?"

"Cops," he said, and shook his head. This time he smiled.

Aloa headed toward home, reluctantly admiring how smoothly Detective Quinn had gotten the better of her. She was getting rusty.

The night was cool, the sidewalks full of pedestrians. She passed a bar known for its tapas and Spanish wines and ducked inside. She would order some food (she'd had nothing since breakfast), get a glass of wine, and think.

There was a long bar, scattered tables ringed with leather barrel chairs, and wrought iron chandeliers hanging from a high ceiling. She found a table in a corner; ordered a Rioja, a small plate of olives, and one of fried sardines; and pulled her notebook from her pack. The bar was populated with men in dress shirts and women in heels. Some of the customers pecked away at their laptops while they sipped their wine. No time for leisure in this city.

She'd just taken her first bite of the salty-sweet fish when a male voice asked would she mind if he shared her table. She looked up to see a guy of medium height with a straight nose, thick brown hair, and a jaw that was just a little too strong to put him in the handsome category.

"Actually, I do," she said.

"I won't bite, I promise," he said. "I've just had a super bad day and really, really need to get off my feet." He swept his arm out to indicate the bar, which Aloa realized had suddenly filled to overflowing.

"All right," she said, "but I've got work to do."

"No problem. Thanks." He settled himself in the chair. "I was in court all day. My wife wants custody of our kid. She ran off last year. With the nanny." He lifted his eyebrows. "I just got over that humiliation. Now I have to deal with this."

Aloa didn't say anything.

"Sorry, it's just hard to talk about this with the guys, you know." He smiled. "Eddie," he said, and stuck out his hand. "Eddie Swafford."

"Aloa," she said, and gave his hand a shake.

"Let me buy you a drink," he said. "It's the least I can do."

"Like I said, I've got work."

In the last two years, it was as if Aloa had taken an unintentional vow of chastity with a bit of cloistering thrown in for good measure. Not that she'd been a wild temptress before. Besides losing her virginity to Jason Meyerson (although their fumbling tryst barely qualified as sex), and Michael, there had been a poet, a criminal defense attorney, the photojournalist, and, finally, the homicide detective Colm, although his darkness tended to exacerbate her own issues of self-worth. None of them had lasted, mostly because she put up walls to prevent them from getting too close, and she wasn't about to start breaking them down now.

She turned back to her notebook, heard Eddie order albondigas, a glass of house red and another of Cava, then blather on with a long story about wanting to move to Seattle but not wanting to leave his kid behind. She shot him a look just as the drinks arrived, and he slid the glass of sparkling Cava in her direction.

Aloa figured she was owed the drink for having to listen to that monologue about how Seattle was so much better than San Francisco and took a sip. The wine was dry, just the way she liked it, which didn't mean she forgave the guy for being so obnoxious.

"Good, huh?" asked her tablemate.

"It's fine. But listen, I need you to stop talking. I've got to concentrate." She gestured at her Moleskine.

"What are you working on?" Eddie asked, leaning over her notebook.

"Nothing I want to share."

"Oh, come on. What is it, the Great American Novel?" he teased.

She fell back in her chair. "Do you follow baseball, Eddie?"

"Sure I do." He grinned.

"Then you know what happens after strike three?"

Eddie nodded, the smile still on his face.

"Right now, Eddie, you've got two strikes."

"What?"

"Strike one, you kept talking even though I told you I had to work. And strike two, you're so boring I'm ready to stab myself with this pen just to end the conversation."

The grin slid from Eddie's face. He took a sip of wine. "You don't have to be such a bitch about it," he said.

"Strike three," Aloa said, and pointed toward the door. "That's your cue to leave, Eddie."

Eddie opened his mouth and Aloa braced herself for an onslaught of male insults. Instead, Eddie suddenly reached over, grabbed her Moleskine, and pushed himself out of his chair.

"What the hell?" Aloa said, reaching for her precious book but missing as Eddie turned from the table.

She jumped from her seat and clawed at him, managing to grab a handful of his shirt as he tried to leave. "Drop the book," she barked.

But instead of obeying, Eddie pivoted and gave her a hard shove that sent her stumbling back into the table, causing two wineglasses to crash to the floor.

"Crap," she yelled.

Patrons looked up.

"Stop him," she hollered, as Eddie, now free of her grasp, pushed his way through the crowd.

A waiter carrying a tray of food yelled something in Spanish as Eddie knocked into him. A woman in beige cried out as Eddie shoved past her, sending most of a glass of red wine onto her chest. Her companion grabbed Eddie's arm and Eddie turned, giving him a frantic punch to the nose before he was quickly on the move again.

Aloa waded through the now-angry crowd. "Stop him," she yelled again, but it was too late. Eddie was out the door and running.

The bartender moved in front of her. "Hold up there," he said.

But whatever journalism gods existed had smiled on Aloa. There on the floor, near where Eddie had punched the defender of the wine-stained woman, was Aloa's notebook, only slightly damaged by splotches of Cabernet.

"What's going on?" the bartender demanded as Aloa grabbed the Moleskine.

It took her a few minutes to explain that she'd gone after a guy who tried to pickpocket her but that she'd retrieved what he'd taken and there was no need to call the police. It was another few minutes before she could get back to her table and retrieve her pack, only to discover Eddie-the-asshole's quick exit had made it so she not only had to pay for the wine and Cava but for his dinner too.

She strode from the bar, angry at men, angry at herself, and certain that Eddie sitting at her table was not a random choice. Who had sent him, and why?

Tomorrow, she would figure out who Eddie Swafford really was, see what connection Baldy had to Tremblay, and try to uncover why a book about an African tribe might be worth killing for.

CHAPTER 29

He stood in the apartment he'd rented for the assignment and looked out the window at the lights of the Bay Bridge. Behind him, a seventy-inch TV above the marble fireplace showed the baseball game while a dinner of steak and roasted root vegetables—delivered twenty minutes ago from Alexander's—sat untouched on the mahogany table.

He couldn't care less about any of it.

He rattled the ice in his scotch and took a sip. He didn't like what that reporter was doing: sneaking off to visit Ethan's climbing partner, finding the ex-roommate, meeting with Michael Collins.

It didn't seem possible that Novo had hired her for a story, but then, a lot of what went on in the world didn't seem possible until it was.

And the call from the detective? That was not good either. He rubbed a hand over his chin.

Killing that mechanic hadn't been part of the plan. He'd only meant to scare the guy into telling him if the girl, Hayley, had left anything with him. But instead of being intimidated, the guy had come at him with a big-ass knife and then jumped on the hood of the truck when he tried to leave. He'd had no choice but to ram the pickup into the wall and hope some rookie would catch the case, but instead, it had been given to Quinn. Quinn was good. He took another gulp of scotch, hardly tasting it.

Then, he'd hired his nephew, a decent kid who'd dropped out of law school, to follow the reporter for a day while he flew to Portland to deal with a problem on another case. The kid had done an OK job—until he went rogue and grabbed the reporter's notebook. It was a gutsy move, and while he would have liked to have seen what Snow knew, the stunt had only served to put her on high alert.

He threw back the rest of the scotch and watched thousands of lights flicker and dance along the cables of the Bay Bridge. He thought of Paris and Shanghai and fine dinners. His clients would give him a .45-caliber lobotomy if he screwed up.

Anger tightened his belly. He sent his mind back through the mission, searching for weaknesses, looking for cracks the reporter and/or the detective might find. Everything had gone according to plan until that idiot mechanic had come after him.

He thought the assignment was still safe, that the walls he'd put up would hold. He would not get rid of the reporter unless he had to.

The bridge lights flowed and ebbed. He tossed his dinner into the garbage and went to pour himself another drink.

CHAPTER 30

Aloa awakened with a groan. Her neck ached from falling through the tree, and now the bruise on her hip was matched with twins on the back of her legs from the previous night's bar scuffle. If this kept up she could qualify as a fourth member of the Blue Man Group. Make that the Black and Blue Man Group.

She pulled herself from bed and started her coffee in advance of what would probably be a full day on her butt.

Her first task was to figure out who Eddie Swafford was. An hour later, she was no wiser. Every Edward or Edwin or E. Swafford who lived within a hundred-mile radius was either not the right age or the wrong ethnicity. No divorce filings matched his name and the court docket for the week didn't list anybody with a moniker even close to his. It was obvious he'd been hired to follow her and find out what she knew, but it was impossible to prove that Hank Tremblay had been behind the surveillance and attempted theft. She got up and looked out the front window. She'd stirred up something, but what the hell was it?

Her next task was a call to an entertainment lawyer she knew in LA who told her whatever media came from a sponsored trip was owned by the sponsor—unless the contract spelled things out differently, and that was unlikely.

Which meant Tremblay probably believed the book Ethan was writing belonged to him. But why kill someone over what you could simply sue for? And yet, people with money and lawyers killed all the time. She'd once written about a Hollywood real estate mogul who had killed his wife because she'd been awarded $30,000 a month in alimony, even though the sum was peanuts compared to what he earned.

Greed clouded the eyes of the rich as well as the poor.

She got up once again and walked through the house, letting her mind reboot as she wiped a smudge from the bathroom mirror, smoothed her bedclothes, and hand-washed a few pairs of underwear. Her brain refreshed, she went back to her desk, where, over the next two hours, she discovered Tremblay was part of a group of developers intent on building some kind of upscale senior housing project with a spa, on-call doctors, and high-class chefs, which could explain yesterday's meeting with Baldy the slimy real estate agent. Still, there had been something about the way Baldy had confronted her at her house that made her wonder if he also served as Hank's hired muscle. He had the air of a street brawler.

She got back to work, clicking through websites, looking for more information on the status of the senior housing project and Hank's finances. She phoned Samantha to see if the RedHawk lawyer who had threatened her looked anything like Baldy, but Samantha didn't pick up. No surprise there.

Finally, she watched a trailer for an earlier documentary the filmmaker Monica Prager had made about a blind climber, and decided to give the director a call. Prager talked like a used car salesman on speed.

"Yes, Jordan and Hayley were very close, in fact there was a moment in the film where the two of them are on a training run and Hayley starts crying and Jordan holds and rocks her, saying women need each other the way a storm needs the wind, which was a beautiful thing to say and why this movie is going to be so friggin' good because even though we lost Hayley, which was a shock to all of us, there's still Jordan, who pulled herself up from nothing, training like a beast in her friend's name, and you know that a story like this, about loss and strength and courage, is going to rip your heart right out of your chest and that's what making movies is all about even though filmmaking is a bitch that tries to eat your soul while starving you out of home and relationships and every penny in your bank account."

By the time Aloa hung up, she thought the filmmaker had missed her calling as an auctioneer.

Her muscles tightening and her brain filling with what felt like cotton, Aloa got up from her desk and went to her room to change. Ten minutes later, she was in her running clothes and loping toward the Ferry Terminal, the air fresh against her skin, the HardE app recording her workout. That was not restriction, she told herself. That's what runners did.

She ran past Washington Square Park, which was neither square nor on Washington Street. Nor did it honor the nation's first president but instead had a statue of Benjamin Franklin as its focal point. Another of the city's quirks. She ran past Liguria Bakery, past Lombard Heights Market, past a nanny pushing an expensive stroller inhabited by two fussy charges. She picked up her pace.

One block later, a guy in a ball cap leaned out his car window, slowed, and yelled "nice ass" as he passed. Did he think that was some great pickup line? Some irresistible witticism no woman could resist?

She gave the guy a middle finger.

"Bite me," he shouted.

"That would be animal abuse," she yelled back as he sped away.

At the two-mile mark, she U-turned and headed for home. Her breath came hard, her muscles strained against the uphill climbs. It felt good to work, to push against what was trying to hold her back, to test her strength. After, she drank a tall glass of water, showered, and sliced up the last of the cheese and bread. She dabbed on mustard and went out and sat on the front porch, eating slowly, deliberately tasting each bite.

It was a way of eating she'd learned after those years of restriction, years when the seeds of insecurity her mother had so carefully planted bloomed into obsession. Michael's call had resurrected all the old feelings of not being good enough—he'd left her, after all—but the fact she had work to do made it easier to ignore the urge to prove herself through starvation. Plus, all that running and interviewing and thinking on her feet had made her hungry. And that was good.

Afterward, Aloa went back to her desk and read articles about adventure athletes like Hayley and Ethan. She found stories of the climber Alex Honnold and runner Kilian Jornet, humans who seemed to possess abilities almost beyond comprehension, as if they were the offspring of god and mortal. And yet, there were also stories of athletes whose lives had been snuffed out when they reached too far.

Aloa wondered what the world would be like if everybody embraced the unknown instead of being afraid of it.

CHAPTER 31

May 30—Fifteen miles, Gazos Creek w/JC. 1:43:17. Cold, rainy. Saw two coyotes, a red-tailed hawk. Legs felt good. Stomach OK. RedH's endurance powder sucks. Tell H.T. Making progress. Cloudrunner on mind. Eight months since lost the tadpole and one month since Ethan gone. He always said, hardship makes it interesting, babe. It's interesting, that's for sure.

June 7—Six miles a.m. 42:23; Twelve miles p.m. 1:38:07. Three weeks to Montana. Slower not faster. What wrong? Change diet? Too much protein? Need to focus. What's more important? I feel like I'm letting everybody down. I don't know if I should keep doing this. If you're there, Ethan, send me a sign. Let me know what to do. Everything is against me. I want to quit but won't.

June 22—7 a.m., double Dipsea, 2:06:01. Iced shins, a little better. Free-radical flush, 64 oz. water, salmon, nuts, egg for rest of week. Must get this done. Will get this done. Finish line still far away but the route is clearer. What is hidden still has power. What others want they will not get. On the move tomorrow. The Hunter will have, the hunted will be safe. Flea.

Aloa rubbed her forehead. Hayley's journal was still mysterious. She'd gone through it again in hopes that what she'd learned would make Hayley's notations clearer this time. But they remained a puzzle of quotes and admonitions and coded thoughts with no mention of a book or threats by Hank Tremblay. She sighed. And was Hayley actually talking about a small biting insect or was she just a terrible speller?

She went over and plucked up the keepsake box, put on some music—a little early Madonna for nostalgia's sake—and went to the couch near the window. The day's edges were beginning to soften, the light cooling, the shadows lengthening.

She opened the box to the owl feather and the bracelet. She lifted the braided wristband with its single red stone and wondered where it had come from and why Hayley had consigned it to a box full of memories. It was a small detail, but it reminded her of how much there was still left to uncover.

She reread the birthday card from Ethan and found an ultrasound photo with the beanlike image of a baby. "Our little tadpole," someone had written in the margin. She quickly put the photo facedown in the box.

She also discovered a note from Ethan that urged "fly on, Puma Girl," a small pink-tinged seashell, a ticket stub for a lecture at UC Berkeley titled "Warm Jupiters Aren't Lonely Tonight," and another for an Alison Krauss concert, along with a gold medal for the first Cloudrunner race.

"What was worth your life?" Aloa mumbled, closing her eyes and letting her mind go free.

The ring of her cell phone brought her quickly back. She sighed, stood, and moved toward her desk, shoving the keepsake box into an open spot in the bookcase behind it.

"Mark Combs," the screen announced.

She wrinkled her nose, accepted the call. "What?" she said.

"The police report said you found the body of that mechanic in Dogpatch." Combs's voice had lost none of its arrogance.

"Congratulations on your reading skills," Aloa said. "Why do you care?"

"Because I saw a short piece we did online and noticed the address was the same as that of Ethan Rodriguez and his girlfriend. The one you're doing a story on."

If he expected her to congratulate him on his deductive skills, she didn't.

"Then I talked to the detective who caught the case, Quinn, and he said Ethan's girlfriend was friends with the dead guy. He said you told him you thought the girl was probably murdered. Wouldn't tell me anything else."

She didn't answer.

"I'm curious about what you've got."

Aloa remained silent.

"What I'm saying is, I'll share my notes. The ones you asked for."

"Too late."

"I've got other stuff too. Sources in the PD, an ADA in Reno I know. I don't mind helping you out. I shouldn't have said what I did."

Aloa knew what Combs was doing. She'd done it herself: ease yourself into your source's good graces.

"I don't need your help," she said.

"I think you might, actually."

"And why is that?"

"Because you aren't exactly a poster girl for the truth, are you?"

"I'm hanging up now," Aloa said.

"No. Wait," Combs said. "Hear me out. All I'm trying to say is that I know you're good, but the only thing any journo remembers is that you made stuff up. How about we work together on this? My name makes the story legit. I put you on as a contributing reporter, people see you can be trusted again, and there you go, you've got a foot back in the business. Maybe we could even do more stories together. That's what you want, right?"

"You're saying you want me to do all the work while you get the credit?"

"No. I'll work on the piece with you. I've got some time right now."

Aloa could hear the tiniest bit of desperation in his voice. Were there changes afoot at the newspaper?

"You know, Mark, as tempting as your offer to hijack my story sounds, I think I'll pass."

An exhale of breath. "I thought you were smarter than that."

"I am," she said, "which is why I'm turning you down."

"I don't need you, you know." Combs's voice took on the ego-driven edge she remembered from the conference they'd attended. "Like I said, I've got sources. I know people in Nevada, plus T.J. trusts me. It's game on, babe."

I'm not your babe, she started to say, but Combs had already hung up.

Aloa swore, slammed her phone onto the desk, and then immediately picked it up again.

She dialed Hayley's mother and left a voice mail telling her another reporter might call but advising her not to talk to any other journalists. "Things are happening," she said cryptically and hung up the phone.

She hoped Emily would listen but also knew that Hayley's mother would be among the first calls Combs would make. She thought he might easily break through Emily's defenses.

She would have to work fast.

Aloa made a pot of French press coffee and returned to her desk. She stared at the timeline she'd sketched in her notebook and the list of questions that needed answering. It was way too long.

She sipped from the mug of coffee and read Hayley's workout journal another time and looked again at the crime scene list. Something tickled her brain but disappeared. She got up, took her coffee outside, and sat at the top of the Vallejo steps. Night had descended on the city, turning it into a montage of light and shadow, of quiet and noise.

Do not think of Combs. Or, as her father used to say, do not let your eyes be distracted by the arrival of other birds. Keep your focus.

She finished her coffee, her sight drifting upward to a scattering of stars. She picked out the Big Dipper, the only constellation she knew, and stared at it for a moment. She cocked her head.

She was up and back in the house in less than a minute, powering up the giant TV and the computer and locating the photos she'd taken in Calvin's shop. She scrolled through the images until she came to the shot she wanted: a photo of Calvin's tiny living space.

She moved the cursor, tapped more keys. There it was: a poster on the wall with an artist's beautiful rendering of a cat's-eye-like planet. The same drawing she'd seen on the ticket stub in Hayley's keepsake box.

She zoomed in again and read the text. A lecture on warm Jupiters would be presented by UC Berkeley Professor of Astronomy and Astrophysics Roland Douglas with an introduction by his post-doc research assistant, Sayat Hunter.

Hunter. The word Hayley had used in her workout diary entry. "The Hunter will have, the hunted will be safe."

A spike of adrenaline sent Aloa to her laptop where she looked up first Sayat Hunter and then Roland Douglas. She read up on their research, on the grants and accolades Douglas had received, and then turned her attention to the personal. Fifteen minutes later, she smacked her forehead.

While there was no address listed for Sayat Hunter, Roland T. Douglas, professor of astronomy, lived in San Francisco. On Uranus Terrace.

CHAPTER 32

Aloa stood next to a corner market and stared down the short stretch of street in the Corona Heights neighborhood. Uranus Terrace. Calvin hadn't been so crazy after all.

She'd taken the bus to get here, knowing that finding a place to park at night in a residential neighborhood would be next to impossible. She consulted her notebook and began to walk.

Lexuses and Priuses lined the street, the block a mix of Marina-style cottages and larger homes that spoke of new money. She searched out house numbers, passing an expensive Range Rover with a license plate that read DROPOUT, and stopped in front of a two-story stucco house with a Mexican palm out front. Four symmetrical windows lined the second story of the older home and two windows marked the first floor. A tiny garage with a Volvo parked in front was located on the other side of a gated breezeway. A bumper sticker on the car read WARNING: OBJECTS IN TELESCOPES ARE FARTHER THAN THEY APPEAR.

Aloa approached the front door, a dot of light announcing the presence of a doorbell with a nameplate underneath it. DOUGLAS, it read in Times New Roman Bold. Beneath it was a small square of paper taped to the wall with the words S. HUNTER written in delicate black ink. She gave herself a silent high five.

A man in rumpled corduroy and a sweater vest answered her ring. He wore slippers and looked to be in his fifties.

"Can I help you?"

"Is Mr. Hunter here?" Aloa asked.

The man glanced at his watch. "Is he expecting you?"

"Actually, I was just dropping by. A mutual friend died. I wanted him to know before he read it in the papers."

"Someone from the college?"

"A friend of a friend." Aloa would have to tread carefully.

The man studied her. "It's ten o'clock, you know how he gets."

"It'll just take a minute."

A moment of hesitation, then: "All right. He's in the cottage. Through the breezeway."

"Thanks," Aloa said.

The cottage sat in the far corner of a shallow yard and looked more shed-like than the title "cottage" would suggest. A slurred "enter" answered Aloa's knock. Aloa wondered if that's what the rumpled professor had meant by his warning: "You know how he gets."

Inside, the structure was hobbitlike, with a narrow bed and a single window on one side of the space. On the back wall was a miniature kitchen: microwave, sink, cupboard. Across from the bed, a Mongolian flag hung above a small rolltop desk and an upholstered purple chair in which sat a dark-haired man in his late twenties. A half-empty bottle of vodka was clutched in his hand.

"Mr. Hunter?" Aloa said.

"If you wish." The man stared up at her. "Who are you?"

"My name is Aloa. Aloa Snow."

"Ah, a woman who is also named for what comes from the sky."

The man's brown eyes were shaded by an epicanthic fold that gave away his Asian heritage, while his dark beard and flannel shirt made him look like the grunge version of Genghis Khan.

"I have also given myself a skyward name," he slurred. "In my country it is Sayatshy or Sayat and then, for America, Hunter, because

Americans must have more of everything. Even more names." He smacked his lips and took a sip of vodka. "In Mongolia, you see, one name is enough. But in order to come here, I had to call myself something, and so I took the name of the noble art my father and others of the Kazakh practiced, a people who hunt with eagles." He sighed. "But that is the failure. I am named after what I am not. But then my father suffered his disgrace so who is the fraud? Him or me?"

Aloa wondered if he was already too far in his cups to be of any use.

He looked at her. "Have you come to talk about my research?"

She shook her head. "I'd like to talk about Hayley Poole, Mr. Hunter."

"Sayat, please."

"She was your friend, wasn't she?"

"She was. She has returned to the stardust from whence she came." He settled the bottle on the floor next to his chair. "I see by the look on your face you don't believe me, but it's true," Sayat said. "The cells inside us, all of us, were made in the cores of stars. So that is what we are and always will be: stardust. I'm an astronomer. I know these things. But in my country there is no money for science now, and so I became an alcoholic." He gave a small burp. "Professor Douglas is trying to save me, but it's probably too late." A frown. "Who are you again?"

"My name's Aloa. I'm doing a story on Hayley. For Novo, a website."

"De novo. Latin. It means 'from the beginning,'" Sayat said. "I like it. Please sit."

Aloa looked around and perched on the edge of the bed.

"I was wondering," Aloa said. "Did Hayley bring you something? Something for you to keep?"

Sayat lolled his head back on his chair. "Ah yes, Hayley. The running woman, the lover of Ethan. Such a beautiful friend." He waved a hand in the air. "He and I met in Ulaanbaatar. He was on an adventure. I was exploring the stars. I would do anything for him." He closed his eyes and Aloa waited.

"Sayat?" she said.

The astronomer startled and sat up straighter in the chair.

"Did Hayley bring something to you, Sayat?" Aloa repeated.

The astronomer smacked his lips and rubbed a hand over his face. "Yes. Yes, she did."

"What did she bring?"

Another slow blink of eyes. "Papers. She asked for understanding and also for protection. I don't have much room, but I kept them for her, for Ethan, for my lionly friend." His words were becoming even looser around the edges.

"Do you still have them, the papers?"

"Do I still have the papers?" Sayat tapped himself on the forehead as if trying to loosen the knowledge. "No," he said finally. "No, I don't."

A tug of disappointment. "What happened to them?" Aloa asked.

He picked up the bottle. "The friend of Hayley came."

Had Tremblay beaten her to the punch? "Who was the friend?" Aloa asked.

The astronomer took a long pull from the bottle and hiccupped twice.

"It was the beautiful bartender. I gave them to her."

"Jordan Connor?"

The astronomer nodded. "Yes. Her very good friend. We were speaking of Hayley and Ethan, and I told her of my promise. I did not want the papers anymore and she took them."

"Do you know what was in those papers?" Aloa asked.

"Bad things." Sayat shook his head. "Very bad things."

"Can you tell me what the bad things were?"

Another slow close of eyelids. "Why do you want to know?"

Aloa made a quick decision. "Because I think it may be connected to what happened to Hayley."

"It was not she who became infertile," Sayat slurred.

The same old reporter who'd taught Aloa about knock-and-talks had told her an open-ended statement would get you further than admitting ignorance. "That's what I understood."

"It was the men." Sayat opened his eyes. "The men would drink the powder to be strong and energetic and later find themselves unable to even summon their members to the task." He took a pull of vodka, swishing the alcohol in his mouth before swallowing.

"Erectile dysfunction?"

Sayat leaned forward. "Worse. Not even desire. They were as babies. Sexless, weak, lying in bed all day."

"Omigod," Aloa said under her breath.

"Ah yes," Sayat said. "The hawk has laid a very rotten egg." He giggled to himself.

"The hawk?" Aloa asked.

"Ethan's employer. RedHawk," Sayat said. "Ethan was going to clip its wings. Then, Hayley." His voice trailed off. He bit his bottom lip and shook his head. "The lie, you see, is the man standing before the tank in Tiananmen Square believing he can stop the gears of corruption. No, they will roll on. They will grind him up. They will eat his soul." He touched his fist to his chest. "I know because that was what was done to Mongolia. To me." His eyes filled. "It's why I drink. Why I live in this closet of a home when I belong on the mountains of my country. I asked what part we play in the universe, and their answer was to destroy me." A fat tear rolled down his cheek. "It is as it will always be."

He scrubbed his face with a hand and Aloa noted the neatness of his nails. "I said the same to the beautiful bartender, but she said she was not afraid. She is a lion of a woman as well."

"So Ethan was going to expose this rotten egg."

Sobriety seemed to be making its last call on the astronomer. "A book to rake the muck, to sound the whistle."

"And Hayley came to you?" Aloa said.

Sayat gave a loud burp. "I have notes, notes in which I attempted to help her in her quest but failed, as is often my story, as is my life."

"May I see them?"

"Even foul water will put out a fire," Sayat said. "Even poison can taste like wine."

Aloa didn't understand but decided to take it for assent.

Sayat pushed himself to his feet. "A man stands up to a hawk and is plucked from the earth," he muttered, swaying. "A friend will protect you, yes."

Aloa jumped out of the way as he stumbled toward the bed, falling facedown onto it, one bare foot still on the floor.

He mumbled into his pillow. Aloa watched for only a second and then began her task. She went to his desk, finding a drawer of manila folders labeled neatly in his hand. CORRESPONDENCE. IMMIGRATION. EXPENSES. TRANSCRIPT. CV.

In a folder marked IDEAS and filled with magazine clippings, scribbled notations, and a wrapper from a Mars candy bar, Aloa found a stapled four-page document. "Hayley P. project," read the title.

Aloa looked over her shoulder at the now-snoring astronomer, stuffed the notes into her pack, and left.

Aloa read the astronomer's notes on the bus ride back to North Beach.

There were lists of tongue-tying chemical names and long equations along with records of scientific papers about endocrine disruptors, nonsteroidal estrogen, and mitochondria. Arrows linked effects like muscle building and energy enhancement to weight gain and profound exhaustion.

Little made sense until the last page, where Sayat had written what appeared to be his conclusion: Six of eight male subjects exposed to a compound made by RedHawk Nutritionals (called Pro-Power 500) began suffering devastating effects after sixty to ninety days of use. At first, the men had a surge of energy and libido. Their muscles grew, their sexual stamina rose. Then, suddenly, their revved-up bodies seemed to crash in on themselves. Their sex drive disappeared, their testicles shrank, and debilitating exhaustion made it almost impossible to work or live a normal life. Their symptoms did not fade when they stopped taking the supplement powder. One of the subjects committed suicide (in front of his gym) and the other five participants seemed to disappear (apparently relocated to undisclosed cities).

"Unknown structure-function relation of above ingredients," Sayat wrote. "Chemical analysis needed. Possible contamination at manufacturing site?"

Aloa looked up as the bus halted and a stooped old woman got on, dragging a battered baby stroller filled with what looked like all her possessions.

"In for the night, Gladys?" the bus driver asked.

"Unless you want to check me into the Fairmont, Bobby," the woman answered, and they shared a forlorn laugh. Aloa had heard of the homeless riding buses in lieu of a dangerous bed on the streets. She guessed these two had shared the same joke many times before.

The bus pulled away from the curb.

Aloa dug out her Moleskine and made notes, the picture shifting but still out of focus: RedHawk develops a new product called Pro-Power 500 (some kind of supplement powder) and gives it to eight men. Marketing? Product testing? For six men, improved health is followed by terrible side effects, but the victims have remained silent. Most likely because of some kind of large cash settlement, and now all but one, the suicide, are living a life of disability and forced chastity, which would be enough to bring down Tremblay's company if the news ever got out. Her pulse ratcheted up a notch.

A mechanical voice announced Aloa's stop and she descended the steps. She checked her phone: 10:58 p.m. Almost too late. She decided to risk it anyway and dialed.

"Yes," came Emily Poole's voice. The single word contained whole paragraphs of exhaustion, of grief.

"Hi. It's Aloa Snow from Novo. Sorry to call so late."

"It doesn't matter. I'm up anyway." She sighed. "I had a bad day."

"I'm sorry." Aloa knew of bad days. "Did you get my message?"

"I did. That means you talked to Jordan, right? You saw how she wanted to destroy Hayley."

"I spoke to Jordan Connor, yes." Keep things vague. "By the way, has anybody called you? Another reporter?"

"No."

"Can you do what I asked and not talk to anybody else if they call?"

"Isn't it better to have more publicity?"

Aloa tried to keep the frustration out of her voice. "Not right now. It could hurt my investigation. Things are happening."

"I knew it. It's Jordan, right?" Emily's voice took on an edge of smugness. "She undermined my Hayley. She got her so far down Hayley couldn't get back up. There are laws against that. I read it yesterday. Like when people on the internet talk somebody into committing suicide. She should be in prison."

Aloa interrupted. "Can you do what I ask, Emily? Not talk to any other reporters."

"I guess."

"I have a few more questions, if that's OK?" Aloa said.

A bicyclist dressed in wizard robes with a cat perched on his shoulder rode past. Another of the city's eccentric denizens.

"Did Hayley ever mention that Ethan was writing a book?" Aloa asked.

A pause. "She told me not to talk about that."

"I'm sure she wouldn't mind if you told me now."

Emily seemed to ponder the statement. "I suppose not."

"Do you know what it was about?"

"Not really. But he had an agent and everything. Edie Brightwood was her name. I remember because I thought that was a sign of the bright future ahead for my Hayley. It was going to be a bestseller."

Aloa jotted down the agent's name. "What about Hayley and Hank Tremblay? How were they getting along?"

Aloa could hear the frown in Emily's voice. "They got along fine. Hank did everything for Hayley. He paid for her rehab. He got her that annuity. It was a big hassle and he stepped right in. He backed that insurance company into a corner. All by himself."

Tremblay had told her the same thing at their first meeting but then amended it to say his lawyers had done the work when she'd pressed him. Which of the two was the lie?

"I heard they had some conflict," she said.

"What? No. Who told you that? I mean, Hayley had distanced herself from a lot of people, but Hank understood that. He said we should just let her have her space. He loved Hayley."

"I understand she broke into his office."

"You can't write about that," Emily sputtered. "That was a misunderstanding. Hayley was drinking. She wasn't right."

"Did she ever say what she was doing there?"

"I don't know. Something about showing Hank he had to pay for his sins. Hank said addicts need someone to blame for their problems and that Hayley obviously blamed him for Ethan's death because he sent Ethan to Africa. He understands those things. He got her into rehab and make sure the annuity came through. She was lashing out at everybody then. Even me. Hank is such a generous man."

"Sounds like it," Aloa agreed. Keep the conversation going.

"But then Hayley got better," Emily rushed on. "She had her movie and her races and she and Hank were back in touch."

"How do you know that?"

"Hank told me. I called to thank him for the Calm-V powder he sent. Valerian root. It didn't help as much as I hoped but I wanted to tell him how much the gesture meant. He said he had something important he needed to deliver to Hayley, something Hayley had asked for, and he asked me if I knew where she was. I told him I didn't because Hayley hardly called anymore."

"When did he call?" Aloa asked.

"I guess it was a few days before . . . before, you know."

"Her death?"

Silence.

"Did Hayley mention anything about RedHawk having a problem with one of its products?" Aloa asked.

"I'm not sure what you mean."

"Like bad side effects. Something that might hurt his company?"

"Why are you going after Hank? He's done nothing but good for people." Emily's voice rose. "I thought you were looking into what happened to Hayley. Not Hank. He's a good man. He watches out for people. He supported Hayley and Ethan. He supported me. He even gave me a loan because I couldn't work after Hayley . . ." Emily broke off the sentence. "You leave him alone."

Aloa kept her voice calm. "Just checking everything."

"Well, there's no need to check Hank."

The window of cooperation was closing. "I have to go, Emily, but I'll be in touch. And remember, don't talk to anybody else."

"Well . . . ," Emily said, and Aloa clicked off the phone.

She stared at the sidewalk. Did Tremblay really have something to give to Hayley or was he looking for her in order to destroy the threat facing his company?

The unlocked front door swung open at her touch.

She frowned. "Tick? P-Mac? Doc?" she called.

A deep thud came from somewhere in the house, and Aloa stepped through the door into the dark hallway. "Are you guys in here?" she called.

She heard footsteps rumble across the hardwood floor, a crash of something heavy. She flipped on the hall light just in time to see a man in dark clothing come out of the living room. He had her old suitcase in one hand, and a ski mask obscured his face.

"What the hell?" Aloa cried.

The man looked up and, for a moment, their eyes locked.

"Drop the bag," Aloa growled.

Later, when she thought back on what happened, Aloa couldn't remember the exact moment when she'd plucked her grandmother's old cane from the umbrella stand, but she could visualize, with clarity, the instant the intruder ran down the hallway, grabbed her prized Aldo Rossi coffee press from its shelf, and hurled it at her. The glass and steel coffee maker flew through the air, and she batted it away with the cane. The container shattered.

"Dammit," Aloa cried as the second culinary missile, her cast-iron skillet, came hurtling in her direction.

She leaped out of the way as the skillet thudded against the wall and then looked up just in time to see a glass jar of coffee beans headed toward her skull. She ducked and heard the container shatter behind her.

"Stop it," she yelled. What kind of burglar fought with kitchen gear? One that didn't have a weapon, Aloa answered herself, and raised the cane above her head.

The man hesitated a nanosecond before bolting for the back door with Aloa pounding down the hall behind him.

The intruder leaped down her back steps, heaved the suitcase over the neighbor's fence, and started to follow it just as Aloa made it outside.

She swung the cane as if the burglar was a piñata at a five-year-old's birthday party. "Oh, no you don't," she yelled, feeling the cane connect with soft flesh.

She heard the intruder curse, and felt the brush of his heel against her ribs as he kicked out at her.

Aloa gave a primal yell and swung the cane again. This time the wood connected squarely with the man's kidneys and he grunted and fell to the ground.

"Shit," he groaned, pulling himself up onto one knee.

Aloa raised the cane over him. "Don't move, asshole," she said.

The man's face was shadowed, his eyes unreadable, and so Aloa did not anticipate what happened next: the hard fist that plowed into her stomach, making the breath leave her body in one quick and painful gasp. She doubled over and dropped to her knees, hearing rather than seeing the intruder take two running steps and vault over the fence. She moaned and curled into a ball on the tiny patch of half-dead lawn that was her yard, knowing, even through her pain-filled nausea, that the burglar and whatever he'd taken were gone.

She waited for the queasiness to pass, rolled to her hands and knees, got up, and limped into the house. Her jeans were dirt-stained, her ego wounded. The remains of her coffee maker shimmered under the hall light.

She pressed a hand against her sore stomach and went into the living room, which looked as if some rock band had decided to throw a party. The rosé chair had been dumped on its side, its bottom slashed to ribbons. The couch cushions had been flung to the floor, each bearing a deep cut in the leather. Her cello stool lay below the huge TV, which was now spiderwebbed with cracks. Gone was her laptop and the new computer. Gone, too, were Hayley's notebooks and papers.

She swore and then did a limping inventory through the rest of the house. Nothing else had been taken.

She debated calling the police, who would tell her how stupid it was to chase a home-invasion suspect (it was) and then they would file a report, which would alert Detective Quinn and bring him knocking on her door.

No, this case was hers.

The only bright spot in the mess was Aloa's habit of handwriting her notes instead of using her laptop. And her Moleskine was still in her backpack.

She dead-bolted her front door, locked the back door, and wedged a chair against it. After, she washed her hands and face, changed her clothes, and set about putting her house back in order.

CHAPTER 33

Aloa knew she would eventually have to call Michael and report his fancy equipment stolen and/or destroyed, but right now she had work to do. She put her notebook, phone, and water bottle in her pack, locked the front door, and set off. She wore jeans, her Timberlands, and a field jacket over a black T-shirt. Her stomach still ached from where the intruder's punch had landed, a reminder of the toll this story had taken on her body. It wasn't the worst she had suffered in the name of journalism. That would be the time she'd gone on a drug raid with an LAPD narcotics team and been clubbed over the head with a beer bottle by one of the suspects who, climbing out a side window, had mistaken her for a cop. She'd landed in the ER with a concussion, and the narcotics guys had awarded her a hard hat that read PRESS in big yellow letters. This was nothing.

Aloa's first stop was Café Trieste, where she ordered a scone and a large Americano. The loss of Hayley's things along with her laptop and her French press had added insult to the injury of someone violating the sanctity of her home. This was personal now.

She blinked and felt grit beneath her eyelids. After she'd secured the doors last night, she'd duct-taped the slashes on the couch cushions, dragged the broken TV to the back door to be put in the garbage can, and cut away the liner that hung in shreds from the rosé chair. Then she'd gotten a damp rag and her grandmother's wood oil, knelt on the old oak floor, and cleaned it board by board.

It had taken until 4:00 a.m. for her mind to stop working and the floor to shine. Afterward, she'd taken a shower, swallowed two ibuprofen, and curled up in her bed, where she slept for three hours.

She made a mental note to buy a bottle of Visine at some point that day.

Aloa found a table near the café window, downing the coffee in almost desperate gulps and picking at the scone. She debated whether to shell out $200 for another Aldo Rossi or settle for a cheaper brand and lousy coffee. Perhaps she could expense the coffee maker as a necessary part of her investigation. She stared into her empty cup, got up, and ordered an espresso.

The café was full: residents arriving for coffee before work, tourists trying to grab a piece of North Beach experience, regulars in their usual places with cups of black coffee in front of them. She made a list of chores in her notebook, located a FedEx store where she could rent computer time, and headed out the door.

The handsome barista lifted his chin in acknowledgment as she left.

Seated before a well-used computer at the FedEx store, Aloa answered her emails, turned down a freelance assignment for an art and wine festival, and looked up Tremblay's donation of a solar-power system to a hospital in Africa. Sure enough, she found an article that described how his generous contribution had provided lights and refrigeration to a hospital where emergency surgeries had often been performed by candlelight. And yet, the same man had allowed eight men to become human lab rats for a dangerous product.

The shop was busy now. Fax machines beeped, copiers hummed and spit. A man in a camouflage jacket ordered a ten-foot banner that proclaimed WELCOME HOME, SON.

Aloa located a number for Edie Brightwood, Ethan's New York agent, and dialed. After talking her way past an assistant, Aloa got confirmation that Edie had been Ethan's literary agent. His death, said Edie, had been a real shame, because the book he was proposing about the

African tribe would have been huge. She pronounced it "yuge." She also said that Hayley had, indeed, called her after Ethan died and said he had started another book while he was in Africa, some memoir-slash-exposé about corporations stealing your soul. "She wanted a big advance. I told her a book like that wouldn't sell even if you tucked a five-dollar bill in every copy," Edie said. "Nobody reads that stuff, and besides, the girl couldn't write. She sent me a synopsis. Like scrambled eggs. I couldn't understand a word of it."

Aloa asked if she still had the synopsis, but Edie said she'd trashed it. Aloa thanked her and hung up.

Next, she typed in a search for "suicide San Francisco gym" and found a short article about an unidentified shooting victim being discovered in front of a downtown workout studio a few months after the supplement experiment had been stopped. The police were quoted as saying the gunshot wound appeared self-inflicted. A later article on the newspaper website gave the suicide victim's name as Dashon Carter. Aloa located an address on Russian Hill and set off.

She did not notice the man across the street who pushed himself away from the wall and began to follow her.

CHAPTER 34

He racked the weights and wiped his face with a towel. The reporter was getting closer.

Lester had delivered the stolen computers late last night and he'd spent four hours going through them. He saw the searches she'd done, the information she'd gathered. He thought about the call from that other reporter and his assertion that Snow believed Hayley had been murdered. He added that to her questions to the dead girl's mother about a bad RedHawk product.

He went into the apartment's gleaming kitchen, got a cold bottle of water from the fridge, and drained it in a single gulp.

He thought of Detective Quinn and what might happen if Snow met with an unfortunate accident. He thought of the mission and the money that was at stake. Killing her was still an option, but he would wait. Dead bodies had their own complications.

He hadn't yet told the clients about the reporter or the detective. It was a delicate balance when it came to them. Speak too soon and they doubted your competence. Speak too late and they wondered about your loyalty.

Maybe matches and gasoline were in order. A message that couldn't be missed.

He pulled another bottle of water from the refrigerator and hummed a few bars from "Burning Down the House." God, he loved the Talking Heads.

He drained the second bottle of water, tossed the containers in the trash, and went back to the weight room. He loaded 225 pounds onto the bar, lay back on the bench, and lifted.

CHAPTER 35

Dashon Carter's widow, Susan, was a stunning woman. She was tall and slender with cocoa-colored skin and close-cropped hair that showed off a beautifully shaped head and almond eyes. But the puffiness under those eyes and the sad set of her lips let Aloa know that the death of her husband was still a raw wound.

Aloa had identified herself as a researcher from Novo who was looking into the supplement industry, and the woman had blanched. She said she didn't want to talk, but she didn't immediately slam the door shut and so Aloa had pressed. She told the widow how the supplement industry was basically unregulated and that there were plenty of cases where people were harmed by products they thought were safe. She said the only way for this to stop was for victims to speak out. When Susan still hesitated, Aloa said she would only use Susan's first name and leave out identifying information in any story she wrote.

"I don't know," the widow had said.

"How about we just talk on background?" Aloa had suggested.

Now they sat on a white sofa in a bright living room with views of downtown. It was a modest apartment with hardwood floors, and yet Aloa knew it probably rented for at least $4,000 a month. The furnishings were spare and tasteful: the couch, a red butterfly chair, a colorful print that hung on one wall, a five-foot-tall sculpture of a dancing woman that dominated the room. Next to Aloa was a lacquered end table with a wedding photo of Susan and Dashon. From what Aloa could see, Dashon was as unremarkable as his wife was beautiful. He wore glasses, had a slight paunch, and his ears stood out from his head. But his eyes were kind, and the way he put his arm around his wife let Aloa know that not only did he adore Susan, he also wondered at the good fortune that had made her say yes to him.

Susan Carter caught Aloa studying the picture.

"Dashon was so thoughtful, so bright," she said. "He worked for a big accounting firm, eighty hours a week sometimes. But he brought me coffee in bed every morning, and on Fridays he always came home with two dozen white roses. My favorite." Her eyes brimmed and Aloa gave her a moment to compose herself.

"He sounds wonderful," she said.

"He is. I mean, was." Susan cleared her throat. "I told him that every day, but he didn't believe me. He always thought he wasn't good enough, that he needed to look like 'we belonged together.'" She made air quotes. "That's why he joined the gym. That's why he agreed to . . ." She stopped herself. "I'm really not supposed to talk about this."

"It's background," Aloa reminded her. "No names."

"I know." Susan twisted her fingers in her lap and looked out the front windows of the apartment. She was even more beautiful in profile. "I signed an agreement," she said finally.

"With RedHawk?" Aloa figured there had been some kind of settlement, otherwise there would have been lawsuits. A castration powder would be a personal injury lawyer's wet dream.

"Not with RedHawk," Susan said. She drew herself up straighter. Aloa cocked her head.

"Hank Tremblay called after Dashon died. He said he'd heard of Dashon's death and that he'd admired Dashon for how he'd worked through his depression and was sorry to hear it had gotten the best of him. He offered me a million dollars as part of what he called payment for Dashon's participation in what was supposed to be a marketing project. He said I could keep doing my sculptures and not have to work." She nodded toward the dancing woman.

"It's beautiful," Aloa said.

"Thanks. I told him I didn't want his damn money and that Dashon's depression had nothing to do with him killing himself and he knew that. I hung up on him."

"Dashon suffered from depression?" Aloa asked.

"He had it under control. He was very good about his medication." Susan's eyes narrowed.

"So it was the supplement, the effects of the Pro-Power 500, that caused him to kill himself," Aloa said quickly.

"That's what I'm not supposed to talk about."

"But if you didn't take the money, you didn't sign a confidentiality agreement, right?"

"Not with him but with somebody else. A few days after that, another guy showed up."

"Who was this other guy?"

The trace of a smile brushed Susan's lips. "They said I couldn't talk about the powder or how much money I got, but they never said I couldn't tell you the name of the man who threatened me, who told me if I didn't accept his offer he would let Immigration know that my mother had come here from Ethiopia without the proper papers. My mother is eighty-three and has lived in this country for fifty years, Ms. Snow. Do you know what an arrest and deportation would do to her?"

"I can't imagine," Aloa said.

"It would kill her." Susan leaned forward. "That's why I took his money. More than what Hank Tremblay offered me, in case you want to know."

Aloa nodded, forcing herself not to appear too eager. "What was the man's name?"

Susan Carter pressed her lips together and seemed to make a final decision. "His name was Radnor Chee, C-H-E-E, and he worked for a company called Pontifex."

Aloa sucked in a breath. *R. Chee,* she thought. *Archie.*

CHAPTER 36

Aloa tried to contain her excitement as she walked toward home. Susan Carter had just established a link between the Archie on the plane— Radnor Chee—Tremblay, and the dangerous powder.

She was entering Chinatown with its brimming markets and cluttered tourist shops when it hit her: T.J. had said the boxes unloaded from the jet had Chinese writing on them. She typed a quick search into her phone. RedHawk's manufacturing plant was in China. Sayat's notes had indicated possible contamination of the powder at a foreign factory.

Tremblay hadn't gone to Africa just to see off his two climbers. He was using the trip as subterfuge to recoup his losses by selling a potentially damaging product in a continent where there were few consumer regulations. He wasn't the first to do something like that. She'd read stories of destructive pesticides and banned drugs being sold overseas by companies who couldn't peddle them in the United States. But there was nothing like this: a supplement powder that chemically castrated a majority of its users.

She could only imagine the ramifications of uncovering something like that—not only for RedHawk, but also for the American people when it was discovered a US company had deliberately sold this crippling product overseas. No wonder Ethan had been so angry when he learned what Hank was doing.

She typed in "Radnor Chee and Pontifex" but got nothing even remotely informative.

She hesitated only a moment before tapping a number from her recent call list.

"How's it hanging, girl?" asked Steve, her source in the State Department who, thankfully, still owed her enough favors for a lifetime of requests.

"It's hanging fine, Steve. Listen, I need you to look up something called Pontifex."

"You mean, besides being the high priest of ancient Rome?"

"Jesus Christ," Aloa swore.

"Some people do say I walk on water," Steve deadpanned.

"No," Aloa said, and stopped in her tracks. "My vic, the girl I'm writing about, told one of her friends that she had to hide the information she had from the High Priest."

"That's some kinda tea."

"What?"

"You know, gossip, information. Tea."

"Oh, sure," Aloa said. "Anyway, could you see what you've got on Pontifex?"

"Hang on, babycakes."

Aloa bit her tongue. She could hear Steve humming, a run of computer keys. She settled herself against a lamppost, the feel of the hunt rising inside her. A clump of tourists, looking unnerved by the sight of duck carcasses hanging in the window of a butcher shop, scuttled past as their tour guide directed them into a restaurant that locals avoided for the high cost of its subpar food. Aloa guessed a few of the unsuspecting visitors would be spending some time on the porcelain throne that night.

"Here it is," Steve said after a stretch of minutes. "Looks like it's some kind of crisis management company."

"Fixers?"

"Something like that."

Aloa knew of the people who made the wealthy's problems go away through favors granted and then called in, through money that dropped into outstretched palms—including those of corrupt rulers and repressive governments. It was a nasty business that balanced somewhere between legal and not and relied on shady middlemen to get things done.

"Any issues with them?" she asked.

Another clatter of computer keys. A few muttered words.

"Looks like something happened to this journalist in Nigeria a year or two ago," Steve said. "Hmm."

"Tell me."

"He died in some freak car accident. Apparently, it was after he started sticking his nose into this skeezy land deal with a copper mining company. A few days later, some guy shows up at the police station with a witness who conveniently says he saw the journo getting hammered in some bar. The reporter was a teetotaler, but you know . . ." Steve's voice trailed off. "Twenty-four hours later, the top cop rules it a drunk driving accident."

"Let me guess. The guy who brought in the witness was from Pontifex."

"Yup."

"Anything connecting Pontifex and the accident itself?"

"Nothing we could prove, but I can tell you this: those homies don't play well with others, if you know what I mean."

"Who else have they worked for?"

"Umm. You got a couple of oil companies, the copper miners, a wheat dealer, some insurance company whose CEO's son was in Thailand and got caught with a quarter pound of cocaine."

"What about a company named RedHawk or somebody named Hank Tremblay?"

"Nothing," Steve said after a few more minutes of searching, "but that doesn't mean it didn't happen. Looks like these guys are flying pretty low under the radar."

"Can you tell me who runs the company?" she asked Steve.

"Hmm," Steve said. "It looks here like it's got some connection to the Pontecorvo brothers, you know, those hedge fund guys from New Jersey? Then there's an ex-CIA agent named Lester Johnson, plus some guy from Florida named Radnor Chee. Goes by the name Archie. I mean, who wouldn't? Radnor?" Steve snorted. "He supposedly runs a boat charter company, but it looks like he spends more time running around the world. Passport shows Kazakhstan, Peru, China, Sierra Leone, Chad."

Aloa pumped her fist silently. "Anything about that Chee guy and a castration powder?"

"What? Holy crap. There's a powder that make your dick fall off?"

"Not literally fall off, Steve, but it's bad."

"Who would make that stuff? I mean, come on." Steve's outrage was bubbling and would soon reach a full boil. "Guys need their dicks. I mean, how could a guy be a guy without one? You'd be a freak, a piston that don't fire. That's some sick stuff, man."

Aloa interrupted his diatribe. "Listen, is there anything you can send me about Pontifex, about that Chee guy?"

Steve fell silent. Sending classified information was not something even he could take lightly.

"Just whatever won't get you in trouble," Aloa assured him quickly. She didn't want him arrested any more than he did.

"I suppose it will be all right. I mean, you could probably find some of this yourself," Steve said finally, "although it would require an IQ of 180 and mad skills."

"I appreciate this a lot," Aloa said, and meant it.

"I still can't believe somebody is jacking guys' dicks," he was muttering as Aloa hung up the phone.

Two minutes later, an email with two attachments arrived from an account she didn't recognize. The first was a report about a fire that had burned down a cutlery factory after its owners had sued Pontifex for trademark infringement. A worker had died, the company had gone out of business, and no one had ever been arrested for the arson. The report included a picture of the disputed image: a sword-crossed Chi-Rho.

The second attachment was a grainy 2001 photo of Radnor Chee having dinner with a guy identified as a former Russian general. She leaned close to the image and felt a startle of recognition. The man identified as Radnor Chee in the picture was none other than Baldy, the rude realtor.

CHAPTER 37

Aloa slipped into her favorite Chinatown hole-in-the-wall café, found an empty table, and ordered a bowl of spicy noodles and a Diet Coke. Thoughts swirled in her head. Suddenly, she was starving.

That Pontifex's logo, a Chi-Rho, appeared on the photo of Ethan's body tied the organization to Ethan's death. And if Tremblay had the photo, then either the company was proving a task accomplished or, as the medical examiner had hinted, it was making a threat. But why would Pontifex threaten Tremblay if he and Chee were working together to dump RedHawk's devastating supplement in Africa? Tremblay hadn't seemed particularly nervous or worried when he'd met Chee at the apartment building a few days ago.

She tugged out her notebook as a fortyish waiter, the brother of the glowering owner/chef in the kitchen, slammed a can of Diet Coke and a glass of ice in front of her. The café was not known for service, but a delicious six-dollar bowl of noodles was worth the indignities that had to be endured.

She decanted the soda and began to sketch a scenario.

The lines ran from Tremblay to Chee to Pontifex to Dashon Carter. Then there was Hayley and Ethan and the Pro-Power supplement powder plus the trip to Africa and Tremblay again. And hadn't she also mentioned Calvin to Tremblay before the mechanic was killed?

When she'd finished the web of clues, two things stood out: Tremblay was in the middle of it all, and Ethan's "terrorist" killers may not have been religious extremists but opportunists hired by Pontifex, especially when you considered their consumption of the expedition's whiskey. Like Steve said, it was hard to stay clean when you ran a dirty business.

Aloa drank her soda as the waiter crashed a bowl of steaming noodles in front of her. She didn't bother to say thanks. This wasn't the kind of place were niceties were needed.

The noodles were perfect, the broth spicy and rich. As she ate, Aloa studied the patterns: Ethan, Hayley, and Calvin dead. A dangerous powder. A fixer providing proof of service. Tremblay saying he had to deliver something to Hayley.

Blackmail. The idea hit her like the crash of a wave on the shore. What if Hayley had been unable to finish the book, had been turned down by Edie Brightwood, and decided to threaten Tremblay with exposure? It would guarantee her money, which she apparently needed, and also allow her to hold a sword over Tremblay's head so that the supplement wouldn't get into anyone else's hands. And if there was a reason to kill, blackmail was it.

She closed her eyes, seeing the pieces fall into place. But in order to prove motive, she needed more than Sayat's notes. She needed either the flash drive or the papers, which were now in the hands of Jordan Connor, who didn't like or trust reporters. Still, Aloa had to try.

She spent the next five minutes finishing her meal and coming up with a plan. She looked through her notes and found the number she'd recovered from the police report just as the waiter appeared at her table.

"How about if you pay right now?" he said, grabbing her empty bowl and nodding his head to a short line of customers waiting to get in.

Aloa got the hint, threw a few bills on the table, and went outside. The street hummed with conversations, a noisy stew of Chinese dialects, English, and a scattering of other languages she couldn't identify. She fished out her cell, remembered the Brain Farm's warning about her phone being tapped, thought of Pontifex and the trail of bodies, and stepped back inside.

The owner's son, a dark-haired boy of about twelve, sat on a stool by the door playing a game on his phone.

"Could I use your cell for a few minutes?" Aloa asked. The boy hesitated. "I'll give you ten bucks," she said.

The kid stared at her. "Twenty," he said.

Aloa sighed and fished a bill out of her pack. Apparently, the customer-service apple didn't fall far from the tree.

She took the phone, told the boy she'd be just outside, and punched in the number.

"Hi, Jordan. It's Aloa Snow," she said when Jordan answered.

"I'm busy," came the quick retort.

"I need to talk to you."

"I can't. I'm on a run." The slap of feet and the cadence of breath proved Jordan was telling the truth.

"How about later?" Aloa pushed.

"I'm busy the rest of the day."

"I want to talk about the papers you got from Sayat."

"What?" From the rhythm of the footfalls, it seemed as if Jordan had slowed and then come to a halt.

"I'm saying those papers you have may be dangerous. There may be powerful people who want them. People who don't mind killing."

"You're freaking me out." Jordan's breath was still coming hard.

"In fact, I think they may be the reason Hayley is no longer with us," Aloa continued. Keep the connection to Ethan's death quiet for now.

A long pause followed on Jordan's end of the line. "Are you saying it wasn't suicide?"

In every relationship between journalist and source, there came a turning point at which the source either walked away or opened themselves up fully. It was always a question of timing and phrasing.

"I'm saying that there are things that suggest she did not take her own life, yes."

"What kind of things?" Jordan asked.

Aloa sidestepped the question. "Let me see the papers and we can talk. If I can get everything out into the open, you'll be safe. Nobody will hurt you then."

Aloa felt a tug on her sleeve as the kid gestured to have his phone returned. Aloa shooed him back inside.

"What do you mean, 'nobody will hurt me'?" Jordan asked, more insistent now.

"Let's talk. In person. This is really important, Jordan."

The line was quiet. "All right," she said, finally.

"Can we meet today? Say, in two hours?"

"Make it an hour. At my apartment." Jordan gave Aloa an address in the Haight, the same one in the police report.

Aloa looked at her watch. It was five o'clock. "I'll be there."

"Does anybody else know about this?" Jordan asked.

"I'm the only one."

"I don't want my name involved in whatever you're doing," she said.

"We'll talk," Aloa said, not wanting to commit. "See you soon," she said, and broke the connection before Jordan could change her mind.

CHAPTER 38

He leaned against the window of the tourist shop, pretending to check his email and watching the reporter across the street. There was no activity on her phone, which made no sense. Who in the hell was she talking to?

He'd listened in on her earlier phone conversation with some friend of hers: the identification of Pontifex, his own name. Plus the visit to the widow Carter's house. A flush of anger spread through him. It was time for Snow to be melted.

A smile cracked his lips. Goddamn, he was funny.

A delivery truck rumbled by and he thought an accident might be the answer. Maybe a tripping foot followed by a quick head-slam into the pavement to make it appear as if she'd simply been the victim of an unlucky fall. Or maybe a nice stab in the belly. He fingered the knife he'd taken from the mechanic. He'd like the feel of that.

If he stole her backpack and maybe even that jacket, the cops would think it was a mugging gone bad. Anybody who knew her would say she was the kind of girl who would fight back. He smiled.

But first he would follow her. See if she would take him to what he wanted: the flash drive with the incriminating evidence on it. Above everything, he needed that.

He watched the reporter shut off the phone, hand it through the front door, and then hurry down the street.

CHAPTER 39

She'd just given the phone back to the kid when she caught a glimpse of a guy leaning against a curio shop and checking his phone. He wore a trench coat, a watch cap, and sunglasses. Not unusual in a city of rapidly changing temperatures. But her father had taught her how to recognize like things (birds of a certain species, of a certain family) and then concentrate on what didn't fit. The man was too casual and studied as he stood amid the crowds of tourists and shoppers hurrying by.

She gave another glance and saw the man look up and turn his head slightly in her direction. She spotted the tiny soul patch under the man's lip and her heart gave a thud of confirmation. Time to move.

She hurried down Jackson and turned into one of the alleys that cut through the neighborhood. Laundry hung from fire escapes above her. An old man sat on a chair reading a newspaper.

She looked behind her. Two stooped grandmothers in black pants and faded cardigans carried the day's groceries. A tourist snapped pictures and a young man unloaded a delivery van, but there was no sign of the guy with the soul patch.

Had she been mistaken?

She turned the corner, counted off three seconds, and then peeked back around the edge of the stucco building. Baldy/Archie was jogging up the alley, his unbuttoned coat flapping behind him. She saw the weapon in a kind of makeshift holster under his arm. Calvin's knife. She hesitated only a second; then she turned and ran.

She sprinted down the sidewalk, darting around pedestrians, her breath coming hard. She looked over her shoulder. Baldy was half a block behind her but gaining ground. *Think,* she told herself.

In the long months after her disgrace, Aloa had often wandered the city as if needing to relearn its ways. She explored its small lanes, its hidden shops. On one of her walks she had discovered a small Chinatown storefront lined with boxes of soy sauce, fortune cookies, and Tsingtao beer. Inside the protective walls of comestibles, a dozen women played mahjongg. Their high-pitched chattering made them sound like sparrows, and Aloa had stood in the shadows, envying their laughter and camaraderie. She returned the next day to watch again and one of the women had beckoned her inside, motioned for her to pour herself some tea and get warm. What Aloa remembered now was the open door in the back of the room and the reason for the boxes of restaurant supplies.

She turned sharply, her boots slapping the gray cobblestones of another of Chinatown's narrow passageways. She glanced behind her, saw Baldy had not yet arrived, and pushed her way into the storage-slash-mahjongg-room.

Hands stilled and eight unfamiliar faces turned toward her, their mouths open.

"Sorry. Just coming through," Aloa said, and skittered between two tables of mahjongg players, ran through the open door in the front of the room, and burst into a narrow restaurant kitchen.

"Hi. Excuse me," she said as she pushed past a dishwasher who couldn't have been more than fourteen.

An explosion of what she guessed were Chinese curses erupted as she squeezed quickly past a potbellied man chopping onions and then slipped past a sweating chef who was at a hot stove.

"Excuse me," she said, not breaking her stride. "Sorry."

The cook shook a spatula at her and pointed toward the front door. The onion chopper was now yelling at the dishwasher, as if he suspected the boy of inviting intruders into his domain.

The edge of Aloa's pack snagged a stack of metal trays and sent them clanging to the floor. The guy at the stove was coming after her now, and she pushed through the swinging kitchen door and into the restaurant, where an old man in a black jacket with a pork bun halfway to his mouth startled with a high gasp.

Aloa hoped she hadn't given him a heart attack.

She ran through the restaurant, squeezing past tables, and then she was out the front door and onto Grant Street. She looked up and down the busy thoroughfare. No sign of her pursuer. She slipped out of her jacket, stuffed it in her pack, and took off at a sprint.

A few pedestrians glanced at her, but that was the beauty of San Francisco. Nobody blamed you for doing your own thing.

By the time she got to Pacific she had slowed to a fast walk, her torso slick with sweat, her limbs shaking with exertion. She hesitated at the star-shaped intersection of Pacific, Kearny, and Columbus, looked in all directions, and hurried to City Lights Books. From there, she thought, she could shield herself among the shelves and still be on the lookout for Baldy from the store's windows.

She crouched down, willing her heart to settle. Her phone vibrated in her pocket, causing a quick startle of nerves. She pulled it out.

"Great job!" proclaimed the HardE app. "Twenty-five thousand steps."

"Are you kidding me," she said, and made to turn off the app, but before she could, another call came in. This one from an unknown number.

She hesitated for a moment, then answered. "Hello?"

"Ink, it's me, Doc," said the voice. "Can you hear me?"

"Of course I can." Aloa let out a breath and sagged back on her heels.

"Are you sure?"

"How else would I know what to answer?"

"Good point," said Doc. "I'm testing out my new iPhone. Tick got it for me. You can't believe the stuff rich white people throw away."

Aloa didn't want to know the details of freegan phone acquisition. "Listen, I can't talk right now."

"Wait, Tick is putting you on speaker."

"Where are you?" came a graveled voice.

Aloa thought of her possibly tapped phone. "I'm with Ginsberg. At Larry's place."

She knew the Brain Farm would recognize her reference to Lawrence Ferlinghetti, who owned City Lights Books, and Allen Ginsberg, the beat poet whose book *Howl* had nearly landed both men in jail on obscenity charges.

"Got it!" Tick said.

She could hear Doc's voice next. "What's going on, Ink? You don't sound so hot."

"Somebody's chasing me. He's with this group of fixers. Out of New Jersey. He had a knife. I think it was Calvin's."

"Don't move. We'll pick you up." It was P-Mac.

"No time. I have to be somewhere at six o'clock," Aloa said.

"Forget the appointment. Your life is more important, Ink," Doc said.

"That's why I need to go. I need proof to stop this thing," Aloa said.

"Wait right there," Tick called. "We can make it, can't we, boys?"

"Where are you?" Aloa asked.

"In the van. Just approaching the Bay Bridge," Doc said.

Aloa did a quick calculation. "There's no time. I'll take the rental car." For the first time, she was glad she hadn't been able to find a parking spot near her house, where Baldy/Archie might be waiting for her.

"Don't be a hero, kid," P-Mac said.

"Who are you meeting and where?" Tick asked.

"I can't say who but it's on the same street as Jerry and the boys." A reference to the Grateful Dead, who had once lived on Ashbury Street in the Haight. If somebody was listening in, she hoped they weren't a fan.

"Roger that," Tick said.

A man in a long coat walked past the window, but he was slender with stringy blond hair that tumbled to his shoulders.

"We can be there in twenty," Doc said.

The pitch of the van's engine shifted so it was nearly a scream.

"I don't want to be late," Aloa said.

"Many calculations lead to victory and few calculations lead to defeat." A Sun Tzu quote from P-Mac. "We're going with you."

Aloa could hear shouts of assent from the other gray-hairs.

"I've got my conker," Tick said.

"And I'll bring li'l Jackie," Doc called out.

Somewhere in his life of monkeywrenching and anarchistic misdeeds, Tick had taken to carrying a tube sock filled with marbles as a weapon. And, as an African American male, Doc knew the only armament he could carry was one that could be denied as sporting equipment. He'd named the bat in honor of Jackie Robinson.

"No need for conkers or bats," Aloa said. "Besides, I think I've lost him." Aloa looked out the window again.

"'When we are near, we must make the enemy believe we are far away,'" P-Mac said. More Sun Tzu. "Stay right there."

"We can make it," Doc hollered.

Aloa thought of the possibility of Baldy/Archie being nearby as P-Mac had said. An unexpected escape in the gray-hairs' van might be her best choice. "All right. But if you're not here, I'm going on my own."

"We got us a mission, boys," Tick cackled. "Radio silence from here on in."

The phone went dead.

CHAPTER 40

Where in the hell did the bitch go?

CHAPTER 41

Aloa squeezed the rental car diagonally behind an SUV parked in the driveway of the gaily painted Victorian that housed Jordan's apartment. That the rental car was blocking someone else's vehicle and resting halfway across the sidewalk was a dispensation allowed under the informal parking code of San Francisco: thou shalt not abandon a spot simply because it might piss someone off. Aloa got out of the car and hurried up the steps to the front door.

When the Brain Farm hadn't showed up at the appointed time, she'd cursed, waited five minutes, then slipped from the store and sprinted to the rental car, driving like a madwoman through tourist traffic in order to arrive at Jordan's apartment ten minutes late. She wondered why she'd believed the Brain Farm could make it to the bookstore in twenty minutes. A golf cart had more chance of arriving on time than that hamster-wheel of a van engine.

She calmed her breath, rang the doorbell, and waited, searching the street for signs of Baldy or anyone who seemed suspicious. The sidewalks were peaceful in contrast to Ashbury Street's history. One of these Victorians, she knew, was where the Grateful Dead had lived from 1966 to 1968 thanks to the generosity of Owsley Stanley, a man who had reportedly manufactured more than a million doses of LSD in a two-year period. There was also the unnumbered house where the Hells Angels once had its headquarters. Now, the formerly shabby homes that had sheltered the 1960s free spirits were priced in the million-dollar range. Yet vestiges of the old neighborhood culture remained. The clock at the corner of Haight and Ashbury was still frozen at 4:20, the universal code for the consumption of cannabis.

Aloa stepped off the porch, examined the house's windows for movement, then went back and pushed the doorbell again. Had Jordan changed her mind?

A European starling fluttered onto the porch railing and cocked its head at Aloa. The species had been brought to the United States by a group of Shakespeare enthusiasts who wanted every bird in the bard's writings to be available for viewing. Now they were everywhere: literature's pests.

The starling fled at the sound of a buzzer and the front door clicking open.

"Finally," Aloa muttered. She grabbed the handle, gave one last look down the street for Archie, and went inside.

Time to see what Ethan and Hayley may have died for.

Jordan answered her door in running tights, a jog bra, and an artfully torn T-shirt. Her hair was pulled back tightly into a bun and she was glistening with sweat.

"Are you by yourself?" she asked.

"I'm alone," Aloa said.

"And nobody followed you?"

Aloa shook her head. She'd kept an eye on her rearview mirror and spotted no sign of a pursuer.

"You freaked me out," Jordan said. "That stuff about people wanting to hurt me. Come in. Hurry up." She opened the door wider and Aloa stepped through. "I couldn't stop thinking about what you said."

The competent Jordan who had climbed trees and run hundred-mile races had faded. She appeared anxious, jumpy. "Want some orange juice? I just squeezed it." She wiped beads of perspiration from her forehead with the sleeve of her shirt.

"Juice would be good, thanks."

A small kitchen opened off the high-ceilinged living space, which contained a black leather love seat, a sleek road bike, and a small table cluttered with framed photos and candles. Exercise equipment filled one corner of the room, and a large American flag hung over the fireplace with more photographs. *Interesting decor,* Aloa thought.

She wandered over to the photos on the table. There were professional-looking shots of Jordan rock climbing, on a road bike, standing on a beach with a paddleboard under her arm. In each, she was dressed in more skin than cloth.

"Do you model?" Aloa asked.

"I've done some catalog work," Jordan said from the kitchen. "Mostly it's social media stuff. I get bonuses for magazine shots, anything that gets over twenty-five thousand hits."

Aloa heard the tumble of ice cubes and went over to the fireplace. The photos there were not the stuff of catalogs or social media. There was a shot of four soldiers in desert camouflage standing next to a dead body in loose Pashtun clothing. Another showed a gathering of dusty soldiers with guns. Some of them were shirtless, some in camo gear and headscarves, all of them grinning and making gestures toward the camera.

Aloa straightened. "These are interesting shots," she said as Jordan came into the room with tumblers of orange juice.

"Friends of mine. They did an important job. If you weren't there, you wouldn't understand." Jordan handed her the juice.

"The dead man?" Aloa asked.

"Al Qaeda."

"How did you know those guys?"

"I don't have a lot of time. Tell me why you think Hayley was killed," Jordan said, and perched on the edge of a weight bench.

"I think Hayley had information. I think she may have been blackmailing somebody. Somebody you know." Aloa settled on the leather love seat, put the glass of juice on the floor, and pulled her notebook and pen from her pack.

"What? Who? How do you know that?"

Aloa studied the athlete. "Why didn't you tell the cops that Hank Tremblay was at the campout?"

Surprise registered on Jordan's face, then flitted away. "When Hayley went missing, somebody called from Hank's office and asked me to tell the cops I didn't know the name of the other camper, that we should say the only name we had for him was Boots. Hank's dad used to call him that, I guess."

"But why?" Aloa asked.

"Hank had blown off some big meeting and the guy who called said if we told the cops Hank's real name, word would get out and he'd lose some big deal he was making. Why does that matter?"

For a moment, Aloa wondered if Tremblay had also bought her silence. "Because," she said, "Tremblay's company was in trouble over this stuff called Pro-Power 500."

Jordan seemed to study the laces of her running shoes. "So you know about that," she said, finally. Her eyes lifted and met Aloa's.

Aloa nodded. "And if Hayley was blackmailing Tremblay over it, which I think she was, well, that's a good motive for murder. RedHawk would be finished if word ever got out." Aloa waited to see Jordan's reaction.

Jordan looked away and then back at Aloa. "But what about the note in her car?"

"The handwriting was never tested, plus the evidence points away from that."

"What evidence?" Jordan asked. She finished off her juice in a long gulp and set the empty glass on the floor.

Aloa weighed her response. "Hank Tremblay had motive, opportunity, and the means to hurt Hayley. That's why he was at the campout."

She decided to play a little hardball. "Withholding evidence in a criminal investigation is a crime, you know."

Jordan got up and moved over in front of the American flag above the fireplace. Her unblinking eyes held Aloa's gaze for just a little too long, a sign, Aloa's detective ex-boyfriend believed, that showed cognitive overload—either extreme stress or a lie.

"How close are you to writing about that stuff?" she asked.

"Pretty close. The papers will just confirm what I know."

"Let me ask this: Do you love America?"

Aloa frowned. "I appreciate the freedoms we have," she said carefully, "but I don't always agree with our partisan politics, the influence peddling."

"You don't think we should have been in Iraq? In Afghanistan?"

"I think the evidence suggests we went there for the wrong reasons." Aloa wondered where the conversation was headed.

"Well, I love America."

"I can see by the flag."

"Hank Tremblay loves America too."

"I'm not sure where this is going."

"God, it's hot in here." Jordan slipped off her T-shirt and mopped her still-perspiring face. Her jog bra was black, her torso so taut it was almost sculptural. "Just because a corporation tries to make money, you think it can't do good things?" she said.

"I didn't say that."

"Hank was doing something noble."

Aloa wasn't sure how to answer. Dumping tainted supplements on unsuspecting people was only noble if you were devoted to the bottom line.

"Hank was looking at the big picture."

"Which is?"

"That America is being threatened and it's up to patriots to step forward."

"I'm sorry, but I don't understand."

"Of course you don't. None of the media does. Neither did Hayley. She was so shortsighted."

Jordan went over and threw open the apartment's front window, letting in a wave of cool air. "Better," she breathed.

And that's when Aloa saw it, the tattoo low on Jordan's back: two angel wings supporting an arch with the single word "sapper" on it.

CHAPTER 42

Aloa calmed her mind, keeping her voice neutral.

"You mentioned patriots. Were you in the military?" she asked.

"PMC. Private military contractor. Two years in Afghanistan." Jordan turned back toward Aloa. "Why do you ask?"

"Your tattoo."

"My fiancé was a sapper. He was killed over there."

"I'm sorry to hear that."

"Charlie was doing his duty." Jordan pressed her lips together. "He was a good man. The only man I ever loved."

"That's his burial flag, isn't it?" Aloa inclined her head toward the red, white, and blue standard above the fireplace.

"I was his PNOK, his primary next of kin." Jordan lifted her chin. "They gave me his stuff."

"His uniforms too?" Aloa knew she was walking a dangerous line.

"What are you getting at?" Jordan's eyes narrowed.

"Nothing." Aloa backtracked quickly. "So tell me, what did you do in Afghanistan?"

"Worked in a prison for high-value targets. We were saving lives, stopping the terrorists, and why are you asking about Charlie's uniforms?"

"Just wondering. What was the name of the contractor you worked for?"

"Atlas TRD."

"It must have been a tough job."

"I did what was needed."

"What kind of training did you get? Weapons, interrogation, psychology?"

"We had six weeks of training," Jordan said. "Psychological, physical, weapons, yes."

"I'll bet you're a good shot."

Jordan moved back toward the fireplace. "Why do you care if I can shoot?"

"I don't." Aloa backpedaled. "I've just heard that women are often better shots than men. We should talk about what's in the papers."

"No," Jordan said. "How come you want to know about Charlie, about whether I know how to use a gun?"

Aloa felt the chill air through the window. "I guess because I was surprised. I didn't know you were in the Middle East. I didn't know you knew your way around guns. That's all. I have a lot of respect for our servicemen and -women, people who do their duty."

The fingers of Jordan's right hand curled and then released.

"I know you're in a hurry. Let me take those papers off your hands," Aloa said. She kept her gaze direct. *Show no worry,* she thought.

"I'm not sure it's a good idea now."

"You changed your mind?"

"I think maybe you're on a witch hunt."

"I just want the truth."

"That's what journalists always say."

"Suit yourself." Aloa rose and shouldered her pack. The tension in the room was ratcheting up. Time to leave.

"What are you doing?"

"There's no reason for me to stay if I can't see the documents. You have my number. Call me if you change your mind," she said.

Aloa measured the distance to the door. Twelve feet, maybe less. She moved toward it.

"You can't make an accusation and just leave," Jordan said.

"I didn't make an accusation," Aloa said.

"It seemed like one."

Aloa was at the door.

"Wait," Jordan said.

Aloa put her hand on the doorknob. She heard a scrape, the fumble of a lid opening.

"Stop right there," came Jordan's voice. "Move away from the door."

In the trials Aloa had covered, witnesses who'd had guns pulled on them could describe, down to scratches on the barrel, what the weapon looked like but often couldn't recall a single detail about the person who held it.

It was that way now. The pistol that Jordan held drew Aloa's attention the way a mirror draws a narcissist. The weapon appeared huge, ugly. Its angry black eye was aimed straight at Aloa's chest. Aloa's heart gave an arrhythmic thump.

"You shouldn't point guns at people," Aloa said. "Somebody could get hurt."

"That's the whole idea of guns," Jordan said. The hand that held the weapon trembled slightly. "Come back here. Sit down."

For the briefest of moments, Aloa considered flinging open the door and running down the stairs, but she knew she couldn't outrun an athlete like Jordan, or a bullet. She let her hand fall away from the knob and moved back toward the leather love seat. She clutched her notebook to her chest like a shield.

"This is a bad idea, Jordan," Aloa said as she lowered herself onto the sofa.

"I think it's a worse idea to let you leave knowing what you know."

"I don't know much, really," Aloa lied.

"It seems to me like you know too much. You know about the blackmail, the Pro-Power 500, about giving it to the terrorists in Africa."

Aloa sagged. "Well, now I do."

"Dammit," Jordan said.

"Why did you tell me that?"

"I thought you already knew."

For a moment, both women seemed to scold themselves for the mistakes that had brought them to this moment in time: Aloa's clumsy questions, Jordan's admission.

"Listen," Aloa said, finally. "I'm just a freelancer. I don't really care about the story. I can walk away. Nobody has to know anything."

"I doubt it," Jordan said. "I googled you. All those prizes."

"I don't care about prizes. I don't care about this story either. It's just a paycheck."

Despite the cool temperature in the apartment, Jordan appeared to still be in the flush of her workout. Or maybe it was adrenaline now.

"And in case you missed it, I got let go for being a bad journalist," Aloa continued. "I have no problem walking away from this story. It means nothing to me. I don't have a stake in it like Hayley did."

"You think I killed her, don't you?"

"I didn't say that."

Jordan lifted her chin. "Sometimes a patriot has to make choices for the greater good."

A chill ran down Aloa's spine.

"Stand up," Jordan ordered.

Aloa hesitated.

"I said, let's go." Jordan came over and pressed the gun into Aloa's ribs until she stood up.

"It's not too late to change your mind."

"Stop talking," Jordan said. Movement seemed to make Jordan more confident. She grabbed a jacket from a hook near the door. "Don't even think of yelling for help."

At that moment, Aloa didn't doubt Jordan had it in her to kill. In fact, if she were a betting woman, she'd wager Jordan had already done that at least once before Hayley's death. War changed people. It turned some into the walking wounded, a few into sadists and killers. Look at the jailors at Abu Ghraib.

Think, Aloa told herself.

She walked slowly down the stairs and out the front door of the house, stalling for time. An old man was walking his dog across the street but he paid no more attention to Jordan and Aloa than he did to the tiny Pekingese straining almost to the choking point at the end of its leash.

"Is that yours?" Jordan asked as they neared the illicitly parked rental car.

Aloa could only manage a nod.

"You drive," Jordan said, and poked her with the gun.

It was then that Aloa saw the rusted motorcycle hidden underneath the steep stairway to the house where Jordan lived, the same one she'd seen at T.J.'s mountain home. "Is that bike yours?" she asked.

"It belonged to my dad. Still runs great, though."

"Did you take it to the campout?"

"Shut up. Get in the car."

Her attention still on the motorcycle, Aloa took a step and stumbled on the uneven sidewalk. She staggered forward, her pack sliding from her shoulder and knocking the Moleskine out of her hand.

What Aloa did next was more instinct than decision. As Jordan grabbed the pack and yanked her backward, Aloa kicked her notebook under the rental car. Maybe some Good Samaritan would find it. Maybe they would see Aloa's name and phone number on the inside cover and connect it to the story of a missing woman on some back page of the *Chronicle*. If something happened to her, maybe someone at Novo would use the notes to figure out the whole story and Jordan would get her due—although that was slim consolation if you were soon to be dead.

"You think you can get away?" Jordan said. "You think you're smarter than me?"

"I didn't say that," Aloa replied, and watched as an angry Jordan retrieved the car keys from Aloa's pack and then ordered Aloa to climb across the passenger seat to sit behind the wheel.

Aloa backed the car out of the driveway and, at Jordan's indication from the passenger seat, steered the vehicle uphill and turned at the first intersection.

The notebook lay on the cracked pavement of the driveway, gathering moisture from a dark-gray sky.

CHAPTER 43

Aloa piloted the car north onto Highway 1. Any thoughts of signaling passersby or causing a crash so she could escape were cut off by the hard metal of the gun Jordan pressed into her rib cage. She imagined the way the bullet would pierce her skin and rattle around inside her, crashing through liver, lungs, heart. As a girl, she and her father would pore over his anatomy book, with the consequence that she was the only kid in fourth grade who could recite the name of every bone and organ in her body.

"So Hayley was messing things up?" Aloa glanced over at Jordan. Her eyes had gone hard. Perhaps it was the gun in her hand. Perhaps it was a shift back into the past where she had learned how to regard her prisoners as subhuman in order to do her job.

"After Hank left the campout, she told me she was going to screw him over. She was going to take the money he paid her and then call a magazine reporter she knew to tell him about what was going on. We got into an argument. She would have ruined everything."

"Which was?" Aloa prompted.

"To make it so the terrorists couldn't fight. To save American lives."

They were entering the Presidio, its serene trees and green lawns belying its more than two-hundred-year history as an active military base.

"With the Pro-Power 500?"

"Of course. You mix it with this flour everybody uses over there, make a special delivery to the jihadis, and after a month or two of eating the stuff, the ragheads are useless and we take them down. It's brilliant."

Only if your sense of right and wrong is skewed, Aloa thought, *because even though it is tempting to want to rid a corner of the world of terrorists, how could you justify killing two innocent people in order to do it?* Not only that, but allowing a small group of individuals to wage their own chemical warfare could have very real, and very dangerous, consequences—especially against those who believed in revenge.

"So Hank dreamed up this plan?"

"He went along with it."

Aloa was quiet as parts of the puzzle fell into place. "Because after Hank discovered the side effects of the Pro-Power stuff, he needed somebody to clean up what would have been a PR nightmare," she said. "So he hired somebody, fixers, and they came up with this idea to kill terrorists with the bad supplement." She paused. "But why Chad?"

"You're not so smart after all, are you?"

Aloa didn't say anything. *Let Jordan feel superior,* she thought. *You might be able to use it to your advantage later.*

"Because there was this diamond mine in Chad that got taken over by a bunch of jihadis, the Holy Army, they called themselves," Jordan said. "They slaughtered everybody and were using the profits from the mine to finance their cause. The fixers, as you called them, got hired to clear them out. So they figured, why not kill two birds with one stone." She snorted. "Actually, they were going to kill a lot of birds. Once the stuff got delivered and those ragheads couldn't fight, a bunch of ex–special forces guys were going to get dropped in and get rid of them all."

"And Ethan and Hayley were going to expose this?"

"Ethan was going to write a book about it. He had a recording of Hank explaining everything."

"But how did you find out?"

"I was there when Hayley got the flash drive with the book and the recording. Ethan wrote that all she needed to do was add the science part and send the book off to the agent."

"That's why she broke into Hank's office. To get the formula and have Sayat help her figure out what went wrong," Aloa said.

"She was on this mission. I tried to talk her out of it but she wouldn't listen. That's when I told Hank."

"Which is why Ethan was killed."

"He wouldn't take the cash they offered. He told them he'd been a slave to corporate greed and now he wanted his freedom."

Aloa's hands tightened on the wheel. "And then you killed Hayley. You ran her into the desert until she died."

"She was going to ruin everything. Think of the other terrorists we could stop with this stuff."

"It was a horrible way for her to die."

"It was her choice. I told her if she'd tell me where the flash drive was, I'd drive her to town so she could get her truck fixed. It quit on her."

Aloa thought of the starter interrupter. "Were you following her when her truck died?"

"What? No. I was trying to figure out what to do when she called me."

"Even though she was angry with you?"

"She said she'd already called that mechanic friend of hers and he was on his way, but she ran out of water and it was hot. She wanted out of there, so I turned around."

Aloa thought of Calvin muttering "finder-minder" at his shop. *Was he actually saying, "find her"?* She pictured him arriving at the empty truck, taking out the offending device, then looking for his friend.

That's why he gave me the starter interrupter at his shop, she thought. *He thought whoever put it in the truck had killed Hayley.*

Aloa glanced at Jordan. "But you argued again when you got to her."

"I told her I'd help her if she gave me the flash drive. She called me a hillbilly loser. I shoved her and she hit her head on her truck. Then she, like, went crazy and attacked me," Jordan said defensively.

Aloa touched the brake as cars slowed in front of her.

"There was a sapper tab found near Hayley's body. You were wearing Charlie's jacket when you fought, weren't you, and she tore it off?"

Jordan pushed the gun a little harder into her ribs. She'd hit a nerve.

"And you fired your gun."

"Only to let her know I was serious. I made her take off her shoes, but she started running anyway."

"And you chased her on your bike. You left her out there to die."

"She could have given me the flash drive and I would have taken her back. It's called suicide when you won't listen to reason."

"No. It's called murder, and two people are dead because of it." Aloa didn't mention Calvin, although she thought his death was also connected to the plot.

"It was more like collateral damage," Jordan said.

"Deliberately killing someone is hardly collateral damage," Aloa said. Below the bridge, ships made their stately way toward ports unknown while a few sailboats bobbed on the pewter-gray water.

"Let me ask you this," Jordan said. "If you could have stopped the planes from flying into the towers by killing one person, would you do it? What's a couple of lives in exchange for our safety, our freedom?"

"It sounds like Ethan and Hayley died for diamonds, not for freedom."

"The diamonds were just a side benefit. They died like my Charlie, in the fight against terrorists. He was a hero. A patriot. I won't let his death be wasted."

Aloa looked over at Jordan. Her lips were pressed into a tight, angry line.

"But where do you stop?" Aloa said. "If it's OK to kill two people like Ethan and Hayley, how about five or fifty? It's a slippery slope."

"You think those jihadis play nice?"

"I'm saying when you deliberately poison people, when you murder two people whose only crime was getting in the way of your plan, you become no different than the people we're fighting against. Our country was built on justice, on morality, not on murder and chemical warfare."

Jordan lifted her chin. "I did what I had to do."

"Only now you're a murderer."

"Shut up and get into the right lane," Jordan ordered.

Aloa looked in the rearview mirror in preparation for the lane switch and saw a sight that nearly made her yelp with relief. Three cars behind her was a sedan with roof lights. Sheriff? Police? Highway Patrol? It didn't matter.

"What are you waiting for? Move over," Jordan said.

Before she'd gone on the reporting trip to Juárez, Aloa had taken a defensive driving course. The instructor had showed her how to swerve without losing control of the car. Aloa did that now, hitting the brakes, jerking the car into the next lane inches in front of an SUV and then accelerating to regain control, her hands firm on the wheel. A cacophony of horns erupted.

"What the hell?" Jordan said.

"You said to change lanes," Aloa answered, and looked into her side mirror, praying to see a flash of red lights, hear the blurp of a siren, but there was nothing.

"Try that again and you'll be sorry," Jordan said.

Aloa could see the telltale spotlight of the patrol car. *Please, please,* she prayed in her head.

"Take this exit," Jordan said.

As Aloa took the off-ramp, she begged whatever higher power there was to have the patrol car follow her. Instead it continued on, the officer behind the wheel talking intently on a cell phone.

CHAPTER 44

"Out," Jordan said as Aloa parked the car at RedHawk headquarters. She pulled the keys out of the ignition and jabbed Aloa hard with the gun.

"Will you stop poking me with that thing?" Aloa said.

"If you don't like it, then you should do what I say," Jordan said.

"Or what? You're going to kill me like you killed Hayley? I already know that," Aloa said.

"Shut up." Jordan came around and dragged Aloa out of the car. "Let's go," she said, and headed toward the stable, hiding the pistol against her thigh.

Tremblay looked up from saddling a powerful-looking horse as they came through the open doors. He wore a pair of striped shorts with a gaudy orange-and-black San Francisco Giants shirt and scuffed brown cowboy boots. His hair was pulled back in a man bun.

He frowned. "What's going on?"

"I need to talk to you, Hank. Right now," Jordan said, and stepped close so that Aloa could feel the threat of the gun.

Hank hesitated, then said, "Buck, take Thunder for a quick trot on the Winner's Loop trail, will you? Warm him up for me."

"Sure thing, boss," said the old stable hand. He put down the rake he was using to clean the stalls and walked the horse outside without looking at Jordan or Aloa. He obviously knew how to ignore what should be ignored. *No help there,* Aloa thought.

"She knows," Jordan said when the stable hand disappeared.

"She knows what?" Tremblay asked.

"Everything," Jordan said. "She knows about Ethan, about the Pro-Power 500, about Africa. You need to call Archie."

Tremblay's face went gray.

"She killed Hayley," Aloa said. "She ran her to death in the desert so she could stop Ethan's book."

"She wouldn't give me the flash drive with your recording," Jordan interrupted. "She was going to blab about the plan."

"You killed her?" Tremblay looked stricken. "Why? I paid her just like she asked. A quarter of a million in a Swiss account, plus the annuity. I gave her the account number when we were camping. She was going to keep quiet."

"She was going to double-cross you, Hank. She was going to call a reporter about what was going on," Jordan said.

Tremblay ran two hands over his hair. Aloa saw the tremor again in his fingers.

"She was going to expose the project, and expose you," Jordan said. "She picked herself over America's safety, over the war on terror. She deserved to die."

Tears brimmed in Tremblay's eyes. "I'm so tired of this," he said, "just so tired." He scrubbed a hand over his face. "When they sent me that photo of Ethan . . . when they threatened . . ." He swallowed. "They're horrible people. All they wanted was diamonds, not peace, and now two people are dead because of what I did."

"And thousands more will live," Jordan insisted.

Tremblay went on as if she hadn't spoken. "It was just that we'd lost so much with the Pro-Power fiasco. The accountants told me we'd taken a big hit; then when Archie told me the plan, I thought maybe some good could come from it." His voice trailed off. "Oh my god, what have I done?"

"Peace requires sacrifice, Hank," Jordan said.

From the corner of her eye, Aloa saw the rake the stable hand had left behind. She would not die without a fight. She moved a few inches toward the heavy tool.

"I'm tired of being afraid of them," Tremblay was saying. "Where are they going to stop? If they killed Ethan, they could kill anybody who didn't agree with their politics or their plans or had oil or diamonds or gold that some company wanted."

Aloa took another slow step toward the rake.

"I can't believe you killed her," Tremblay said.

"She was a problem," Jordan said. "Hey!" She lifted the gun from her side toward Aloa. "Get back here."

Aloa froze.

Tremblay's eyes darted from the gun to Aloa and back again. "What the hell are you doing, Jordan?"

"I'm fixing another problem," Jordan said. "We need to get rid of her."

Every neuron, every nerve in Aloa's body was firing. "Even if you kill me, it won't end. There'll just be more reporters. They'll dig like I did. It won't take them long to figure out you were there when Hayley died," Aloa said.

"I don't believe you. Shut up." Jordan lifted the gun so the muzzle was aimed directly at Aloa's face.

What happened next was a blur: A shout from Tremblay, a sudden move, an explosion of noise. A heavy weight fell against Aloa, knocking her to the floor. She was pinned by a soft heaviness she couldn't explain. It was claustrophobic, cloying. She scrabbled from beneath it.

In front of her lay Hank Tremblay, a bloom of red staining his flamboyant shirt.

"You shot him," Aloa cried.

"He grabbed the gun. It went off." Panic tinged Jordan's voice.

Aloa touched a finger to Tremblay's neck, searching for a pulse. Nausea rose in her throat.

"Get away from him," Jordan barked.

Aloa thought she felt a flutter of heartbeat under her fingertips but she couldn't be sure. Blood pooled on the brick floor.

"Look what you did," Aloa said, anger building.

"Stop talking."

"He's going to die, Jordan."

"I said, be quiet."

"You know what? I don't think you're a patriot," Aloa said, getting slowly to her feet. "I think you just used that excuse to hide the fact you wanted revenge for Charlie, for his death."

Aloa measured the distance to the rake.

"You're not even a real soldier," Aloa went on, holding Jordan's eyes with her own. "If you were, you'd know soldiers don't kill innocent people." Aloa moved toward the rake. "What you are is a rent-a-cop playing games. Games that got out of hand."

Another few inches.

"Everything is falling apart," Aloa pressed. "You'll spend the rest of your life in prison. Only this time you'll be the inmate and not the guard." She pointed at Tremblay's body. "Look at him."

Jordan's eyes shifted toward Tremblay, and that's when Aloa made her move.

She leaped across the stable floor and grabbed the rake, swinging it at Jordan in a fierce arc.

The tool's heavy tines struck Jordan's wrist, causing her to cry out and the gun to fall and skitter across the brick floor.

The two women's eyes met for a moment, and then Jordan darted for the pistol. Aloa stabbed the rake toward the athlete as if warding off a rabid dog. They circled. Jordan lunged. Aloa thrust the rake again.

"You can't win," Jordan said, breathing hard.

"We'll see about that," Aloa said, and jabbed the tool into the athlete's chest, knocking her backward to the ground.

Aloa sprang toward the gun just as Jordan scrambled to her feet. The runner threw her weight into Aloa's legs and Aloa fell hard, feeling twin stabs of pain in her knees. Now the two were grabbing and kicking. Their fingers raked faces, their feet connected with flesh. Then, suddenly, a fist was in Aloa's hair and she felt her forehead slam into the bricks. For a moment, she saw stars.

Aloa groaned and rolled over, blinking at the pain. Jordan stood above her, the gun in her hands, her eyes wild. "This is what you get for hating America," she said, and aimed the gun at Aloa's chest.

Aloa couldn't help it. She threw her arms over her face and squeezed her eyes shut.

But instead of a gunshot, she heard Jordan say, "What the . . . ?" followed by a grunt, a thump, and the muffled sound of something hitting the floor.

Aloa opened her eyes to find Jordan lying on the ground with Tick standing above her, his breath coming in raspy pulls, his conker—the dangerous tube sock—still swinging in his hand.

"Jeez, Ink, you scared the hell out of us," Tick said.

"Yeah," said a voice, and Aloa turned to see P-Mac and Doc behind her, both silhouetted in the glare coming through the big stable door, each holding a baseball bat.

"What the hell were you thinking?" Doc said.

CHAPTER 45

Aloa sat in front of the editor's desk at Novo's headquarters, Michael sprawled in a chair next to her. He rested his chin on his fingers as Aloa recounted to the editor, Dean Topper, her desperate drive to RedHawk's headquarters, the car accident that had slowed the Brain Farm's van on the bridge, and their discovery of her damp notebook in Jordan's driveway. They'd used Doc's new iPhone to hack into Aloa's HardE app and used the passwords Tick had stolen from her computer to track her to Tremblay's headquarters. Thank god for the obsessive little app and for the Brain Farm's nosy ways. Her knights in rusting Volkswagen armor.

"Once we heard the shot from the stable, we knew we had to move," Doc had said to Aloa after the police swarmed the concussed Jordan and a coroner's van drove off with Tremblay's body. Paramedics had been unable to revive him.

"P-Mac came up with the ambush plan," Doc had said.

"Simple distract and attack," P-Mac had grumbled. He didn't like hero labels.

"Don't forget who did the conking and who hacked the gate code," Tick had said.

"Li'l Jackie and I scared the hell out of her," Doc had added. "Six-foot-five black guy with a bat? You should have seen her, man."

"My god," said Dean, the editor. "Maybe we should make those guys a sidebar."

The first installment of Aloa's three-part series was ready to go live. Day one covered the Pro-Power 500 fiasco, Pontifex's history, and the

Africa plot. Day two was the trip to Africa and Ethan's death at the hands of hired killers. (Combs would be tearing out his carefully styled hair when he saw that.) Day three was the triggering of the starter interrupter, which, although it had been coincidental, had led to Hayley's murder, Tremblay's death, and eventually the charges facing Jordan Connor, along with sources who confirmed the diamond mine had been retaken around the time Tremblay was killed. (Detective Quinn was close to linking Calvin's death to Radnor Chee, but no charges had been filed yet.)

Chee was nowhere to be found. A flight to New Jersey had brought Aloa to an empty office in Toms River, where Pontifex had supposedly been headquartered, and Aloa guessed he had left the country, although Steve Porter could find no passport record for him.

The PR flack for the Pontecorvo brothers insisted Pontifex was an independent company that had handled a minor problem with a security breach at one of its international branches but that the firm's work had been unsatisfactory and the relationship dissolved. The brothers only met Chee once, the flack insisted, and they knew nothing about a diamond mine or a plot to kill terrorists. The Pontecorvos were backpedaling so fast they'd wind up disavowing their mother if this kept up, Aloa had thought.

The missing flash drive, which included Ethan's book along with photographic and audio evidence of the plot to poison the extremists at the diamond mine, had been found by Aloa, tucked into a false lid on Hayley's keepsake box, which had been mercifully overlooked by the burglar, tucked away as it was on Aloa's bookcase. Smart girl, that Hayley.

"Would you like to see the page before it goes live?" Dean asked.

"I guess." Aloa's heart gave a skip.

Dean touched a few keys and a stark photo montage of mountains, a hooded assassin, a map of Africa, and Hayley and Ethan standing atop a boulder appeared as a banner across her series.

SHADOW WAR, read the headline. AN INVESTIGATION INTO MURDER, LIES, AND A SECRET PLOT TO STOP THE TERRORISTS.

BY ALOA SNOW.

Aloa felt a prick of pride but also nerves. She never thought she'd see her name on a story like that again.

"Well?" Dean asked.

"It, um, looks good," Aloa said.

"Good? It's terrific," Dean said. He glanced over at Michael. "In fact, I owe you both an apology for thinking the story wasn't worth anything."

"Thanks, Dean," Michael said.

Aloa only nodded.

Dean grew serious. "You know this is going to raise a ruckus— and not just because some wackos decided to take war into their own hands." He looked at Aloa. "There's going to be blowback. People are going to come at you from all kinds of directions."

Aloa knew the truth of it, but having Dean say it aloud made it seem more real somehow.

"They'll be bringing up the nail salon story, your resignation, anything they can to discredit the story. People are going to be scrambling to put out the fires this thing is going to set off."

"I know," Aloa said.

"We can handle this however you want," Dean said. "Usually on a story like this, we'd have a reporter available for talk shows, interviews, what have you. But in this case, maybe you'd rather lay low for a while."

"I think laying low is a good idea," Michael said.

"I can handle it," Aloa said.

"I just worry that you'll be the story, instead of the series," Michael said. "That's how those guys operate."

"He's got a point," Dean said.

"You could come to Montana for a few weeks while Dean handles things here," Michael said, turning toward her. "We could hike, go into town. There's a great little burger joint. You'll like the place. Lots of open space, plenty of birds. A fine front porch." His eyes searched hers. "We can spend a little time catching up."

Aloa looked out the editor's window at the afternoon sun. September was a fine time to be in San Francisco, the air crisp, the tourists departed.

"I think I'll stay here and take the heat," Aloa said, and held up a hand toward Michael. "I don't want to run. I already did that once and it didn't work out so well."

"Good for you," Dean said. "We're behind you all the way."

Aloa stood. "I'll do whatever you need me to do, Dean. Answer calls, do interviews. I'm guessing there will be follow-up pieces."

"For sure," Dean said.

"I've got to go, but I just want to say thanks for giving me a chance." Aloa moved toward the door.

"No need," Dean said.

Michael got to his feet. "Wait. Could we talk for a minute, 'Lo?"

Aloa looked at him, remembering the way he'd looked out on the raft on the lake so long ago, the way he and her father would sometimes play catch in the backyard, both of them so content, so happy. "Maybe some other time, Michael. Right now, I have an appointment I can't miss."

Guillermo brought out a coconut curry cake covered in pecans and raisins and set it grandly amid the detritus of what had been an incredible meal.

Aloa had arrived at Justus at the appointed time of six o'clock to find the Brain Farm clustered around a center table and Erik shooing out two German tourists who, pink and peeling from overexposure to the California sun, had wanted a beer and were insisting the sign proclaimed the bar open until 1:00 a.m.

"I'm sure it's one o'clock somewhere," Erik had said, closing the door firmly behind them. He swept closed the curtains and hung a sign on the front door that proclaimed SHUT FOR PRIVATE PARTY.

He flung open his arms. "Let the wild night begin," he said.

Guillermo brought out the first of many courses to come—a pot of mussels in a fiery sauce—and they proceeded to celebrate the heck out of the fact that not only was Aloa alive but, they believed, she would win what Tick insisted on calling "the pullet surprise."

She watched the old men chew and slosh wine and wipe bits of food from their wrinkled lips and felt affection for them, her mismatched and ill-fitting tribe.

Around ten, she lifted Baxter from her lap, where he'd feasted on bits of Japanese steak, and allowed Erik to talk her into letting him walk her home.

"Somebody messes with you and I'll rip them a new seam," he said.

"I'm fine," she told him, "but company would be nice."

They walked through the neighborhood and climbed the hill to her house. The evening hinted at the arrival of winter, but right now the air was warm.

Erik went up the stairs ahead of her and plucked a bottle from the top step.

"Glenlivet," he said. "Somebody knows their scotch."

A business card had been rubber-banded to the bottle and he pulled it off. "Hmmm. The card seems to belong to one Rick Quinn of the Major Crimes Unit at SFPD, and it says, 'Nice work, Snow.'" Erik lifted his eyebrows.

"I gave him some information on Radnor Chee. It's a thank-you scotch."

"Believe whatever fairy tale you want, honey, but scotch isn't a thank-you note. It's a party invitation." He kissed her on the cheek. "Now go inside and lock the door."

Aloa did what he said and went to the front window. Erik stood protectively on the sidewalk.

She lifted a hand to let him know all was well, and he lifted his in return.

Then he turned, and she watched him lumber off.

ACKNOWLEDGMENTS

A writer may write in solitude but there are a whole lot of people behind her when she does. Huge thanks to my agent, Heather Jackson, for taking me (and Aloa) under her very competent and wise wing, and to Liz Pearsons at Thomas & Mercer, whose support, intelligence, and enthusiasm have made all the difference.

Thanks also to editors Heather Lazare and Faith Black Ross for making this book sing, and to the entire team at Thomas & Mercer for their talent, care, and passion for books.

Loud applause to my writing groups, who taught me so much about the craft and who kept me at my keyboard when I was tempted to wander off: Kathleen Founds, Karen Joy Fowler, Elizabeth McKenzie, Liza Monroy, Micah Perks, Melissa Sanders-Self, Susan Sherman, Jill Wolfson, Wallace Baine, Jessica Breheny, John Chandler, Richard Huffman, Richard Lange, Vito Victor, and Dan White. Also, thanks to Martha Mendoza for her insights on investigative reporting, to Gail Michaelis-Ow and Claudia Sternbach for their unwavering encouragement, to Kayla Isenberg, Shelly King, and Carolyn Lagattuta for making me look good on social media, and to Mary Bisbee-Beek for helping get the word out. Thanks, too, to Todd Newberry for teaching me how to really see birds and to Randy and Mary-Jo Lomax for the seaside cottage. Huge thanks go out to all my family (Henry, Regina, Chris, Jack, Mary, and Garren) for their love and encouragement, and to Cody Townsend and Elyse Saugstad for teaching me so much about facing fear and embracing every minute of life.

But most of all, I have to thank my husband, Jamie, the love of my life, who is not only my sidekick on every single one of my research trips, but has always believed in me.

ABOUT THE AUTHOR

Photo © 2017 Carolyn Lagattuta

Peggy Townsend is an award-winning journalist whose stories have appeared in newspapers around the country. She's chased a serial killer through a graveyard at midnight and panhandled with street kids. In 2006, the USC Annenberg Institute for Justice and Journalism awarded her a Racial Justice Fellowship. Peggy is a runner, a downhill skier, and a mountain biker. She currently lives on the Central Coast of California. Follow her on Twitter @peggytownsend or on Facebook at www.facebook.com/peggytownsendbooks.